SWEATPANTS SEASON

DANIELLE ALLEN

Editor/Proofreader: Nerdy Girl Editing
Cover Design: Q Design
Cover Photo Credit: Shutterstock

Sweatpants Season

He has a big…smile.

It was the first thing I noticed that day until he stood. His grey sweatpants hung off his hips and I didn't want to look. I really didn't.

I'm a feminist.

I don't believe in objectifying men. I don't catcall men. I don't ogle the bodies of men. I don't view men as objects of my affection rather than complex people with feelings, wants, and needs of their own. I don't treat men the way society often treats women.

I treat men the way I want to be treated as a woman—with respect!

So, when Carlos ran into me while I was reviewing my interview questions in the park, it surprised me to see my photography classmate out of context. I was also surprised to see as much of him as I did.

It wasn't just that it caught my eye. It was the fact that it held my attention.

It wasn't just that it was large. It was the fact that it was visibly large.

It wasn't just that it was Carlos Richmond. It was the fact that I am Akila Bishara.

And I am not seduced by anything other than intelligent conversation, witty rapport, and meaningful actions.

I am not seduced by a dick print.

I am not.

Seriously, I'm not.

Dedication

To everyone who knows there is no compromise between right and wrong.

And to Tarana Burke.

Prologue

"So, what we've learned is that all women—" City Boy started, his voice rising with amusement.

"Not all women," Country Boy interrupted, his deep voice countered.

"All women," City Boy yelled, doubling down on his claim.

"Oh god, here we go," Country Boy muttered as he laughed.

"All women who wear lowcut shirts are doing it so that we can check out the fun bags! They want us to look. They are showing so much skin that they are basically begging for the attention. So, VanDamn645, you are not wrong for looking at your classmate's cleavage. She has them out for a reason."

"VanDamn645, what I will say is that you may not be wrong for looking for a second, but you're wrong for staring. There's a difference between an appreciative glance and a full-on creep move. Don't be a creep," Los Cabos chimed in.

"Los Cabos is always riding the fence," City Boy complained cheerfully. "I say fuck it! Be a creep! Just don't touch. But if she got them out for you to look at them, look! The saying goes 'look, but don't touch' not 'look for no longer than three seconds and don't touch' okay, VanDamn645?"

"If you're out there listening, VanDamn645, don't let City Boy get you caught up in some bullshit," Country Boy laughed.

"Better yet, VanDamn645, don't listen to City Boy period," Los Cabos laughed.

"Okay, that's it for tonight. Tune in next week and we'll answer more of your emails. We'll also have a special guest that you won't want to miss. I'm City Boy—"

"I'm Country Boy…"

"And I'm Los Cabos."

"And this is Date Night with the Lost Boys," the three of them said in unison.

I turned off the podcast and looked at my best friend, Meghan Parks, and my younger sister, Alexandria Bishara. Shaking my head, I waited.

"This is what's wrong with a lot of the men at Hamilton University," Alexandria snapped, crossing her arms over her chest.

"This is what's wrong with a lot of men in this society," Meghan amended, pouring the rest of her wine into her mouth.

"Exactly! Thank you!" I threw my hands into the air as I rose to my feet.

"I'm pretty sure a bunch of guys on campus listen to this. Who are these idiots?" Alex asked as she reached for the bottle of wine we'd been drinking since we returned from dinner.

"They're a group of dimwitted, egomaniacal, frat boys and assholes," I replied, sitting back. "According to the description, Date Night has been around for a few years. They built a cult-like following feeding bad advice to *boys* aged eighteen to thirty-five." Rolling my eyes, I emphasized the word boys.

"Please tell me the bio on these assholes didn't say boys. Please," Meghan groaned.

"No, it said men, but no one who actually takes advice from The Lost Boys could possibly be a grown man. They have to be adult children like the on-air clowns," I pointed out.

"Definitely clowns. You have to admit it was a little funny when they were answering the question about how to flirt with women at a party or in a bar," Alex giggled, dribbling some wine onto her shirt. "Shit! Some of the advice was terrible, but there were a couple of funny moments."

I looked "They are the enemy." The show was cringe-worthy, but decently humorous." She shrugged as she blotted the wine spot.

"None of that shit was funny because men actually take and utilize this advice." I narrowed my eyes. "Is that my shirt?"

Alex's eyes darted to Meghan before returning to me. "Nooooooo."

I put my hands on my hips. "Yes, it is!"

She scrunched her nose and her eyebrows crumpled in confusion. "Is it?"

"Alex! It's bad enough you stole my shirt, but you spilled red wine on it," I scolded my little sister.

"Well, in my defense," she started, holding her hands up. "I took it from Meghan's closet, so if anyone stole it, it wasn't me…"

My jaw dropped. Shifting my eyes from my sister to my best friend. "Meghan!"

"In my defense, I bought that shirt for your birthday, and Alex had it on all night and you're just now noticing." Meghan leaned forward, her platinum blonde wig framing her face. "So, really, should I be offended?"

My jaw dropped. "Are you kidding me?"

As hard as I tried, I couldn't contain the short laugh that escaped me once Alex laughed.

"Okay, fine!" I pointed at them both. "But leave my stuff alone," I warned them as firmly as I could.

Alex rolled her eyes and Meghan saluted. "Yes, Kiki," they said in unison.

"I can't stand you two," I chuckled. "Anyway…" Shaking my head, I continued pacing the living room of the apartment I shared with Meghan. "I referenced Date Night with The Lost Boys as poor examples of the dating pool in a piece for the Lifestyle section of Richland Times Dispatch."

"Wait? I didn't know about this!" Alex squealed. "When did this happen? What's the article about?"

"Oh! I thought I told you!" I grinned. "I pitched it to The Herald, but they weren't interested. So, when Richland Times reached out last week about a summer recap piece they're doing in the Lifestyle section, they asked me to do a colorful commentary about being single in the city. So, it's basically about me being single and enjoying single life. And they wanted me to touch on why I'm single and on the dating culture and—"

"But don't you have to be dating for that?" Alex quipped, interrupting my sentence.

I opened my mouth to respond, but Meghan cut in.

"And Kenneth, Jamal, and Zack don't count," she teased.

Putting my hands on my hips, I glared at the two people I was closest to in the world. They giggled, but I resisted the urge. "Those do count!" I paused. "Just because I took time out to focus on me and my career doesn't mean my dates don't count."

"They don't," Meghan confirmed.

I looked between them with my mouth agape. "Just because I didn't feel the magic with these guys, doesn't mean the dates don't count."

Alex shook her head. "No…"

"And why not? I went on dates with all of them!"

Meghan rolled her eyes. "Yeah, but if it's been over three months since your last first date…" She lifted her shoulders with her palms up.

"You guys know that my bank account required me to focus on my career and not dating for a few months! But that's neither here nor there; I'm going on a date in two days," I argued. "And the article is being published the same day so it's not a lie. I am single and dating. It's just that the dating pool is full of..." With my eyes bulging, I gestured toward the speakers. "Lost Boys parading around as grown ass men."

"Well, if nothing else, those Lost Boys provided you with tangible references to point out the fuckboy behavior that is alive and well. If you would've said you didn't go on many dates because men say shit like what they said, there would be someone in the comments section of the online version of the article saying 'not all men' and calling you a lying bitch," Meghan pointed out, using air quotes and shaking her head.

"Okay, before you two get started, can we toast?" Grabbing her glass, Alex lifted it waiting for me and Meghan to follow suit.

"Here's to my big sister's big news—" She paused for effect. "—her date! Lord knows it's been too long."

Letting my head fall back, I laughed loudly.

"No, but seriously, here's to a great article," Alex continued, giggles making her voice flutter. She gulped the last of her wine. "And most importantly, the real reason we went out tonight… here's to beginning that photography class with Luca Romano's sexy ass."

"I'll drink to that!" Meghan sang, leaning forward and clinking glasses with Alex and then me. "Congratulations, Akila!"

I smiled. "Thank you both for going to the club with me tonight. Over the next few days, I'll have an article featured in the paper, and I'll have my first date in months. And Monday, I'll get to hone my skills as a photographer with a legend. And the week after that, I have an interview with Re-Mix Magazine. And then I'll launch my blog."

Bringing the glass to my lips, I couldn't help but smile.

I can do all things.

Chapter One

*T*here was a slight chill in the air as the sun set on the city. A beautiful backdrop for what hoped to be a beautiful night. Wearing a shade of marigold yellow that made my skin glow, I sat at the rooftop bar of the busy restaurant, Koi, waiting for my date. I stared at my reflection in the mirror behind the rows of alcohol bottles and rolled my bare shoulders backward.

Just a few more minutes.

It was the first week of September and still very warm on most days. I brought a cute black jacket with me just in case the temperature dropped unexpectedly like it had the day before. But my dress was hot and needed to be shown off. I'd waited all summer for a reason to wear it and thought my date with Niles was the reason I was waiting for.

The sweetheart neckline was both sexy and sweet and the fitted material showcased the width of my hips and the roundness of my ass. My dark, tightly coiled hair was brushed into a high ponytail that sat on top of my head like a crown. My gold hoops and bracelet sparkled in the sunlight as I slipped off my gold rimmed sunglasses. I completed my look with sexy heels that hurt my pinky toe, but made my legs look fantastic. Smiling at my reflection, I was pleased. I hadn't been on a date in months and I wanted to bring my A-game.

Two minutes after Niles gets here, the jacket is going on. But he has to see the full effect—oh! I love this song.

Moving in my seat, I rocked to the music, watching myself in the mirror.

"Hi, I'm Brad. Would you like to dance?" A man asked as he slipped onto the barstool next to me. He looked like one of those good-looking frat boys you'd see in an R-rated comedy about nothing.

"Oh, no thank you…" I flashed him a smile. "I'm waiting for someone."

"Well, why don't you let me buy you a drink while you wait for whoever was stupid enough to leave you unattended at the bar?"

"I'm actually here on a date," I replied, my lips still turned upward. "But thank you for the offer."

"Come on… Anything you want, I got you covered." His eyes slid down my face, lingering on my breasts for a second before he leaned a little closer. "You know I own this place, right?"

"No, I didn't. But that doesn't change anything."

He silently stared at me for a second before standing up and straightening his tie. "No need to be stuck-up about it," he responded, sneering. Turning to the bartender, he barked out a drink order.

My jaw dropped. "I'm stuck-up because I said thank you and turned down your offer?"

"You didn't have to be a bitch about it."

I recoiled, my lip curled in disgust. "Who are you calling a bitch?"

"I didn't call you a bitch. I said you were acting like one."

"Honestly, the only person at this bar acting like a bitch is you," I snapped.

"You're not even that cute anyway."

Shrugging, I smirked. "I was cute enough for you to ask me to dance and to buy me a drink." I rolled my eyes dramatically. "And my eyes are up here."

"You have your fun bags out so clearly you wanted me to stare at them. You got them out for me to look, so I'm looking." He made a point to look at my cleavage even harder and with even more intensity.

Did this asshole say fun bags? That's that same lame shit The Lost Boys said.

"Who taught you that lie? The Lost Boys? Because let me tell you something... I can wear whatever I want and that doesn't give you a right to objectify me."

Ignoring me, he continued. "And if I wanted them, I'd have them in my hands. If I wanted you, I'd have you in my bed."

"Come on, let's not fool ourselves... you couldn't have had this on your best day."

"You'd be lucky to suck my dick."

"You'd be lucky if I could find it."

Tossing money at the bartender and snatching his drink from the bar, he muttered something under his breath and stormed off.

"You are such a badass," the bartender commented as she gathered the dollar bills that he threw at her. "That prick comes here all the time, and he's an asshole."

"Why hasn't he been kicked out and banned from this place?"

"He's the owner's son."

I rolled my eyes. "Of course, he is."

"He's disgusting and rude. He's used to picking up any girl he wants. And when you said no, it was probably the first time he'd heard that in a long time. I wanted to laugh out loud." Her blue eyes danced gleefully as she made a drink. "Let me get you another mojito."

I waved her off. "Oh no, I'm fine."

She walked down the bar and handed a man his order and then made her way back to me, grabbing things to make the minty concoction. "I insist. As a thank you for putting a chauvinistic pig in his place, it's on me."

I smiled appreciatively. "Thank you."

A hand settled on my shoulder and my eyes darted to the mirror behind the bar. Smiling, I turned to the man I'd met at a writing retreat a couple of months prior.

"The beautiful Akila," he greeted me.

"Niles!" Standing, I embraced him. "It's so good to see you."

"It's always good to see you." He backed away and whistled appreciatively. "And you look even better than I remember."

Grinning, I spun in a circle, so he could get the full effect. "Thank you! How are you? You look great!"

He ran his hand down the front of his black button-up shirt. "My dad-bod is still holding strong."

As I sat back down on my stool, I lifted my newly refreshed glass. "The dad-bod is sexy."

"Between that and the new beard craze, I'm in high demand," Niles joked.

"I believe it. I'm glad you were able to squeeze me into your busy schedule."

He chuckled, sitting on the bar stool next to me. "Speaking of which… what made you decide to take me up on my offer? I believe I asked you in April if you wanted to get a drink…"

I cocked my head to the side. "You know…" I took a long sip of my drink. "You questioning my being here makes me question my being here."

Holding his hands up in surrender, he grinned. "Akila Bishara, you are something else."

"Can I get you something to drink?" the bartender asked as she handed a drink to a woman on the other side of Niles.

"Whiskey, neat, please," he answered immediately. "And a refill for the lady."

I stared at his profile and smiled.

Niles was handsome, funny, and a talented writer. We got along well and when he first asked me out, I considered it. But as much as I wanted to feel something with Niles, I just didn't. He was a good guy. We exchanged emails regularly and proofread each other's work. I'd hoped not seeing him for a few months would make the heart grow fonder, so I sent him a response to his unanswered question out of the blue. He quickly jumped on the opportunity, and I found myself looking forward to the night. But as I sat beside the handsome, intelligent man who made me laugh, I didn't feel anything.

We talked nonstop for an hour and a half about the most random topics. I laughed hard and often. He was so funny. Wiping the tear that had welled in the corner of my eye, I sighed with contented amusement. I wanted to feel something other than friendship for him. On paper, we worked. We had a ton in common and we were a lot alike.

"Now, be honest… career wise, what are you scared of?" Niles asked, wiping his mouth. "Your website should've been up and running by now."

I whistled, finishing with a good-natured smile. "You're asking the heavy hitting questions, aren't you?" I took a swig of my drink and then sighed. "Honestly, I'm scared of failure. You know how it is… freelancing can be hit or miss. I'm trying to upgrade my photography skills so I can make my website standout, and maybe that'll also make my writing standout."

He nodded. "I understand."

I gave him the short version, but it was more than that. I wasn't just scared of failure. I was scared of failing the thing I wanted most. The Re-Mix opportunity was a much bigger deal than I let on. It wasn't just a good career move, it was *the* career move. The series writer position was more than just a job for me. Working for Luna Daniels would be a dream come true. I knew my loved ones were aware that I wanted the job. But I didn't want to tell my parents or Alex or even Meghan that I was scared I wasn't going to get it. I didn't want to speak that into existence, but I'd subconsciously pinned my hopes and dreams on the Re-Mix opportunity.

"Freelancing isn't easy. Not many people get that." He paused. "Not many people get the newspaper either so…" He made a face, cracking me up.

"I haven't laughed like that in a long time," I acknowledged, sipping my water.

"Well, now that I'm going to be around here more often, maybe we should make this a regular thing…?"

"Oh, so you were holding out on the real news, I see! If you're going to be here more often, I take it that your editor liked your opinion piece on the football scandal?" I asked, changing the subject.

His eyes lit up. "He loved it! I was offered the permanent position."

Squealing, I clapped excitedly. "I'm so happy for you. You're a damn good writer, and you absolutely deserve this! That's awesome!"

He took a swig of his brown liquor. "You're just saying that because you like me."

"I'm saying it because it's true. And because you're my friend."

Shaking his head, he chuckled to himself. "Friend, huh?"

I gave him a tight smile as I nodded. "Yeah."

He dropped his head for a second before giving me a boyish grin. "You realize I asked you on a date tonight, right?"

Cringing on the inside, I took a sip of water and braced myself. "Let me pay."

His smile dimmed. "I can pay for our meal, Akila."

"I wasn't implying that you couldn't. I just didn't want you to feel like you had to since—"

"Since it wasn't a real date?" Annoyance dripped from his words and turned down his lips.

Not shying away from his eye contact, I wanted to be clear, firm, and kind. "Like I said, I'll pay. I have no problem paying."

"I asked you on the date, so I'll pay for it. I'm just wondering why you accepted knowing I was asking you on a date."

"I said yes to drinks and dinner because I knew we would have a nice time," I answered honestly.

"We could've just hung out as friends and had a nice time." He poured the rest of the contents of his glass into his mouth and then sat back, eyeing me. "Why did you wear that and agree to go on this date?"

I sighed. "Niles…"

"No, I want to know. I'm curious."

"Honestly?"

"Honestly."

I sat back in my chair and looked at him. "I've always thought you were attractive. And on paper, you and I make sense."

He smiled but said nothing.

I cleared my throat. "After a dateless summer, I thought maybe I wasn't feeling that vibe with anyone because I wasn't making good dating decisions. So, I thought about what I wanted in a man, and I thought about the conversation we'd had about your article…which made me think about the fact that you asked me out." I shrugged. "So… I accepted."

He squinted his eyes as though he was trying to make sense of what I was saying. "So, I'm what you're looking for in a man, but…"

Tilting my head to the side, I gave him a look. "I don't feel it."

"What's *it*?"

I paused for a second, trying to put it into words. "Magic. Chemistry." I lifted my shoulders innocently. "Anything."

His eyebrows shot up. "Well, damn."

"I know."

Shaking his head with a smile, he flagged down the bartender. "You are cold-blooded."

"I know."

Before the bartender reached us, Niles had already started speaking. "I just got friend zoned, so that'll be two checks please."

My jaw dropped as a shocked laugh fell from my lips.

The bartender looked back and forth at us in shock. "Oh, okay, okay…?" She looked at me as if she were waiting for permission to bring two checks.

I was at a loss for words, but I was also deeply amused. Holding in my laughter, I nodded my approval.

"I'm kidding," he assured us as he started to chuckle. "But the next round of drinks is on her because she really did friend zone me."

The bartender laughed uncertainly, but she printed only one check and handed it to Niles tentatively.

"Are you sure?" I asked, slowly reaching for the check.

Slapping my hand away lightly, he pointed at me. "Stop!"

After Niles paid, he turned to look at me. "Do you want to know what I think?"

"What's that?"

He chuckled to himself. "I think that you are holding out for something that doesn't exist."

I groaned and playfully rolled my eyes. "Here we go."

"Now hear me out…"

Smiling, I rolled my eyes. "Mm hmm."

"You said it yourself, we work on paper."

I nodded.

"But somehow you don't feel any chemistry between us."

"Correct," I murmured, unsure of his point.

"You know most marriages fail, right? Lasting relationships are built on compatibility." He leaned closer to me, searching my eyes. "Compatibility. Not chemistry."

"I agree. But mutual chemistry and interest are necessary." I paused, cocking my head to the side. "You've been thinking about marrying me, huh?"

Running his hand down his face, he tried to cover his amusement. "You wish." He sat back in his chair and crossed his arms. A smirk graced his handsome face. "I just wanted to ask your overdramatic ass on a date and of course, you blow it out of proportion."

"Blow it out of proportion?" I giggled. "You went from compatibility to marriage real quick!"

With a laugh, he countered, "I brought up marriage as a standard and comparison, not as a proposition and an offer!"

"Yeah, yeah, yeah," I teased, bumping my knee against his as I turned in my chair. "Man, Niles… I forgot how hard you can make me laugh."

The genuine smile on his face spoke volumes. "And I forgot how easy it is to be around you."

"If only we had that spark, that chemistry, that pull…"

He rose from the barstool. "I never pegged you for the romantic type. Usually you're a little cynical—"

"Hey!" I interjected, glaring at him. "I'm not cynical!"

"The last couple of articles you sent me weren't at all…romantic."

"They weren't supposed to be!"

Niles took my hand and helped me off my barstool. "Uh… they were about dating." He made a face. "You didn't even try to be optimistic."

"They were about the culture of dating!"

His eyes widened comically. "Yeah, okay."

"And it's journalism, not my diary," I argued. "If a man wrote those same articles, you wouldn't have thought anything of it. I can't believe you of all people would—"

He put his hands on my shoulders and forced his face close to mine. "You are a fantastic writer. Look at me! You are an excellent journalist."

I tried to turn my head, but his whiskey-soaked breath and pleading eyes held my attention. Rolling my eyes, I relented and looked at him, waiting for him to continue.

"You know me, and you know I'm not saying, 'because you're a woman, your article should've been frilly and romanticized' or any sexist shit like that." He seemed to realize that I wasn't going to turn away from him anymore, so he dropped his hands from my shoulders. "All I'm saying is that your work, even in its early drafts, never really gave me the impression that you were the type to value feelings over facts. I've never known you to value emotions over practical considerations."

I was quiet for a second. "Isn't that the markings of a great journalist?"

He smirked. "Yes. But you told me your goal is to do more opinion pieces on the dynamics between men and women and how it plays in heterosexual relationships and dating culture. Earlier tonight you said you wanted to create your own brand with your blog. With your blog you have to bring a little more of who you really are into it."

I nodded. "I want my website to have links to articles that I enjoy as well as my original content and think pieces. I want to create a dialogue," I affirmed passionately.

"I know. And I know you're going to do excellent work. All I was saying is that with your writing and your attitude about dating, I would've never guessed you were a romantic."

I shrugged. "I just don't wear my heart on my sleeve."

"And you don't have to. But you have a voice, and on your platform, you are free to use it. Never forget that."

"You're great, you know that?" I gazed up at Niles. His earnest eyes and encouraging tone filled me with appreciation. "Thank you."

"For what?"

"For being my friend."

Niles looked around, cupping his ear. "Did you hear that?"

I shook my head. "Hear what?"

"That was you locking the friendzone door with a damn deadbolt." He held his hands up in surrender. "I mean damn, I get it. We're friends. Just friends. Nothing more."

I tossed my head back and laughed.

Chapter Two

"*Aww*, Akila, it sounds like you have a crush," Jennifer teased, cooing in what seemed to be a mix of baby-talk and the staccato tone of her speaking voice. "Sounds like you liiiiike him."

I was irritated for three reasons. One, Jennifer and I did not know each other like that. Two, she was loud as hell. Three, I did find him attractive.

"No…" I kept my voice leveled and low. "All I'm saying is that from his work to his interviews, Luca Romano is a legend. From what I can tell, he's a lot like his work. He's talented, introspective, forward-thinking… His eye and perspective are one of a kind," I gushed about our photography instructor as his assistant handed out the assignment. "I don't know him to like him. I just… I'm excited to learn from him. I'm excited to study under him. Getting into this workshop was…" I shook my head as my voice trailed off.

Getting into that workshop was a true blessing.

"And he's so hot!" Jennifer squealed. "I can't wait to study under him—and not the way you meant it." She wiggled her eyebrows. "I'm glad you don't have a crush on him because I'd hate to hurt your feelings when I get my hooks in him. He's about to be taken."

I felt my face twist in confusion at the woman that I'd just met fifteen minutes prior. "What?"

"I don't know his work, but I know he's hot. And not just regular hot. He is lick-him-from-head-to-toe hot. He just oozes sex, and his ass is perfect. So, I call dibs. And I will get him. His ex-girlfriend was a celebrity trainer and yoga instructor, so…" She unzipped her jacket, gesturing to the tight, black yoga pants and sports bra she was wearing. "Here I am."

"I'm confused."

She flipped her blonde hair over her shoulder. "He's a catch. He's the definition of tall, dark, and handsome. He travels the world. He speaks another language. He's well connected. And he's hot. Someone like that needs something pretty on his arm." She winked. "And I plan to be that something pretty."

Stunned silent, I just blinked.

"I mean, fuck photography—I'm trying to fuck him! Right?" She tossed her head back and laughed.

I stared at her blankly.

I immediately thought about how many people—people, including my sister—didn't get the opportunity to get into the work-shop because someone like Jennifer wanted to use the career defining opportunity as a dating opportunity.

"What?" she snapped, her voice indignant as she zipped up her jacket. "Don't judge me!"

I lifted my hands. "I'm not judging you. I'm just shocked that you spent a thousand dollars for an exclusive photography workshop taught by a legend because you are hoping he wants to date you. You don't really know the man or his work, and people like my sister were so disappointed to not get into this class."

"Whatever! I do know his work," she argued.

You literally just said you didn't know his work two minutes ago.

I sighed, feeling the energy drain from me. Between the conversation and the thought of being partnered with her for the entire class, I considered switching seats. Sliding the assignment closer to me, I skimmed the instructions. "Okay. Let's just do this."

As I was writing, she decided to continue her argument. "I do know him and his work. He's talented. I looked his work up online once I got confirmation that I'd gotten in the workshop. And yeah, he takes great pictures. But I'm looking for a great man. And since he's single, I think I should be his muse. There's nothing wrong with that, and I'm not going to let you make me feel bad about it."

I shrugged. "I never said you should feel bad. You should feel however you want to feel about it. You asked me a question, and I was just saying that I was shocked your only reason for wanting to be here was for a hookup. You could've just waited for class to be over and *bumped into him* in the hallway since you knew the workshop was going to be taught here today. And you could've done that for free. A seat could've gone to someone who really wanted to be here, and you still could've tried to date him."

"It's a little more complicated than that," Jennifer snapped irritably. She crossed her bony arms over her chest.

I shrugged. "Honestly, what you do doesn't matter to me. You asked me a question, so I answered it. I was surprised, but I wasn't judging you. Anyway, do you have anything you want to add to the list?" I asked, changing the subject and focusing on the assignment.

She grumbled under her breath as she read over what I'd written. "You forgot to add thin to the list."

Her snarky tone and haughty look wasn't lost on me, but my eyebrows flew up because that aspect of her personality was in sharp contrast to the bubbly woman I'd first encountered.

I frowned. "No…"

"It's going to be a long class if you can't compromise, Kia."

I inhaled deeply and then exhaled slowly, calming myself down. I cocked my head to the side as I eyed her. "Okay, first of all, my name is Akila," I corrected her before saying it slower and phonetically. "Ah-key-la."

"That's basically what I said," she argued, fingering her short blonde bob and rolling her eyes. "Kia, Akila, same thing."

Ignoring her, I continued, "Second, and most importantly, I don't have to compromise on that."

Her brown eyes widened indignantly. "What?!"

"I don't have to compromise," I reiterated calmly, watching as our instructor spoke with a student outside of the classroom.

"Yes, you do!" She jerked her hands through her hair irritably.

Glancing at my watch, I regretted arriving to class early and flashing a friendly smile to Jennifer as she walked into the room.

My smile was lethal.

It was as warm and welcoming as it was seductive and flirtatious. With a single parting of my lips, I've made women want to be my best friend and gotten men to do my bidding. I never mean for it to happen and it never was an inconvenience until it happened with men I didn't want to date or women I didn't want to be friends with. Which incidentally, happened often. So, I should've guessed that Jennifer would take my smile as an invitation to sit in the empty seat beside me.

Even though it was not.

I sighed. "The directions on this paper clearly state that we are to get with a partner and write five characteristics of a beautiful woman that 'both partners agree on'. The 'both partners agree on' part is pretty specific."

"Exactly." Jennifer threw her arms up in exasperation. "We have to compromise."

I furrowed my brows. "No, we have to agree…" I glanced at the door as several people streamed in. A few of them found seats, but a group of four crowded around Luca's desk, waiting. Not wanting to make a scene, I lowered my voice slightly. "And I don't agree with this bullshit."

She gasped and recoiled. "How dare you call my list bullshit! This is my opinion!"

I pointed at her list and then met her eyes unflinchingly. "Your opinion is your opinion. It is not our opinion." I looked around the room, most of the seats were filled. "It's your opinion. And I can accept your opinion as yours, but I'll be damned if I cosign on an opinion I don't believe in."

"Just because you are a little on the heavy side doesn't mean that thin shouldn't be on the list, Kia."

My head snapped back to Jennifer as I glared at her.

She knew my name. *But two can play this game.*

I picked up my pen and scratched out her name on my paper. Standing, I grabbed my notebook and my handbag. "You can put whatever you want to put on your list, Jeanine." Gesturing between the two of us, I smirked. "Because this isn't going to work. Perhaps your new partner will agree with you."

"What?" Panic filled her eyes. "But we're already partners!"

I lifted my shoulders as I held up the paper with the line through her name. "And now, we're not."

"Whatever, it's for the best anyway," she snapped, throwing the words at my back as I walked off. "Your feelings wouldn't be so hurt if you lost a few pounds. Just twenty or so around the hips."

Shaking my head, I didn't bother to look back. "Okay, Janet."

She grumbled under her breath as I made my way to the back corner, closest to the window.

I had two options for a new partner—a talkative woman in the front row and a man who appeared to be sleeping in the back row. Without even thinking about it, I'd realized that I'd made the decision to go for the least obvious choice.

The man with his head down on the desk was turned toward the window so I couldn't see his face. His broad shoulders and head were completely covered with his hoodie. I couldn't tell what he looked like, but there was something comforting and nonthreatening about someone who arrived to class before anyone else and was comfortable enough to take a full-blown power nap in the back.

He either has too much time on his hands or not enough, I mused as I took a seat beside him as quietly as possible. *And if he needs a nap, he's less likely to talk my head off.*

After placing my bag on the table, I opened my notebook and glanced over at the man in the oversized hoodie. I waited silently until the clock at the front of the room said it was one minute until six o'clock before interrupting his slumber.

Clearing my throat, I gently tried to rouse my new partner awake. "Excuse me?" I whispered, my hand hovering over his back. I hesitated to actually touch him, so my hand just hung in the air above him before I brought it back to my lap. "Sorry to wake you, but we have an assignment to complete in the next eleven minutes."

He didn't respond.

Knocking on the table in front of him, I spoke a little louder. "Hello? Time for class to start. We have an assignment."

He still didn't respond.

"Come on, Sleeping Beauty. Wake up please," I muttered defeatedly.

I looked around and just as I considered going to find another partner, the instructor stood in front of his desk. In a pair of dark denim jeans, a plain white t-shirt, and black, leather boots, the photography phenom Luca Romano greeted the class. "Welcome to Visual Storytelling."

I stopped mid-thought.

Oh wow.

It was a little irritating that Jennifer was right, but there was no denying my attraction to my teacher. His thick, Italian accent was sensual and immediately had me smitten. I was already taken with his talent, but I could've listened to him talk for hours.

There were stories in books, TV shows, and movies dedicated to someone being hot for the teacher. But that was never my experience. I'd never in my life had a teacher fantasy because I'd never in my life had a teacher that was worth fantasizing about. There weren't any teachers in high school that I had a crush on. There weren't any professors in college that I was infatuated with. There weren't even any teacher's assistants that I had sexual thoughts about. But the tall, dark, and handsome man who greeted the class with the sexiest accent I'd ever heard in person captured my attention immediately.

"Good evening. Welcome to Photography 250: Visual Storytelling. My name is Luca Romano. Before I get started, please understand that this workshop is unlike most adult education classes offered through the Department of Parks and Recreation. This is a hybrid class. We only meet in the classroom today and in five weeks on the final day. Between now and then, I will give you virtual lessons, and you'll submit assignments online. My priority will be to show you how I create art and hope that it inspires you to find your eye and create art for yourself. I'm not a teacher in the traditional sense because that's not my skillset. I am an artist. I am a storyteller. My goal is to make you an artist and a storyteller. Understood?"

"Yes," I breathed, eyes glued to him. Each word out of his mouth made my body take notice.

"Is everyone in the right class?"

"Yes," I answered again as if he were speaking only to me.

Licking his lips, Luca's gaze settled on me momentarily before it skirted around the room. "I'm going to give you a quick overview of how our classes will work and then you will start with your icebreaker activity. Every Monday I will post your weekly lesson. Your homework will always be to capture your own version of what I taught you and submit it, unedited, within five days. There will be a partner component for the first and last assignments and I will touch on that when the time comes. But for right now, I want to make sure you understand the basics." He clapped his hands and then rubbed them together. "Sounds good?"

Sounds really good, Luca. Can I call you Luca?

He flashed us a grin. "Are you ready to get started?"

"Yes…" I was pretty sure I moaned.

"Something you may not know is that you are all writers. Every single one of you are writers, creators, storytellers. You were partly chosen because of that fact. All of you are talented writers—from personal bloggers, travel bloggers, fiction writers, journalists, poets, lyricists. You are in this room with people who are in the same field as you on some level. Now, turn to the person you are sharing a table with—that's your partner. Get familiar with them. They will be your partner for the duration of this course. Your first and last in the field projects will involve the person sitting next to you. So, look at your neighbor… this is who you will be working with. Any questions?"

I shook my head.

He looked around and smiled. "I see some of you have already gotten started, so I'll give you ten minutes to complete the assignment that was sitting on your desk when you arrived, and then you will share. As you begin to combine lists, remember—both partners must agree on every adjective used in the five words you present."

I couldn't help but smirk in Jennifer's direction as soon as those words came out of his mouth.

Sighing, I turned toward my sleeping partner, ready to shake him awake, and abruptly stopped.

Soft, brown eyes framed by the longest, darkest lashes I'd ever seen blinked over at me.

"You scared me!" I yelped, my hand flew to my chest.

His eyebrows furrowed, and his full lips pulled upward. It wasn't quite a smile, but he appeared moderately amused. "How? I was here first."

"I wasn't expecting to turn around and have you staring at me with those eyes."

"Were you expecting me to be staring at you with someone else's eyes?" His flat tone and slight tilt of the head was so on time, it felt scripted.

I let out a slack-jawed giggle, more out of the shock of his response than anything else.

I couldn't tell if he was a sarcastic gentleman or a charming asshole. He managed to be warm and inviting, but his tone was unchanged, and his facial expression remained blank. He didn't follow his rhetorical question with a laugh but based on his relaxed body language and the glint in his eyes, he didn't appear to be serious. He was hard to read, but his vibe felt good to my soul. He was a host of inconsistencies, and that was both interesting and irritating at the same time. But I kind of liked it.

Not to mention his voice sounds like sex feels…

Shaking the thought out of my head, I rolled my eyes and replied, "No, I was expecting you to still be asleep."

"I was never asleep. I was resting my eyes."

"Yeah, okay," I scoffed playfully. "So, what's your deal? I got here early, and you were the only one here, sleeping. Who can sleep in a classroom full of people you presumably don't know?"

"I wouldn't know. I wasn't asleep." He gave me a look. "What's your deal? Who calls a grown ass man Sleeping Beauty?"

I blinked rapidly, trying to think of something to say. "So, um… you heard that?"

"You can't be aware of your surroundings if you're asleep." He winked. "I was resting my eyes."

"Sorry…" I made a face. "When I called you Sleeping Beauty, I didn't mean any disre—"

He shook his head, cutting me off mid-sentence. "Don't worry about it."

"Thanks," I mouthed sheepishly.

"But let me ask you a question… why are you here?"

"Because Luca Romano is probably the best photographer on the East Coast, maybe the world," I gushed, bringing my hand to my chest. "I remember the first time I saw one of his photographs. It was of an old woman and I felt like I could see her wisdom. It was so vivid, so real, and so powerful that I felt like he was able to capture everything that she'd ever learned in the course of her life. I felt like I knew her. I'd never seen a photograph like it! I told myself that in everything I do, I want to evoke that kind of emotion. I want to tell a story with my work."

"Oh, okay," he remarked with an approving nod. "Sounds like you're serious."

"Very serious… about this class and about my love of his work." Realizing how intense I probably sounded, I cleared my throat and picked a nonexistent piece of lint from my pantleg. "What about you? Why are you here?"

"If I'm going to be the best, I have to learn from the best. I'm working on a collection of essays that I want to publish. Adding photos that correspond with the essays on my website will help it stand out."

"Oh, wow!" I was impressed. "When are you looking to publish?"

"The website will launch next month. I'm releasing the book in January." He glanced up at me from what he was writing. "That's why I wanted to know if you were serious. If I have to be partnered with someone for the next five weeks, I need it to be with someone who is taking it as seriously as I am."

"I'm right there with you," I agreed earnestly, scanning what I could see of his face, trying to get a better look at him. In every one of his slight movements, his confidence poured out of him. I was curious about the mystery man who was now my partner. "One hundred percent."

"Just looking and listening, I know there's at least a couple of people who are here just to say they took this class." He lifted his hands and shrugged. "I'm not judging, but I'd rather work alone than to have anyone get in the way of my growth and progression."

My eyebrows flew up. Hearing him echo my sentiments emphasized that I'd made a great decision. But hearing the passion in his voice stirred something within me.

"Yes... I agree wholeheartedly." Taking a glimpse at the clock, I gave him a quizzical look. "Speaking of..." I slid my list to the middle of the table. "Where's your list?"

He put his paper right beside mine and then ran his hand over his beard contemplatively.

Tearing my eyes away from him, I noticed his paper didn't have his name on it. Before giving his list a complete onceover, I met his eyes again. "What's your name?"

He stuck his hand out to shake mine. "Carlos Richmond."

My smaller, softer hand slid into his larger one. "Akila Bishara."

"Akila Bishara... that's interesting." He held my gaze and my hand for a beat too long.

"I'm interesting," I returned, removing my hand from his.

"I'm sure you are." Sitting back in his chair, he eyed me. His laser-like vision moved over the elongated strands of my naturally coiled hair. "Interesting for sure."

I knew instinctively that he was playing with me, even though his emotionless face and slightly sarcastic tone said otherwise. There was a familiarity in the way he interacted with me. It was playful, but not overtly so. I couldn't really explain why I was so intrigued by him, but I wasn't ready to let him know that yet.

I narrowed my eyes at him, trying not to smile. "You're not wrong."

"I know." His eyes danced as he licked his lips. Slipping his hands in the pockets of his hoodie, he pulled out a cell phone. Checking it briefly, he placed it on the table in front of him and then directed his attention back to me. "I'm never wrong about people."

His cryptic response intrigued me even more.

"What's that's supposed to mean?"

"It means exactly what it sounds like—I'm never wrong about people. You can tell a lot about a person if you look and listen."

I lifted a perfectly shaped eyebrow. "This is true," I agreed, biting my lip to keep from grinning. "But I imagine that's hard to do when you're sleeping."

He shook his head, turning toward the window, away from me. Although he did his best to hide it by scrubbing his face with his hands, I caught the corners of his mouth turning up into a smile. When he turned back toward me, his face was once again expressionless. The fact that I amused him amused me and for the first time, I embraced the connection I felt with him.

He tried to give me a serious expression, but his eyes were sparkling with laughter. "You're funny. I was awake." There was a glimpse of something that I couldn't quite describe that changed the way he looked at me. After a brief pause, he added, "You're definitely interesting."

Folding my arms over my chest, I lifted an eyebrow. "And what is that supposed to mean?"

"Just an observation. You're interesting…different…unique. Your name is unique. Your style is unique. Your look is unique." He shrugged. "That's all."

"You don't know me, Carlos Richmond."

"But I have eyes and ears, Akila Bishara." Looking at my paper, he jotted my name down on his paper and then returned his eyes to mine. "I've never seen Akila spelled like that. Honestly, I've only seen Akila spelled on the movie poster about the little girl and the spelling bee."

I suppressed a giggle and nodded. "Mm-hmm."

A slight smile played on his lips as he continued. "Your style is dope… or you spilled something on your work shirt and that's all you had in the car. Either way, anyone who wears grey dress pants and a black Biggie t-shirt is a woman who is about her business and who knows what's up. I don't know what the hell is going on, but it works."

I laughed. "Oh, okay. Thank you." I paused, twisting my lips into a dubious grin. "I think."

Staring at me thoughtfully, he concluded with a shrug. "And your look is different., interesting. You're pretty, but there's something interesting about it, about you—and that's what makes you beautiful."

I felt my cheeks heating. "Thank you," I whispered, holding his gaze.

The way he said it was unlike any other time a man had ever called me beautiful. It didn't seem to be coming from a place of desire or lust. It didn't even seem to be coming from a place of attraction. His words and the look he gave me to accompany those words seemed to come from an artistic place. And for some reason, that compliment was ten times more powerful.

"You have one more minute to compare your lists," Luca announced.

He slid the hoodie off his head, exposing a perfectly lined haircut that faded into a sexy mid-length beard. Blemish-free skin, full, sexy lips, and straight, white teeth accompanied the gorgeous, brown eyes to create a face so handsome that it caught me off guard.

Oh, hello!

Spiritually, my energy was already attracted to him. Intellectually, I was attracted to his conversation. But after seeing his whole face, I was also physically and sexually attracted to Carlos Richmond.

I glanced up at Luca Romano and realized the stark difference between thinking someone is attractive and being attracted to someone. Luca was attractive, and I momentarily had a crush on his talent. But what I'd felt with Carlos was unprecedented.

Turning back toward my partner, I was again struck by how attracted I was to him. The endorphins were flooding my system, and it was too much too soon. Clearing my throat, I pulled my eyes away from his and stared at our lists. I tried not to beam as my eyes moved over how he defined beautiful.

"That's crazy," I murmured.

His list was not at all what I expected, but somehow, very much what I should've expected from him.

"We have a couple of the same things." He pointed at his paper. "As you can see, interesting is at the top of the list."

I looked down at his paper, hoping to hide the fact that my cheeks heated as I smiled again. "So, we both wrote down kindness, confidence, and intelligence"—I circled those on both of our papers — "I agree with your interesting so that's four. And you don't have a fifth one."

"If a woman is interesting, kind, confident, and intelligent, she is beautiful," he replied.

"But what attracts you to a woman?" I asked more for my own general curiosity than for the assignment.

He licked his lips. "The assignment asked what makes a woman beautiful. That's not the same as attraction."

I ignored the flutter in my stomach. "So, what attracts you to a woman?"

He opened his mouth to answer but was interrupted.

"Okay, class!" Luca clapped his hands together, getting everyone's attention. "I want to quickly go around the room and hear your thoughts on what makes a woman beautiful. Then, I'm going to give you an assignment associated with that list." He looked around and his eyes landed on me. Gesturing to us, he smiled broadly. "So, we'll start in the back. You don't have to introduce yourself yet, just read your list."

I looked over at Carlos. He gave me a nod.

"The characteristics of a beautiful woman: interesting, kind, intelligent, confident, and…" I glanced at Carlos as I tapped the last word. He nodded. "And passionate."

"Perfect! Yes, yes," Luca exclaimed, nodding his approval. "Okay, next."

I tried listening to the other people in the class give their lists, but I felt Carlos staring at me.

"I like that," he whispered.

His words washed over me, and I felt the heat creeping up my neck, flushing my cheeks. "What?" I replied discreetly, glancing over at him.

"Passionate." He paused, capturing my gaze and reeling me in.

I swallowed hard. *Is he flirting with me?*

"I think I will add that to my personal list."

No, he's just being friendly… I think.

He licked his lips, but that time was slower, sexier. My body woke up.

I think…

Realizing I hadn't responded, I nodded quickly. "I think you should."

He's definitely flirting…right?

He stared at me, into me, without saying a word. The sound of photography students rattling off their lists faded into nothing.

I swallowed hard.

"You seem okay, Akila Bishara." He scribbled a number down on my paper and then sat back in his chair.

Typing his number into my phone and then sending him a text, I bit my lip to keep from grinning. "You too, Carlos Richmond."

"Looking forward to this partnership." And as if we didn't just have a moment, he turned his attention to one of the last pairs reading their lists.

Wait, what?

The internal record scratch caused my entire body to stop abruptly.

Did he give me his number because we're partners, or did he give me his number to get to know me on a personal level?

I liked to know how I'm being approached so I could counter it appropriately. If a man wanted to be friends, and I wanted to be friends with him, we could move forward knowing the limits and boundaries of friendship. If a man wanted to pursue me, and I wanted to be with him, we could move forward knowing the limits and boundaries of dating. I didn't like the grey area.

The grey area was where feelings were hurt, friendships were ruined, jobs were lost, etc.

But as I stared at my mysterious partner, I had no idea if he even wanted to be friends, let alone if he was interested in me romantically. But the pull I felt between us was undeniable and not knowing where he stood made me a little nervous.

What am I doing?

I couldn't help silently laughing at myself. Somehow, I'd let Carlos Richmond get in my head and the feeling, that elusive feeling he gave me, had me all mixed up. I smiled ruefully as I decided to just loosen up.

He glanced at me, catching me in the exact moment that I happened to be eyeing him.

I froze.

We sat there staring at one another, and I didn't know if I should be embarrassed for getting caught looking at him or if I should be flattered that I caught him looking at me.

I swallowed hard.

"You're staring at me," I blurted out breathily.

He licked his lips before easing into the sexiest smile I'd ever seen. Leaning forward, his mouth was right next to my ear and the heat of his breath caused my entire body to tremble. My breathing hitched slightly when I inhaled his cologne. The hair on my arms stood on end. I'd never had that reaction to anyone before.

The only sound I could hear was my heart thumping against my chest. I held my breath and I waited, anticipating what was next.

"I was staring..." His deep voice sexily held my attention. "Because I could feel you staring at me."

I rolled my eyes, but my cheeks were still warm from his nearness. "Whatever, dude," I giggled.

Chapter Three

"Your assignment for today is a quick one," Luca Romano announced, sitting on the edge of his desk. "You have thirty minutes to go outside the classroom and capture the best examples of a beautiful woman. You and your partner must capture two different images of two different subjects. And no, you and your partner can't take a picture of the same woman and call it a day."

The class hummed with laughter.

"Once you've both completed that task, you will return and upload your photo digitally. When both raw, untouched photos have been uploaded, you and your partner have officially completed the assignment. These submissions will give me an idea of where your individual starting point is so don't think too long and hard about it. You only have thirty minutes so let's get started. Grab your cameras, grab a few consent forms… The time starts now!"

I pulled my camera out of my bag. "Are you ready?" I asked Carlos who was fitting a different lens on his camera.

"Yeah, I'm ready." When he looked over at me, I could see the excitement in his eyes even though there wasn't a hint of a smile on his face.

Standing, I smirked. "I'm starting to figure you out."

He stood, gesturing for me to walk before him. "Is that right?"

"Yes."

No, not at all.

"I can see right through you," I added.

I had no idea.

Glancing over my shoulder at him, I continued, "I think you—"

"Stop," Carlos commanded, gripping my waist and pulling me back.

I gasped as my back hit his chest and my ass hit his thighs. Turning my head, I looked around and then down.

"Oh, sorry," Jennifer apologized in a saccharine sweet voice that dripped with insincerity and disdain. "You almost tripped over my bag. You should watch where you're going."

My blood boiled as I stared at her smug face in shock.

Did she really just try to trip me up?

"That was a bitchy thing to do, Jennifer." I started moving toward her, but felt a hand flex against my hip, reminding me of his presence and preventing me from going anywhere.

"What?!" Jennifer shrieked, causing the last few students in the room to look our way.

The slight movement of Carlos's hand sent a wave of activity through my entire body. I didn't mean to swoon. I wasn't even sure if I did swoon. But everything slowed down except for the flutter in my belly and the heat of his hand that scorched my skin through my clothes. I let out a small breath instead of the angry growl I was going to give Jennifer's petty ass.

"Did you just call me a bitch?!" Jennifer yelled, catching the attention of Luca Romano.

"What's going on?" our instructor asked, making his way across the room as Jennifer continued yelling about me verbally attacking her.

I looked at the legend up close as he approached us, and my tongue felt heavy and too big for my mouth. Cotton had lodged itself in my throat. I opened my mouth and no words came out at first.

"Luca, Akila called me a bitch," Jennifer whined as she batted her eyelashes.

He looked at her and then looked at me.

Shifting my gaze away from the handsome instructor, I focused on the grown ass woman who was acting like a little ass kid.

"I did not call you a bitch. I said that you trying to trip me up was a bitchy thing to do, but I didn't call you a bitch," I corrected her. Turning my attention to Luca, I swallowed hard. "Because I've been a fan of your work for a while now and I have the utmost respect for you, I wouldn't disrespect you or your class like that."

He held my gaze for a beat too long before turning to speak to Jennifer. "I wasn't here when it happened, but I do see some belongings in the walkway." Redirecting his attention to me, he assessed my face silently before his eyes dropped to the strong hand that was still firmly holding my hip. Carlos released me tentatively as Luca continued. "You don't have very much time to complete your assignment. Head on out."

I nodded, giving him a soft smile as we started heading out the room.

We'd only managed to get three steps away before I heard Jennifer's voice. "Thank you for protecting me from her…"

"What?!" I screeched, turning to look over my shoulder.

"Let it go," Carlos commanded, wrapping his arms around my shoulders and ushering me out of the room. "Don't feed into her shit. You're in this class for a reason. You want to get something out of it. Don't worry about her."

Inhaling his scent, I closed my eyes briefly and allowed him to lead me down the hall. With my lungs full of the sandalwood and vanilla cologne he wore, I exhaled my words. "But she's lying on me."

"And everyone knows that."

"But Luca—"

"Come on now, Akila…" Carlos removed his arm from around my shoulders and gestured for me to walk through the door before him. When we were walking side by side again, he didn't look at me as he continued. "If you think Luca gave a damn about what that woman had to say about you, you weren't paying attention."

I stared at the strong profile of my partner. His chiseled jawline clenched as we made our way out into the courtyard of Hamilton University.

My stomach twisted.

"What do you mean?" I asked, somewhat sure I understood exactly what he meant.

He slowed to a stop and looked at me. "You're…" His voice trailed off as we held each other's gaze.

I swallowed hard. "I'm what?" I whispered, my belly fluttering in anticipation.

"Look out!" A woman screamed as the clunking sound of a rouge skateboard barreled toward us.

"Umph," I grunted as my body slammed into Carlos's chest. He'd grabbed me and pulled me into him, out of the way of the skateboard. Our faces were close, too close.

My eyes widened as I looked up into his. My lips parted as I attempted to say something, anything. I wanted to thank him for saving me from falling on my face twice in a five-minute period. I wanted to make a joke to get him to show me those pearly white teeth. But all I could do with those beautiful eyes staring into mine was gape at him. A breathy sigh escaped me as he continued to hold me against him.

"I'm sorry!" Stealing our attention away, the woman ran up to us, throwing an apology over her shoulder as she scooped up her skateboard from the grass a few feet away. "I'm so sorry!"

Carlos let me go and looked down at his watch. "We have twenty, twenty-five minutes."

I turned my head, looking around the courtyard, so he wouldn't see how severely his touch affected me.

Still slightly shaken from the rush of endorphins that flooded my brain while in his arms, I pulled myself together. "So, what were you saying? I'm what?" I asked again, my voice back to normal. "And if you say something shitty, I'm going to kick your ass."

A smile played on his lips. "You'll kick my ass?"

"Yes."

"Well, lucky for you, I don't fight women."

"Lucky for you." I shrugged, pursing my lips. "So, I guess you better not say anything shitty, so you won't have to meet your match."

"You're what? Five feet, seven inches? I think you're tough, but you're not tough enough to kick my ass. I'm seven inches taller than you and twice your size. So, even with me not fighting back, you wouldn't be able to kick my ass. Not without some help anyway."

I stared into his eyes. "I don't need help." Raising the arm that didn't have my bag strap slung over it, I flexed my muscle. "I just need my guns."

Finally, the sound I'd been waiting for danced against my eardrum.

His deep, rolling chuckle was intoxicatingly sexy. It drew me in with each inflection and as hard as I tried not to, I smiled. Without warning, my smile turned into a small giggle.

"Put your weapon away," he laughed, pushing my arm down.

I looked at the ground as his fingertips seemed to burn their way into my skin.

"All I was going to say is that… you're beautiful."

My eyes met his unintentionally and just when I was about to melt, he continued.

"And beautiful women tend to rise to the top of the class with teachers like Luca Romano."

I stopped mid-swoon. Furrowing my brows, I asked, "So, I can't be attractive and talented? You don't think I could excel in the class on my own merit?"

He gave me a look. "I didn't say that at all. My comment is less about you and more about him." He shrugged. "Maybe if you paid any attention to the way he was looking at you, you'd understand what I'm talking about."

"He wasn't looking at me any kind of way."

"Okay." He shook his head, turning to watch the people around us. "Excuse me, miss," he called out to the woman with the skateboard, moving into her path, but keeping a safe distance away. "Hello, I'm Carlos."

Beaming, she bit her bottom lip. "I'm Ava."

"Hi, Ava," Carlos's voice was seductively smooth.

A pang of displeasure tugged at my gut. I wasn't quite sure why it rubbed me the wrong way that he was speaking to her like that, but it did. I wasn't jealous or anything. It just felt wrong.

"I'm taking a photography course and our first assignment is to find a beautiful woman and capture that beauty on film." He handed her the release form. "Would you be interested in being photographed?"

Ava barely read over it before she stared up into Carlos's face. "I don't do nudes—well not for anyone I'm not dating." She swayed back and forth. "But for you, I'll pose however you want me."

I almost threw up in my mouth.

Rolling my eyes, I turned my back on the flirtatious display in front of me.

"Really now?" Carlos sounded amused. "Well, I just want to get a couple of fully clothed shots of you..."

I tuned them out. Casting my gaze around the courtyard, I searched for any woman that stood out to me. I didn't see anyone that really caught my attention, but I heard a laugh that caught my ear. Following the sound, I eyed the most stylish woman on campus at that moment.

In bright blue, wide-legged pants, a white and black polka dot top, and a black leather jacket, she stood out in a sea of casual wear. But it was her big, curly hair, musical laugh, and undeniable confidence that drew me to her. She had three men and one woman surrounding her as she told a story. As I got closer to her, I noticed the black spiked heels and the impeccable makeup.

She was perfect for the assignment.

"Excuse me," I interrupted as the men were exchanging good-byes with the beautiful woman.

"Hey!" She flashed a sparkling smile.

"I don't know if you're familiar with Luca Romano, but——"

"I'm familiar with the fact that I prayed to the gods that I'd get into his class and wasn't selected," she interjected with a laugh. "I'm guessing you were one of the lucky ones?"

I smiled. "Yes. But if it's any consolation, my sister wanted this more than anything. She loves his work and she didn't get in either."

"So, she feels my pain?"

"I imagine she does." I laughed along with her. "Speaking of his class, our first assignment is to photograph someone beautiful"—I handed her the form— "and with your beauty and your awesome style, I thought you'd be the perfect person for this quick assignment."

She read over the paper quickly as she spoke. "Well, thank you. I love it when women compliment other women. But I have a question?"

"What's that?" I pointed to the bold print on the form. "Just so you know, your photo won't be used for anything outside of this assignment."

"Yeah, I read that part, and I'm willing to do it," she replied, scribbling her name at the bottom of the form. "But I was going to ask for something in return."

"What's that?" I asked slowly.

I silently prayed she didn't ask for financial compensation. Time was running out and I'd have to be back in class shortly. I couldn't go back with assignment number one incomplete. Failing the first assignment was not an option.

"Would you give Luca Romano my card?" She pulled a card out of her pocket. "I'm a stylist, model, and budding photographer."

"Oh, yeah." I nodded, relieved. Taking her card, I glanced at the name and the headshot of her that covered the entire back. "This is gorgeous! I can definitely get this to him," I agreed, before putting it in my bag with the consent form she'd signed.

"And what's your name?"

"I'm Akila."

After we shook hands, I positioned my camera to my face and snapped a bunch of shots. In the two-minute photoshoot, I didn't give her any direction because she knew her angles, she knew how to pose, and she effortlessly slipped into model mode.

"Got it," I said as I looked at the screen of the last shot I'd taken. "You made this easy."

"Thanks! And I appreciate you giving THE Luca Romano my card. A campus wide email went out asking us to respect his space, but a secondary email went out to the School of the Arts basically asking us not to embarrass Hamilton University by throwing ourselves and our portfolios at him."

I giggled. "I get it. So, what I'm going to do is rave about my model and give him your card casually once he raves about the pictures here."

She grinned. "Perfect!"

"Okay, I have to head back to class, but thank you, Serena."

"No, thank you!"

Turning, I was only a little surprised to see Carlos standing a few feet away, watching me. As I approached him, I could see the way he searched my face.

"You walked off…" He pointed out as he fell into step with me.

"Well, I needed to find my subject. You seemed preoccupied with yours and I didn't know how long it was going to take." I had more bite in my voice than I intended, so I tried to soften my statement. "We're down to the last ten minutes or less, and we still have to upload and choose the best photos to submit."

"I spent more time waiting for you than I did with Ava."

It took everything not to roll my eyes. *Ava.*

"Did you get your shot?" I asked.

"Yeah. I thought it was going to be difficult to convince people to participate." He opened the door to the building, gesturing for me to go before him. "But looks like after they see the Romano name on the paper, it's easy."

"Did you say she was easy?" I asked, knowing it was in fact not what he said.

Carlos smirked knowingly. "I said it was easy to convince someone to be photographed."

"Oh okay." I looked away, a little irritated that he could see through my statement so quickly. "She was obviously interested. I had to walk away when she presented herself to you. Our society conditions women to instinctively present themselves as sexual objects to men."

"She didn't present herself as an object," Carlos pointed out as we approached the classroom. "She offered herself as an object. There's a difference."

"What?" I scoffed, secretly loving that he challenged me.

"There's a difference," he repeated as we walked into the classroom. "It's in the intent. You can be attracted to someone and want them to be attracted to you so you present yourself as desirable. You can be attracted to someone and want them sexually so you offer yourself to them in hopes of being desired." He winked at me. "I minored in Women's Studies, too."

I couldn't help that my lips turned up slightly. "My point is that she's beautiful—all women are physically, uniquely beautiful—so if she wanted you because she wanted you, cool. But I hope she didn't offer herself up to you because she thought she had to—" I stopped in my tracks. "Dammit!" I swore under my breath as I saw that almost everyone was back in the room.

"Come on. We still have time," Carlos assured me, placing a hand on my elbow as we rushed to the other side of the room.

"This one is free!" I spotted a student getting up from one of the computers and claimed it for us.

We quickly uploaded our photos onto the computer, dropping it in the Beautiful Woman Assignment folder. As we returned to our seats, I smiled.

"What are you smiling about?" Carlos asked.

"We just submitted our first assignment for this class. We submitted photos for Luca Romano to critique." My smile grew. "Life is good."

He stared at me. "It is."

I exhaled. "What's up with you? You keep giving me these looks and if we're going to be partners for the duration of this class, we need to make sure we're on the same page."

His eyebrows furrowed. "What do you mean?"

"I'm not going to let a man distract me from my goals."

"Who is trying to distract you?" He lifted his hands in surrender. "I was looking at you while you were talking."

"And you kept finding reasons to touch me…"

"Do you mean when I kept you from falling on your face or when I kept you from being hit by Ava's skateboard?"

Rolling my eyes to mask the uncertainty I was starting to feel. "Well, you also called me beautiful."

"You are."

He was so matter-of-fact about it that my lips snapped shut. I was quiet and so was he.

We just stared at each other as the seconds ticked by.

I cleared my throat. "Don't tell me you don't feel like there's a thing happening here."

"No, I feel something between us, but you're the one making a big deal about it. You must've been thinking long and hard about it. Must've been on your mind the entire class." He paused before winking at me. "But I don't mix business with pleasure."

"Don't do that." I shook my head and kept a straight face. "Don't wink at me again. Unless you have something in your eye or you're blinking, don't even close your eyes rapidly around me."

We both laughed heartily as Luca began class.

"Okay, now that everything has been submitted, you have made your introductions with your work. Let's talk about beauty." He flipped a switch, and the projection screen eased down. With a few clicks of a remote, a picture of a woman flooded the screen. She was older—with wrinkles and crow's feet. Her hair was a mixture of black and grey strands that framed her round face. There was a sparkle in her eyes that drew the focus.

"Look at the eyes," the photography legend directed. "Beauty is in the eye of the beholder. Beauty is in the eye of the photographer. And lastly, beauty is in the eye of the subject."

Nodding, I jotted that down in my notebook. Sneaking a quick glance at Carlos, I saw that he was also writing down the quote. There was something so sexy about his personality. My lips turned upward into a smile slightly before I looked away and continued taking notes.

For the next forty-five minutes, Luca explored the idea of beauty and how we limit it through our own filters and through societal definitions. He showed us various photos he'd taken of beautiful women and then he showed us the photos we had taken. Without disclosing whose photo was whose, he offered praise and a suggestion for improvement.

Turning the projector off, Luca walked around to the front of his desk and sat. "Now we'll conclude class with formal introductions." He looked around the room and smiled. "Everyone had to write an essay explaining why they wanted to be here. Of those submitted essays, a lottery was conducted to choose who would be offered a seat." He paused dramatically. "And here you are." He opened his arms widely. "You randomly sat beside your classmate who is now your partner for the duration of this workshop. But as we will find over the course of the semester: nothing is random."

I could feel Carlos's gaze on me, but I kept my eyes forward. Biting the inside of my cheek, I kept myself from smiling. Unfortunately, there was nothing I could do about the butterflies in my stomach.

"Your partner is the person that will push you to be better," Luca continued. "Look at your neighbor… part of your grade will be influenced by this person." He clapped his hands and rubbed them together. "So, let's find out who you are."

He began the introductions on the other side of the room. As people introduced themselves, I discreetly pulled Serena's card out of my bag without disrupting Luca engaging with students during their introductions. Once I had it in front of me position where Luca couldn't miss it, I leaned back in my seat with a satisfied smile.

"What are you doing?" Carlos whispered.

"Minding my business," I retorted, pursing my lips with sass.

He smiled. "Oh, I thought maybe you were thinking about how there's something here." He gestured between us.

"It was…until you winked," I murmured under my breath, trying not to get caught talking. "Now you've lost all your allure."

"You're not a good liar."

I grinned at him. "We have a connection and I brought it up

because I think it'll help us work well as a team for this course. But I wasn't saying it like I was trying to date you."

"I wasn't either."

"You're not a good liar."

He smirked but said nothing.

The connection between us was undeniable and the energy we exchanged was electric.

"Last, but not least..." Luca called out, interrupting the moment and breaking the trance I was in.

I tore my eyes from Carlos to find our teacher glowering in our direction.

"Tell us your name, your occupation, and why you're here," he directed, folding his arms across his chest.

Damn! I cursed internally as I rose to my feet. *Now he's going to think I'm some kind of rude, disruptive slacker. Maybe I can redeem myself...*

"Hi, my name is Akila. I'm a freelance writer. I'm a fan of your work and a fan of photography so being here is an honor. My hope is that I can capture the essence of what I write and tell a story with my photos. And I can only learn that from a legend."

"Very nice, Akila." Luca's eyes lit up as he flashed me a pearly white smile. "Very nice, indeed. I've read an article of yours, and it's excellent. I look forward to seeing that passion in your photography."

My cheeks heated under his approving words.

Carlos cleared his throat. "I'm Los. Right now, I teach high school English—ninth grade. But I'm working on my first book of essays and building my online brand. I'm going to be posting original content, including pictures, and I'm here because if I'm going to put out the best, I need to learn from the best."

Luca nodded. "Good, good." He paused. "I've listened to your podcast. Very entertaining."

"I love podcasts! What's the name of it?" The man sitting next to Jennifer called out from across the room. Everyone's interest seemed piqued.

Luca gestured to Carlos to respond.

He ran his hand over his beard. "I co-host a show called Date Night."

"What?" I gasped horrified. My stomach plummeted.

Carlos gave me a weird look before he told the class where to follow The Lost Boys on social media and how they raise money for some cause.

I couldn't hear him clearly over the sound of my mind being blown.

"Are you kidding me?" I hissed under my breath as soon as the photography powerhouse moved on to conclude the class.

"What?" Carlos appeared completely oblivious.

"I just…" I shook my head, glancing at Luca to make sure we weren't being overhead. "I guess I had you all wrong."

"What are you talking about?" Carlos asked, just as chairs started scraping against the floor and students started packing to leave.

"I have to go." Standing, I grabbed all my belongings. "I have to go."

He didn't say a word.

Chapter Four

The long bubble bath, calming candles, and soothing music didn't clear my mind of Carlos Richmond. So, when my best friend came home, I told her everything. The conversation resulted in us sitting in stunned silence on the couch.

"He was perfect…" I murmured with a shake of my head. "He was perfect for me. Or so I thought."

Another three minutes of silence descended upon us.

"Wait a minute… this is him?" Meghan asked as she poured over online photos she found on Carlos's social media pages.

I nodded.

We sat side by side on the couch, but she still dramatically jerked her body forward, turning her head from her phone to me and back to her phone again. "This is your photography partner?!"

I looked over my best friend's shoulder and eyed the picture of Carlos that was on the small screen. Dressed in a pair of jeans and a plain white shirt, he was casual yet sexy as hell. Whoever took the picture captured the smile that had turned my insides into mush when I saw it for the first time.

"Yep. That's him," I sighed.

She let out a sigh of her own. "Wow… He's sexy."

"Yep."

"And you two had a crazy connection?"

"Yep."

"And there was definitely a moment?"

"Yep."

"And he's part of The Lost Boys?"

"Yep."

She cocked her head to the side as a new picture of Carlos speaking in front of a group of students appeared on her screen. "Is he a teacher?"

"Yep."

"So, he's a sexy, educated, creative, passionate man who gave you butterflies and called you beautiful?"

Letting myself slump back into the couch cushion, I closed my eyes. "Yes."

"Are you sure he's a Lost Boy?"

"He's the one they called Los Cabos."

"Wow."

"Yeah."

The front door opened, and I barely peeked between my lashes to see my little sister fly into the room. I heard her footsteps stop abruptly.

"What's wrong?" Alexandria asked, forcing me to open my eyes all the way.

My lips parted, but words never passed them. I shook my head in confusion and disbelief. "Everything and nothing at the exact same time."

"What?" Her eyes bounced from me to Meghan and back to me again. "So, is anyone going to tell me what's going on? I'm starting to freak out!"

"You know how your sister always says she's waiting to feel that magic with someone," Meghan started before looking at me to see if I was going to speak.

I dramatically closed my eyes and let my head drop in shame, so she continued.

"Well, she felt the magic tonight."

"With who?" Alex squealed. "Luca Romano!"

"Well, that's another story." Meghan bumped my shoulder with hers and laughed. "But while there may have been a mutual attraction with Luca, she felt the magic with this guy."

"The magic? Oh, damn!"

I opened my eyes in time to see Alex marveling at the physical godliness and model good looks of Carlos Richmond.

Meghan nodded. "Damn is right."

"The fact that he looks like that was secondary," I sighed. "What got me was the fact that he had this energy about him. It was peaceful and alluring, strong and comforting, sexy and confident. I was attracted to him even before seeing how attractive he was—does that make sense?"

"Not really," Alex mumbled, still clicking through the few photos Meghan had found on the internet. "Because anybody with eyes can see that he is attractive. There's no way you can look at him and not see that he's sexy."

Meghan nodded. "Amen to that."

"So, what's the problem?" Alex asked. "He didn't like you back? He has a girlfriend? He's married? He chews too loud? What could possibly have you acting like this after feeling magic with this man?"

"He's a Lost Boy," I answered, feeling confusion wash over me again.

It was such a disappointment. The man I met was intelligent, kind, respectful, passionate, and he didn't openly objectify me or any other woman that I could tell. He was the opposite of everything I'd heard in that podcast.

"He's a 'lost boy' as in he doesn't know what he wants to do with his life?" Alex wondered.

"No, he's a Lost Boy as in he's one of the assholes who does that dumb ass weekly podcast giving out dumbass advice to dumbasses around town," I griped.

"He's a Lost Boy? He…" Alex pointed at the screen. "He's a Lost Boy?"

"That's not a boy, that's a man," Meghan commented, shaking her head.

I laughed on the inside, but I was still too stunned to laugh out loud.

"How did you end up falling for a Lost Boy?" Alex asked as she made her way across the living room and into the kitchen.

My eyes widened. "I didn't fall for him," I said quickly, denying the claim vehemently. "I-I had a mild interest, but clearly, that was a mistake, and the interest subsided."

"Okay…" Alex turned around and looked at me. "It doesn't sound like the interest subsided." She lifted her hands and backed her way toward the refrigerator. "But I just walked in. What do I know?"

I narrowed my eyes at my little sister. "Exactly. Why are you here?"

She laughed before taking a sip from the bottle of water she grabbed. "I have a date tomorrow, and I wanted to know if I could borrow something."

"Of course—"

"From Meghan," she continued.

Meghan laughed. "What do you need?"

"That red dress with the cut-outs on the sides." She clasped her hands together in prayer. "Pleaseeeee!"

Meghan took a screen shot of the image on her phone before rising to her feet. "I don't know, Alex. I love you like you were my own little sister, but that dress is one of a kind."

"I know! That's why I wouldn't ask if it wasn't a special occasion," Alex replied, a slight tremble in her voice. "Your style is impeccable, and that dress is such a statement piece. I don't have anything that has the same wow factor. I met this great guy who has a pretty cool first date planned, and I want to wow him. Please."

My sister knew how to lay it on thick. I'd seen the same tactics work on our parents for twenty-one years, so I knew my best friend was going to relent as they made their way down the hall toward her bedroom.

"Who is this guy and where is he taking you?" Meghan asked before they disappeared from my sight.

My phone vibrated, and I pulled it from my pocket. When I

opened the message from Meghan, Carlos Richmond's photo filled my screen. Even though my stomach twisted, and my body heated with the memory of the way he touched me and held me close, my head hurt, and my heart sank at the memory of the most recent Lost Boys podcast.

Pushing myself off the couch, I felt like I was going to be sick.

"Goodnight!" I yelled as I entered my room, closing the door behind me.

I heard their muffled response as I climbed in bed.

A few minutes passed, and my mind was still racing. I was exhausted, but I couldn't get Carlos out of my head. It didn't make any sense that someone who was so captivating and appealing to me was somehow also a supporter of misogyny and fuckboy-ish ways.

"Akila?" Alex called out as she lightly rapped on my door. "Kiki?"

"It's open," I replied, turning on my side as I pulled my sheets up to my chin. "What's up?"

Alex cocked her head to the side and stared at me. "Are you okay?"

"Yeah, just tired." I eyed the garment bag in her hand. "I see Meghan gave in to your pleas."

She smiled. "I love her. She's the nice big sister. You're the grump."

I let out a short chuckle.

Her lips spread wider into a grin. "There's that smile. Are you still thinking about Carlos?"

"No," I lied, not wanting to get into it.

"You're a horrible liar." She took a step into my room and leaned against the wall. "But I have a question for you... you had no idea when you met him and talked to him that he was a Lost Boy, right?"

I shook my head against the satin pillowcase. "I honestly had no idea."

"So, if the man you met was essentially the perfect guy for you—"

"I never said that!"

"Meghan said it." She paused. "And your reaction said it."

I rolled my eyes but didn't say anything else.

"Like I was saying… if you met him and you felt the magic, maybe you should have a conversation with him about it. What did he say when you asked him about it?"

"Well… I didn't."

"You didn't say anything to him about it?" She laughed. "That's not like you. At all. You have something to say about everything."

Groaning, I pulled the comforter over my head. "Go home-eeeeeee."

She giggled. "Kiki…?"

"I didn't really have a chance. I was mad. So… I just kind of… stormed off and left."

"So, you didn't even ask him about it?"

"What was there to ask?" I questioned, frustrated since I'd had the exact same conversation with Meghan an hour earlier.

What were they missing?

"He is on a show that told a guy that if a woman is wearing a low-cut top, she must want her breasts stared at, and to openly stare. What else is there to know about him?"

"Yeah, that's pretty shitty. But he didn't say it, so you should at least ask him why he's on the show."

I sighed. "Yeah, I will. I mean, I'm stuck with him for the rest of the class so…" I shrugged, pulling the covers from my head. "I kind of have to."

"Kiki…" Her voice was soft and sounded eerily like Mom as she used the family nickname for me. "Just hear him out. You described that guy you went out with last week as nice. You said you had a nice time with a nice guy. You called him nice looking. And while that's very…nice. You said Carlos was like magic."

"Alex——"

"Magic, Akila! Talk to him. You called him magic."

"I said there was magic between us, not that he was magic."

She shrugged. "Same thing."

"Like I told Meghan, it's not that I don't plan to talk to him. I will next week. I have to. He's my photography partner so I can't avoid him. Some of my assignments and therefore the overall impression I'll leave on Luca Romano depends on it. But as far as the magic goes, there's nothing else to talk about with it. He's a Lost Boy, and I'm a grown ass woman. There's nothing magical about that combination."

"That's true. But you didn't know about it until he told you, right?"

"Luca asked him about it and he said the name of the podcast. He never really told me specifically. He announced it to the class like it was something to be proud of." I closed my eyes. "I was just so mad, I couldn't speak."

"You were mad at the fact that he was a Lost Boy or were you mad at him?"

I was quiet for a moment. "Well… I guess, both."

"Why?"

"Because he…" My voice trailed off. "It's hard to explain."

"He didn't lie to you, did he?"

Letting out a rough sigh, I shook my head. "Can we discuss this tomorrow?"

"Of course. Love you, Kiki."

"Love you, too, Alex."

She shut the door behind her and I heard her footsteps make their way down the hall.

As I settled against my pillows, I tried to clear my mind. But Carlos had gotten under my skin and I couldn't shake it.

I was mad at him. Even though I wasn't lied to, I felt like I had been. Even though I wasn't tricked, I felt like the rug had been pulled from under me. I was mad that he was exactly the type of man I could've seen myself falling for. I was mad that he had drawn me in, and somehow, he got his hooks into me. I was mad that he seemed one hundred percent himself. I was mad that he made me feel something for him. I was mad that he made me like him. I was mad at him.

I tossed and turned for hours until I had to confront the truth that kept rattling around in my head.

I wasn't mad at him. I was mad at myself.

I almost fell for the enemy.

The phone vibrated loudly against my nightstand and I startled awake. I wasn't sure when I'd fallen asleep, but I knew immediately, I hadn't gotten enough of it.

"Hello?" I answered the phone groggily.

"Hi!" a voice chirped in response. "May I speak with Ms. Akila Bishara, please?"

Rolling onto my side, I cleared my throat a little. "Speaking…?"

"Good morning! This is Luna Daniels with Re-Mix Magazine. How are you?"

I sat up straight. *Luna Daniels?!*

"Hi, hello!" I cleared my throat, attempting to make myself sound more cheerful than I had when I answered the phone. "I'm well! How are you?"

"I'm fantastic. Thanks for asking." She paused for just a second. "Akila… beautiful name, by the way."

"Thank you."

"So, we called you in for the interview because we read your writing samples and articles and knew you were a gifted writer. But what we were looking for was a series proposal that would wow us." She paused. "And your proposal did just that!"

Kicking my feet against the pillowtop mattress, I silently released all the pent-up tension and nerves that invaded my mind and body from the moment she'd said her name.

Re-Mix Magazine likes my work—correction loves my work!

"Akila?" Luna's voice cut through my silent celebration and I realized I hadn't spoken a word out loud.

"Oh my god," I squeaked, scared my level of excitement would turn her off if I let it all out at once. "I-I'm-I don't know what to say but thank you. Oh wow! I appreciate the opportunity to submit my work and then to find out that you loved it. You loved it! I'm just— I'm speechless. I'm just…wow!"

Luna laughed lightly. "Good to know! I thought I had lost you there for a minute."

"No, no, no, no, no," I giggled, shaking my head profusely even though she couldn't see me.

"I wanted to call and personally invite you to the second interview with me on Friday. Full disclosure, there are only two candidates that we are moving to this round—you and another. I don't usually meet with candidates until the final round, but the notes I received from your interview warranted me meeting both of you myself."

"Oh wow." I didn't know if that was a good thing or a bad thing. I was flattered to be moved to the next round, but knowing the other candidate was also just as impressive was daunting. "Thank you."

She told me she'd email me the information and we said our goodbyes.

"Oh my god!" I whispered, nerves and excitement making my stomach flutter. And then it hit me. My dream job called to invite me for an interview. Flailing my arms and legs, kicking my bedsheets from my body, I squealed, "This is it! Oh. My. God!"

Leaping out of bed, I scrambled out of my room and down the hall. Knocking on Meghan's door, I only momentarily waited until I heard her respond before pushing my way in.

"Apparently, I killed my interview with Re-Mix because they called me today!"

Without missing a beat, Meghan immediately started a celebratory dance with her wig in one hand and her brush in the other. "Ahhhhhh!" she screamed, jogging in place and waving the red hairpiece above her head.

I grinned at my best friend. "I know!"

"I thought you said you didn't do your best at the interview. Tell me everything!"

"I thought I could've done better. I definitely didn't think I was going to get a call back! I thought—I thought I was okay, but I didn't feel like they liked me. I thought I was too eager, too excited, too much, I guess."

"You're never too much for the right people," Meghan pointed out with her sage wisdom.

I clasped my hands together. "Amen!"

Meghan turned to face the mirror as she slid her wig onto her head. "So, let's recap for a minute. You came home from the Re-Mix interview and ate the rest of my ice cream as you lamented about the interviewers not liking your ideas. You questioned and doubted your ideas and your abilities. And now…" She pursed her lips. "Mmm hmm."

Covering my face, I let out an overwhelmed giggle. "I don't know what is even going on right now!" I slid my hands down my face and to my chest. "I knew they took the interview because they liked my writing. But the position is for a series writing position that could turn into a permanent staff writer position if the series is popular. I pitched two original ideas and they looked at me like I was insane. No one reacted like I thought they might. I referenced my most recently published work in the Richland Times Dispatch and…nothing." I shook my head in disbelief. "I really thought they didn't like it, Meghan. I really thought I'd blown the interview."

"See… you never know how you're going to be blessed."

"That's not even the best part." I paused, watching her brush her hair. "The magazine's CEO and Editor in Chief called me herself."

Spinning toward me with her hair flying around her, Meghan's mouth was agape. "Oh my god!"

Dancing, I spun around in a circle. "Luna Daniels called me herself! Luna Daniels wants to meet me! Ahhhhhhh!"

"Ahhhhhh!" Meghan shrieked as loudly as I did. "Kiki! That's your role model! That has to mean you have the job!"

Reality stopped my celebratory dance in mid hip thrust. "Well…" I made a face. "It's between me and another person. Luna basically said that she loved both of our ideas, so she was going to meet with both of us on Friday and see who she likes better."

"Wipe that look off your face! You are going to go in there and kill it. The other person is good, but you're better. So, on Friday, you're going to go in there and have her fall in love with you. You know why? Because you're Akila muthafucking Bishara!"

A small laugh escaped me as I exhaled. "You're right." I shook off the nerves. "You're right."

"Say it like you mean it!"

"You're right!" I repeated myself, louder and more forcefully.

"Say it again!"

"You're right!"

After one final glance in the mirror, she walked over and put her hands on my shoulders. "You got this."

I wrapped my arms around my best friend's waist, careful not to wrinkle her pristine work attire. "Thank you for the pep talk."

She squeezed me back. "You're welcome. Now, I have to run because someone moved my two o'clock meeting to ten o'clock."

My eyebrows flew up as I glanced at the time. "What?"

"Yeah…" She stretched the word out as she grabbed her handbag. "So, I won't be stopping for coffee this morning."

"Well, that sucks. But hopefully the meeting will turn into a huge project."

"Yes. Fingers crossed. Because sitting in my office playing this dumbass trivia game is getting old."

I laughed, following her down the hall, toward the front door. "Yes, because if I have to decline one more invitation to play Trivia Time, I may have to just go ahead and move out."

Cackling with laughter, she said goodbye.

Chapter Five

---

*R*e-Mix Magazine was housed on the second floor of the Empire Building at Empire Park. Known as a hub of creativity and artistic expression, the Empire building was a creative person's sanctuary. The first floor was comprised of art classes, writing rooms, small offices, studios, and performance spaces. The second floor was Re-Mix Magazine.

Owned and operated by Luna Daniels, Re-Mix Magazine was an East Coast staple in the artistic community. There wasn't a creative person from Virginia to New York that didn't know about the seventeen-year-old entrepreneur who started her own magazine and grew it to be a powerhouse in ten short years. Luna Daniels wasn't just the woman with whom I had an interview, she was who I aspired to be.

My interview was in less than twenty-four hours and I needed to calm my nerves. It was a gorgeous day, so even though I'd hoped for a quiet park experience, I wasn't surprised by the amount of people exercising, playing, and enjoying the feeling of fall being around the corner. People roamed the small park enjoying the beautiful day. But I sat motionless on the park bench late Thursday afternoon and took it all in.

Staring at the building, I prayed, hoped, and wrote for hours. I was in the zone, and it wasn't until I finished tweaking my series idea for my follow up interview that I realized the sun was starting to set. With the notebook resting in my lap, I inhaled deeply.

I was ready.

Rays of light cascaded around the building and heated my skin. I felt like I was basking in the glow of a new season. Autumn was in the air and a new opportunity was on the horizon. For the longest time I just sat there, taking it all in. I wasn't just ready for the interview, I was ready for my new job.

I got this. I scanned the park before letting myself relax into a huge smile. *This job is mine.*

"Look out!" a man yelled from somewhere behind me.

Instinctively, I flinched, covering my head. A football hit the back of my bench and I yelped, jerking my body in an attempt to take cover. My notebook flew in one direction, my phone and pen flew in the other. Even though my eyes were closed, I heard the pounding footsteps of someone approaching from behind. I heard a man's voice, but I couldn't make out what he'd said because of the sound of the blood rushing in my ears.

"You scared the shit out of me," I growled with my eyes still closed as tightly as my clenched fists.

"Sorry about that. Are you okay?" he asked, his voice causing my heart to skip a beat.

My eyes flew open.

Even though his head was down as he picked up my belongings, I knew who he was before he looked up at me. The deep, gritty voice that stroked each word with the care and concern of an English teacher while still managing to speak to the most intimate parts of my body could only belong to one man.

"Akila?" Carlos said my name with a surprisingly soft tone. His facial expression showcased his surprise, but his tone said something else. There was something about the gentle way his smooth voice wrapped around my name that made it sound like he was talking to himself but calling out to me.

"Carlos." I silently prayed he didn't notice the slight hitch in my voice as I said his name. Clearing my throat, I tried speaking again. "What are you doing here?"

Still crouching down in front of me, he handed me my belongings. His white t-shirt stretched over his broad shoulders and his muscular arms, and I did everything in my power not to notice. I was attracted to his aura, his mind, his voice, his face, and his body.

Dammit, I cursed to myself. He was the entire package.

An indescribable look darkened his brown eyes and nerves fluttered in my belly. I shifted my weight from one side to the other as I waited awkwardly for him to answer me.

Stop staring back at him, I silently coached myself as I took a deep breath. *Shake it off and end this whole conversation before you embarrass yourself.*

Ignoring the desire that churned between my legs, I opened my mouth to tell him that I was just leaving. But when he wet his lips and I caught a glimpse of his tongue, that yearning deep within me caused me to have a temporary lapse in speaking ability.

For the first time, he flashed those pearly white teeth into a full-blown smile. I fought the urge to smile back.

Wow, I thought as I bit the inside of my cheek.

I had to rip my eyes away from him in order to keep myself from getting too caught up in the feelings he brought out of me. It was a dangerous mix of desire, lust and familiarity. It was the kind of feeling that snuck up on me and gripped me tight.

"Thank you," I murmured, pretending to wipe the nonexistent dirt and grass from my notebook so I could collect myself.

"And to answer your question, Date Night records in a studio here."

My eyes darted to his and narrowed. Everything stopped. The butterflies he'd given me disappeared. That warm feeling he filled me with ran cold. And I remembered why he was off limits.

"Wow," I scoffed. I was mad at myself for forgetting who he really was in the first place. Shaking my head, I muttered, "I can't believe I forgot."

He didn't say anything. He just remained kneeling before me, watching me in that way of his.

My stomach flipped under his gaze.

I don't like him, I lied to myself as his stare pierced through me.

I couldn't withstand his gaze any longer. "I can't believe you're a part of that trash," I muttered, curling my lip in disgust.

"Trash?"

"Yes. Trash. Any podcast that thrives on the objectification of women is trash. Any man who goes on air and promotes the objectification of women is trash. And the fact that you're on it says a lot about you."

"The show is a stepping stone and I'll admit, it's a little crass, but I wouldn't call it trash. And I don't objectify women." He paused. "Why would you think that?"

I sat back against the bench and maintained eye contact. Remembering the exact words I used from their podcast in my article for the Times, I cleared my throat. "'All women who wear lowcut shirts are doing it so that we can check out the fun bags.' And that's a direct quote."

"Oh… I know what you're talking about." He shook his head. "That's not a direct quote from me. But I do know what you're talking about and I'm not going to defend it. He was out of line. But not all the shows are like that. Live shows can go wrong quickly, but he understands that he can't say that anymore."

"You and your friends promoted the objectification of women." I made a face. "Obviously the show has been doling out problematic advice for a while now. And if that wasn't bad enough, his wack ass called breasts fun bags. He's obviously trash."

He stared into my eyes. "I don't know what Bryant was thinking. He was out of line. He was—wait… is that why you ran out of class like that?"

I didn't say anything.

"Do you think I objectify women? Did you think it was me who said that?"

I shrugged. "I know that it came from a show you're on, so even if you didn't say it, you support it."

"No." He stood. "You're not going to lump me in a…"

Holy shit.

I was eye level with the most impressive dick print I'd ever seen in my life.

My heart thumped against my chest with reckless abandon and my face felt flushed. A desire deep within my core stirred dangerously as I saw the outline of his dick against his grey sweatpants.

As Carlos lectured me, my eyes darted around the park. I looked everywhere but at him. I was embarrassed that I noticed it. I was embarrassed that my body noticed it. I was embarrassed that he would figure out that I noticed it. Focusing on the beautiful building in front of me, the lush green of the park, or the random joggers jogging, I ignored Carlos Richmond with everything I had in me.

"...Are you even listening to me?" Carlos barked, jolting my thoughts back to his words and my eyes back to his. "You're looking all around and—you know what? Think what you want, Akila." He stormed off.

My words were lodged in my throat and I couldn't speak. My mouth opened and closed as he walked away from me without another word.

Turning on the bench, I watched his back as he retreated. He didn't look back at me once, not even when his friend pointed at me and said something. He just continued walking until he disappeared around a large decorative fountain.

When I was no longer able to see him, air rushed from my lungs, and I struggled to catch my breath. Swallowing hard, I quickly gathered my belongings. I rose to my feet and felt unsteady. Discombobulated, I tried to shake off what I'd seen and what I'd felt.

"I need to get it together," I muttered under my breath as I started walking toward the Empire Building. "I have an interview to prepare for."

It wasn't like I'd never seen a dick before. I didn't understand why I was reacting as if it was the first time. My throat felt like it had closed. My heart raced and my skin tingled. But even more concerning, my brain seemed to have misfired as well. I wasn't able to speak, and I couldn't remember hearing a word Carlos said.

My phone vibrated.

"Oh my god," I whispered even though no one was around to hear me. "Meghan, can you hear me?"

She paused. "Are you at the library?"

"No, I—"

"Then why are you whispering? I can barely hear you!"

"Hold on." Looking around, I took off running in the direction of my car and didn't stop until I was safely inside with the car started. Breathing heavily, I put the phone against my ear again. "Hello?"

"Hey…?" Meghan stretched the word out into a question. "Is everything okay?"

"No, I don't—I don't know. Um…" I let my head fall against the headrest and closed my eyes. "Shit…shit shit shit shit shit."

"What's going on? Breathe!"

I sucked in a huge breath and then let it out as gently as I could. Even though my panting had started to subside, my heart was still racing. "Carlos," I huffed.

"Carlos from your photography class?"

"Yeah." I put my free hand over my heart until it calmed down.

"So…? What happened? Did you see him? Did you talk to him?"

"Yeah." I swallowed hard. "I told him that his show and his friends were trash. I think he probably assumed I thought he was trash too because of the company he keeps."

"Oh wow!" A shocked laugh echoed on the other end of the line. "I can't believe you said that."

"Why not? You would've said it, too!"

"Yeah, but if I'm forced to work with him for the rest of the semester, I would've waited until the last assignment was turned in." She laughed. "You're still partnered with him and you called him trash."

I groaned. She was right.

"Well, shit." I sighed, realizing how easily he got under my skin. I wasn't usually reckless, but Carlos just brought something out of me.

"Yeah…" Meghan stretched the word out in agreement. "You need to be able to get along with the man if you're stuck with him for the next few weeks."

"I know. I just got so irritated."

"Where are you? Did you decide to go to the University instead of the park to prepare for your interview?"

"No! He was here! At the park!"

"Really? Wow, small world."

"Well see, that's the thing…" I started, my mind drifted to thoughts of him in those sweatpants. "There was nothing small about it."

"What?"

My eyes widened. *Did I say that out loud?*

"What?" I responded quickly.

She laughed. "Are you okay?"

I shook my head and groaned again. "No, I'm not. I'm sorry. What did you say?"

"I said it was a small world," she repeated slowly.

"Oh yeah, it is. And come to find out, Date Night records at the Empire Building."

"What?"

"Yeah. So not only do I have to see him in photography class, if I get this job, I might see him in the lobby or in the park."

"When you get the job."

I smiled at her correction. "When I get the job, I'll run the risk of seeing him, and I just need to minimize my contact with him."

Meghan laughed.

"What is so funny?" I huffed indignantly.

"I'm sorry, but this man has gotten under your skin and I've never seen you like this before."

"I've never seen you like this before," I mocked her, imitating her voice and making her laugh harder. I tried not to smile. "I can't stand you right now."

"He is in your head."

"No, he's not!"

"Akila! You like him."

"Meghan, I hate him," I argued, sounding like a child.

"No, you don't," she laughed heartily.

Whining, I squeezed my eyes shut, trying to block out the image of his gorgeous face, his muscular body, and his impressive dick print. "No, I don't hate him, but I want to."

"Awww… I know you do." Her tone was pacifying, yet amused. "Poor thing."

"Why did he have to be…?"

"Charming? Intelligent? Educated? Handsome?" she offered, filling in the blank.

"…part of The Lost Boys!"

"His one fatal flaw."

"That we know of."

"You're right. Because he could have a weak sex game or a small dick."

My mouth became dry as the thought of sex with Carlos caught me off guard. I licked my lips and muttered to myself, "It's definitely not that."

"What?" Meghan squealed. "What was that?"

"Uhh…" I stalled, not sure what to say without losing my ground.

"Did you have sex with him and forget to tell me?"

"No, of course not."

"Then when, where, and how did you see his dick?"

And as if the words couldn't wait to escape my mouth, I blurted out everything that happened. When I was done, I took a breath. "They say the devil comes to you as everything you want, and lo and behold." I paused, staring in the direction that he'd left. "How dare he?"

"Yeah," Meghan agreed. "How dare he be everything you ever said you wanted in a man?"

"Except for the fact that he is one of The Lost Boys."

"Sounds like he is the full package," she deadpanned.

My jaw dropped, and the giggle rolled out. "What is wrong with you?"

"Did you hear what I did there?"

I tried not to laugh along with her as I shook my head. "You are the worst friend and comic in the world."

"Oh, come on! It was funny!"

"Was it?" I asked with a chuckle.

"Whatever. It was hilarious! Anyway, you have a *big* day ahead of you tomorrow. This opportunity is a *long* time coming. You have to make a good *impression*."

Every time she emphasized a word, I laughed harder.

Wiping the tear that had formed in the corner of my eye from laughing so hard, I sighed. Letting my giggles completely subside, I took another deep breath. "Thank you."

"Feel better?"

I smiled. "I do."

"Good. Unexpected big dicks are a pleasant surprise, but put Big Dick Carlos out of your head and finish getting ready for your interview. We have a job to secure."

Laughing, I said goodbye and we got off the phone.

Rolling my shoulders back, I drove out of my parking space. I knew I had to deal with one thing at a time, so I blocked out everything except for the fact that I was meeting Luna Daniels in the morning and I needed to be prepared.

"Goodbye, Re-Mix. See you tomorrow," I whispered after another deep breath.

I got this. I can do all things.

Sixteen hours later, I was in the same parking spot outside of the Empire Building. Wearing black pants, a sheer black shirt, and a red and black blazer, I felt sexy and powerful as I strolled into the building. I made a beeline for the elevator and blocked out thoughts of Carlos and The Lost Boys as I heard voices, music, and other noises behind the closed doors I passed. I didn't even want to look around. I had to stay focused. I knew if I saw the studio—or Carlos—I wouldn't be at the top of my game, so I kept my head up, my eyes trained on the elevator, and my heart steady.

I got this.

I let out a deep, calming breath as I hit the button for the second floor.

I can do this.

I stared at my reflection in the chrome doors of the elevator as I rode to my interview. Repeating my mantra silently, I squared my shoulders and I slipped into a power pose. I looked strong. I felt strong. I was ready.

I can do all things.

I exited the elevator car with a purpose. My red pumps clicked the marble tile floor as I approached the circular desk.

Smiling warmly at the adorable, grey-haired woman, I calmed my nerves. "Hi, I'm here for an interview with Luna Daniels."

"Your name please?" she asked.

"Akila Bishara," I announced with more confidence than I truly felt.

With a smile, she nodded. "Have a seat. She'll be right with you."

Five minutes later, a fashionable dark-haired beauty emerged from down the hall.

"Good morning, Ms. Bishara. I'm Luna Daniels," she greeted me with a smile and an extended hand.

Rising to my feet, I took her hand and shook it confidently. "Hi, Ms. Daniels."

"Call me Luna." She gestured for me to walk beside her and I fell in line.

"Oh, okay...Luna." I smiled to keep myself from freaking out. "Thank you for meeting with me."

Our heels clicked in unison as we walked down the hallway to an office at the far end of the hall. Once we were in her office and seated at opposite sides of her desk, Luna reclined back in her chair. We sat in silence for the longest minute of my life.

"I won't take much of your time. You already went through the long interview, so this is more informal. I just want to talk, get to know you, and see how you fit with the vision I have for my magazine. So, tell me a little about you."

I told her about graduating summa cum laude from Hamilton University with a double major in Creative Writing and Journalism. I told her how I aspired to write in a way that moved people and made them think. I told her that she was a personal hero of mine and that I'd been reading Re-Mix since it published. I even told her that I was so dedicated to my writing career that I took a photography seminar in order to take my own photos to accompany my writing.

She nodded along with me. She smiled and laughed when appropriate. She seemed impressed and commented on the information I was telling her. It felt more like a conversation than an interview and at some point during the dialogue, I no longer felt like I was talking to Luna Daniels, powerhouse, boss, CEO. I felt like I was talking to Luna, my friend.

Until she moved papers in front of her and gave me a serious look.

My heart sank instantly.

"I knew you were a good candidate," she started. "That's what makes this hard." She shook her head slowly as she picked up a pen and tapped it against her papers. "I want you to know that I kept going back and forth with my decision."

I swallowed hard and fought back the tears that pricked my eyes.

Oh…

Preparing myself for the worst, I exhaled slowly and watched her face. The silence that hung in the air felt like my future dangling on by a thread. It was in that moment that I realized how much I wanted that job and how much the opportunity meant to me. I knew I would do almost anything to get it.

"First, let me say…" Luna broke the silence slowly, drawing out the suspense. "Your stuff is really good. I loved it!"

Unable to contain the grin that eased onto my face, I took a second to bask in her praise. "Thank you." The words came out in a rush. "Thank you so much."

"I was going over the notes for your proposal ideas, and I love them both so much. But as I was reviewing this"—she handed me a copy of my article that ran in the Lifestyle section of the Richland Times— "something really stuck out to me."

I glanced at the article and then back at Luna, trying to play it cool. "Oh?"

"This is the direction I want for the series." She pointed her sharp nail at the printed article. "The passion, the wit, the personal touches. This is just what the magazine is looking for in a series writer. For our magazine, a series writer isn't just a columnist, but a storyteller. A conveying of information that is personal and relatable. And what you did here is compelling."

"Wow, thank you so much." My cheeks burned with happiness as I listened to her praise.

"This right here is a perfect introduction to a new series writer. This could be the hook that draws people in—not just for the series, but for you as a regular…"

As I watched her mouth moving, I felt like I was going to burst with excitement. My breathing became slightly erratic as I tried to contain my joy. My muscles were tense as I held everything in that was screaming to leap out of me. It sounded like she was saying what I thought she was saying, but I just needed her to say the words.

"…great opportunity! So, here's what I'm proposing for you…" She stood and walked around her desk to a large table in the corner. Grabbing a folder, she took a seat next to me. "I want to offer you the position of series writer but under one condition."

I knew I was going to say yes, but to not sound desperate, I asked, "What's the condition?"

"I want to pair you with the other candidate. I want to put you both in situations and get both of you to write your unique perspectives for the series."

My eyebrows lifted as I waited for the rest of what she was going to say. "That's it?" I asked slowly.

Luna laughed. "Yes. That's it."

"Oh!" I laughed along with her. "I was just expecting your condition to be along the lines of 'work for free' or something else devastating like that."

She shook her head. "No, no, nothing like that. This is a job, the salary you discussed during the first interview is still valid. I didn't turn this into an internship position." She chuckled to herself. "I just know the job description indicated that the position would be for *a* series writer. But I think the collaboration of two different perspectives will be a better fit for my vision. So, while I believe you are talented, this is the direction I want to take my series, so you agreeing to work as a team on this series is contingent on it."

Nodding profusely, I exclaimed, "Yes, I'll do it! Of course, I'll do it!"

"Great!" Luna handed me the folder.

"I met with the other candidate this morning just before you arrived, and they should be finishing up the tour. I want you two to meet before everyone leaves."

"Do I have to write with them or…?"

"No, not at all. You two are going to be put in the same dating environment and then write about the event based upon your particular experiences. The articles are going to run side by side, spanning two pages."

I nodded. The idea sounded good—great even. I just couldn't get the little thought that niggled at the back of my mind.

What does this mean for the permanent position?

I didn't want to get ahead of myself, but I had to know.

"I'd love to meet them," I commented, mustering up the courage to ask what I really wanted to know.

With a smile, she gestured for me to follow her to the door. "Come with me. We'll get you two introduced and then I'll let my team take you on the tour."

I stood and crossed the room. "But I have a question… during the interview, I was under the impression that the position could turn into a permanent one. Because there's two of us, is that still an option?"

Luna smirked. "You are definitely a go-getter, Akila. You remind me of myself." Once I reached the door, a couple of feet from where she stood, she continued. "To be honest, I don't know. We'll have to see how the series pans out."

I nodded. "Understood. I'm happy for the opportunity and if it turns into something permanent, I'd be ecstatic. But working on this series with Re-Mix and working under you for however long I have the opportunity, I am appreciative."

She put her hand on my shoulder and giggled. "No need for all of that. You already got the job."

I laughed as I followed her out the doorway. "I'm serious!"

A thin, blonde woman was easing into the room at the end of the hall. Suddenly, having a flashback to my original partner from photography class, I prayed.

Dear Lord, please let the other writer be someone I get along with. I need this job, and I need this opportunity, so please let the other writer be someone that I work well with. Please Lord. Please. Amen.

"Ann!" Luna called out to the blonde.

Ann turned around and smiled. Waiting for us at the door, she waved. "Hey, Luna!"

Once we got to her, Luna gestured to me. "Ann, this is our newest member of Re-Mix, Akila Bishara. Akila, this is Ann Carson."

I reached out to shake the blonde's hand. "It's nice to meet you, Ann."

"It's great to meet you, too! I look forward to seeing you around the halls of Re-Mix."

"I look forward to working with you," I replied, relieved to meet such a warm person.

Luna beamed. "Akila will be the other series writer."

"Oh! That's you! That's awesome," Ann exclaimed with so much sincere excitement and glee that I felt my cheeks heat. "That's such a fun idea. It's going to bring a lot of extra traffic to the magazine."

"I'm really looking forward to it," I admitted. "And after meeting you, I'm even more excited to get started on our series."

Ann's head tilted slightly, and confusion squinted her eyes. "Oh, no. I'm Luna's assistant. We just finished the tour and your series collaborator is in here."

Luna giggled. "I'm so sorry. I didn't realize… I apologize." She shook her head and looked at Ann. "I told her we were going to meet her co-series writer and then I introduced her to you. That's completely my fault."

Pushing the door open, Luna walked in the room, followed by

Ann. I pulled up the rear and as soon as I was fully in the office, I froze.

My jaw dropped as I stared.

"Akila, this is your series collaborator … Carlos."

Chapter Six

My eyebrows flew up and I watched Carlos blink rapidly as recognition hit him. He rose to his feet slowly. Even though the thick, dark hair of his beard covered his jaw completely, I could still tell it was clenched as his eyes narrowed.

"Akila Bishara, let me introduce you to your co-series writer—Carlos Richmond. Carlos, this is Akila," Luna Daniels introduced us with bubbly excitement.

I didn't know what to do. I didn't know how to react or respond. My mouth opened, but words didn't come out.

"Hello, Akila," Carlos greeted me with a forced smile.

Squaring my shoulders, I decided that since he didn't bring up our meeting, I wasn't going to mention it either. "Hi, Carlos," I replied, stretching my arm out stiffly.

The moment my hand slid into his, my heart skipped a beat.

Luna looked between us. "Do you know each other? Have you two met?"

"We're in a photography seminar together," I answered.

Looking into my eyes, Carlos elaborated. "But we don't really know each other."

His words cut deeper than expected.

Tearing my eyes from his, I looked at our new boss and smiled.

"Richland is such a small city sometimes," she mused, giving us both a skeptical look. Turning to her assistant, she continued, "Ann, get them settled in here. I might as well go over the assignment with them both and then you can take Akila on the tour." She checked her watch. "Get them beverages, I'll be right back."

We sat on opposite ends of the conference room table and after Ann handed us bottles of water, we were left alone.

I looked around at the framed editions of Re-Mix that decorated the room. I lasted a solid sixty seconds before my vision felt pulled in his direction.

Don't look. Don't look. Don't—oh shit.

He was staring directly at me.

Correction, he was glaring at me.

It was penetrating.

His brown eyes almost glowed with the intensity and my breathing hitched when our eyes met. The energy between us was electric even if the glances between us were hostile. As soon as my heart started to flutter, I reminded myself of who he was.

"What are you doing here?" I hissed, trying to ignore the feeling he gave me.

He waited a few seconds before speaking. "Building my brand."

"The aspiring author brand or The Lost Boys brand?" I asked with narrowed eyes.

He shook his head. "You are not at all what I thought."

Giving him a pointed look, I lifted an eyebrow. "Neither are you."

His perfect mouth formed a hard line. "And what's that supposed to mean?"

"It means that when I met you, I met Carlos—a funny, charming, driven, insightful high school English teacher and aspiring author. Then I find out that you're actually Los—a member of a problematic group of trash spewing frat boys. It means that I thought you were…"

Perfect.

Well, no one was perfect. He wasn't perfect. Even before I knew what he really was, I knew he wasn't perfect. But I'd always imagined that the man who made my heart flutter, my body react, and my mind spin would be perfect for me. And clearly, the man who did those things to me was indeed not perfect for me.

I rubbed my temple in frustration and opted not to complete my sentence honestly.

"You thought I was what?" he questioned softly.

I licked my lips, trying to think of something to say. Opening my mouth, I began, "I thought——"

Luna Daniels burst back into the room with two folders.

Startled, I shifted my attention to the fashionable woman.

"My two new series writers." She handed me a black and gold folder and then handed one to Carlos. Sitting at the center of the table, she grinned. "I'd planned to give you both this summary after your individual tours, but since you already know each other, I think it's better to give you an overview together."

I looked down at my folder and felt my lips turning upward. Even though I was thrown off my game by having to work with Carlos, I was thrilled to work at Re-Mix.

"The idea behind the series was actually inspired by something you submitted, Akila," Luna turned to look at me. "Your work and your series ideas were incredible. You're a strong writer with a strong point of view so I knew you'd be a good fit with the magazine. But what inspired my idea was Akila's piece for the Times regarding being single in the city. In it, she referenced Date Night with The Lost Boys as the antithesis of the quality dating experience. So, I listened to a couple of podcasts of Date Night and found their point of view to be…"—she quirked an eyebrow— "interesting, to say the least. And then it hit me."

Turning to Carlos, she smiled. "I researched and found out you guys record downstairs and asked if you would be interested in a unique opportunity…"—she turned to me and smiled— "To be honest, I didn't expect them to be as eloquent as they were, but Carlos… his work rivaled some of the official submissions we'd received."

I glanced over and noticed him beaming with pride. It took me a few seconds to realize I was smiling along with him. When our eyes met, I looked away.

"So, believe me when I say this... this assignment was created for the two of you," Luna declared with excitement and certainty. "Open your folders."

The first thing I saw when I opened my folder was the printed version of my Times article. The next piece of paper was a flyer for a Singles Trivia Night at Pop's Bar.

"You two are going to write about your experiences at different area hangouts. It's going to be more than just singles in the city. It'll be a reflection of how technology has altered how people communicate in person. It'll be a peek at what it's like to put yourself out there and interact with people outside of dating apps and social media."

"So, we're going on dates?" Carlos asked.

"With each other?" I quickly followed up for clarification.

Did I sound funny when I said that? I mused as I avoided eye contact with him.

"No, no, no. You two won't be dating at all. You will be socializing. You two will be writing the articles for the series completely independent of one another. I don't want you two to have even read the other's pieces until after it's submitted and published. It will be two completely individualized experiences centered around the same event. It'll be two fifteen-hundred-word articles featured side by side." She paused dramatically, holding her hands in the air in front of her. "He Said, She Said."

"Sounds like a lot of fun," I admitted, cautiously glancing over at him.

"What about you, Carlos?" Luna asked, grinning his way.

"I'm in. I think it'll be good to have two different perspectives." He flicked his eyes to me before adding. "Wouldn't want a one-sided account of what's happening."

"Now, now... let's save it for the articles," Luna chastised playfully. "A difference of opinion is going to be great for readership." She nodded. "This is going to be great, I promise."

"Oh, I believe you. I'm just a little surprised since I'm just now seeing Ms. Bishara's article and the line where she describes The Lost Boys as 'peddlers of toxic masculinity' stuck out."

The corners of my mouth turned upward. I was quite proud of that line. "It's a great line."

There was fire in his eyes. "Paints an unfair and untrue picture of The Lost Boys."

"I disagree."

He paused, shifting his gaze briefly to Luna before adding, "As an English teacher I can admit it's a great line."

"Noted." Not wanting to appear to be the difficult one, I added, "And my assessment was based on one show in particular. I'm sure there are less crass episodes that I hadn't gotten to yet."

He ran his hand over his beard. "Maybe if you took your time and fully researched, it would add validity to your article, and you would have a better idea of how to characterize The Lost Boys."

My lips parted slightly, but I stopped my jaw from dropping. *Did he just question my research abilities and the validity of my work? Did he just call out my work in front of Luna Daniels?*

We silently glared at one another.

"What's this?" Luna looked between us. "What's going on here?"

Rounding my shoulders, I flashed a smile. "I think my word choice may have offended The Lost Boy Los, but I promise it won't interfere in our work."

"If anything, it'll make our work better," Carlos chimed in with a charming grin.

I smirked. *I'm in your head, Carlos.*

I ignored the fact that he was in mine as well.

Luna eyed us with amusement. "We're going to see how this first article goes and then we'll make adjustments as needed."

She went over some other important details and Carlos and I remained silent. We didn't say anything else to one another for the rest of the meeting.

He was the definition of aggravating. From the way he defended the garbage his show promotes with a deep, sexy rumble in his voice, to the way his beautiful, brown eyes had so much passion even though the rest of his handsome face was expressionless. Because I'd seen him relaxed, I could tell there was tension in his shoulders even though he appeared to be calm. I had gotten under his skin. Even though my article was the truth, the fact that he had the audacity to be offended by that truth rubbed me the wrong way.

"Okay, Carlos, you are free to go. I know it's early in the semester and your students are probably missing you. Thank you for being able to come in this time of day." Luna turned to me. "Akila, Ann will take you on your tour of the office now. I'll bid you adieu once you return."

I nodded. "Thank you."

My eyes shifted to Carlos, who was already staring at me. Exchanging visceral glances behind our new boss's back, neither of us said anything. Holding the door open for Luna, Carlos followed behind her and exited the room. The moment the door closed, I finally felt like I could breathe again.

I was irritated at him, but I was even more irritated at myself for being affected by him. Fortunately, Luna seemed more amused by our dynamic than anything, but it could've easily gone the other way. The energy between us was electric when we first met, but even more so in the conference room. I was lost in thought when Ann walked in to show me around.

My tour was quick, and I met a few people, but I didn't remember anyone's name. It was all a whirlwind and by the time I got to my car, the only thing I could do was cry.

I landed my dream job. My dream fucking job.

Drying my eyes, I started my car and drove home. I was happy —overwhelmed but happy.

"Did you get the job?" Meghan asked as soon as she answered my call.

The tears filled my eyes again as I maneuvered through the light mid-morning traffic. "Yes! Yes! Yes!!"

"Oh my god!" She squealed before lowering her voice and repeating herself. "Oh my god!"

"I know!" I giggled giddily.

"You did it!"

Checking my blind spot, I moved to the fast lane and sped up. "I work at Re-Mix!"

"You work for Luna Daniels!"

"I work for Luna Daniels!" Letting out a scream, I swiped at my eyes. "I'm so happy. I'm crying right now. Tears of fucking joy!"

"Hold on, I'm going to leave my cubicle and go to the bathroom because I want the full story," she whispered. When the noise around her got further away, I heard a door close. "Okay, tell me everything."

"Well…" My hands tightened against the steering wheel and I sighed. "I'm the co-series writer. And you will not believe who I'm sharing the position with."

"Uh oh, that was a mood shift," she commented with a little laugh. "Who?"

"My new arch nemesis."

Meghan giggled. "Who? That lady in your photography class that basically told you that you had a big ass?" She laughed harder. "Like that's a bad thing!"

I would've laughed if what I had to say didn't fill me with anger and other emotions. "Carlos," I told her. Even saying his name made me feel a certain way.

Her laughter died instantly. The dramatic gasp on the other end of the line was over-the-top, exaggerated but exactly what the moment called for. "What?"

"Yes." I nodded, even though she couldn't see me. "Carlos."

"Photography class Carlos?"

"Yes."

"Dick print Carlos?"

"Yes!"

"Oh my god!"

"Right? I'm not overreacting, right? It's crazy, right?"

"Oh. My. God."

"I know!"

"Akila," she sighed, and I could almost hear her shaking her head. "Crazy doesn't even begin to describe it."

"That's not even the craziest part. Luna didn't go with any of my proposal ideas. She was inspired by that article I wrote for the Times about being single in the city. She wants to do a series called 'He Said, She Said' and have two different opinions of the same singles' events. She reached out to The Lost Boys because of what I wrote and got a writing sample from Carlos. The idea is to have two completely different points of view."

"That's actually a really cool idea."

"I know. I love the concept of it and how she plans to roll it out over the next month. If she likes the first one, she has three more planned for the online magazine and if they do well, a big spread in the actual magazine."

"I hear you saying it's a good thing, but your voice sounds like… I don't know. Do I hear a but coming?"

"Luna had a copy of the Times article in our folders and Carlos saw the stuff I said about The Lost Boys." Flashing back to the look he gave me, I let out a dry laugh. "He wasn't pleased, to say the least, and he actually defended the show. He defended who they are and what they said. And then he called me out for basing my whole anti-Lost Boys viewpoint on one episode."

"Oh shit, he called you out?"

"Yes!" I exclaimed, increasing my speed and changing lanes. "And this is the crazy part… Not only did he call me out, he did it in front of Luna. And he was so articulate with it that if I wasn't sitting there feeling the energy he was giving me, I would've taken it as constructive feedback and not the professional well-played attack that it was." I took a deep breath. "We're co-series writers because it's called He Said, She Said. But once the series is up, she's likely only keeping one of us around to do other series. So, to have him question my writing in front of our boss just infuriated me even more."

Meghan let out a low whistle. "Oh wow…so not only are you two working together, it's kind of like you're competing against each other as well?"

"Pretty much." I exhaled roughly. "And lest we forget, I still have to be partners with him for our photography class."

"That's so crazy."

"I'm going to ask for a new partner. I shouldn't be forced to work with him in both my professional and personal life." My voice was elevating with each word, and I knew I sounded unnerved, but just thinking about Carlos Richmond twisted my stomach into knots. He literally made my stomach hurt. "I don't like him."

She mumbled something that I couldn't quite make out.

"Huh?"

She giggled. "Just take a deep breath and calm down. You are going to be fine."

"I guess so." Realizing how fast I was going, I checked my mirrors for police and decreased my speed. "It just sucks because even though Luna raved about me, she raved about him too, so her decision could go either way."

"Aw man, I'm sorry. But hey, think about it this way, you were selected and hired for the position. She only contacted him because she was inspired by your work. She's basically doing He Said, She Said because of you, and she reached out to The Lost Boys because you referenced them. So, it all comes back to you."

"True. But still, it could go either way. There are no guarantees."

"I don't think you should worry about that at all."

"I'm just going to focus on writing my best work and whatever happens happens."

"Exactly. What's meant to be will be," she agreed. "But what I want to know is how did it feel to see him?"

"I don't like him."

She paused for an extended period of time before sarcastically replying, "Okay."

I huffed indignantly. "What's that supposed to mean?"

"The lady doth protest too much, me thinks," she teased, quoting Shakespeare.

"Whatever, I'm serious. He's an ass and I'm not into assholes. Stop laughing!"

"Okay, Akila."

I was trying not to be amused by the way she said it. "What are you trying to insinuate with your tone?"

"You're trying to convince me, your best friend in the entire world, that you're not at least attracted to the good looking, smart, gainfully employed, ambitious, big dick having man that you admitted made you feel magic."

My stomach twisted again. "I'm not attracted to him." I swallowed hard. "That's exactly what I'm saying. I don't like him."

"Even though you never say you feel the magic with anyone?"

"Okay, you know I felt the magic before I knew he was part of The Lost Boys!" I threw a hand up in frustration, smacking the steering wheel. It was like she was purposefully forgetting the most damning thing about him on purpose. "You heard the podcast, Meghan! And on top of that, the stunt he pulled in front of Luna Daniels makes us mortal enemies!"

"I understand that being the reason you don't want to date him, but…"

"But nothing!" I argued, although I was curious as to what she was going to say.

"Okay."

"Okay then." I pulled into my parking spot and then let out a loud wail. "I'm sorry. He just gets under my skin. What were you going to say?"

"If you don't admit that you're attracted to him, you are going to end up making a rash decision."

"What do you mean?"

"You said you were going to see if you can get another partner for your photography class. But on Monday when you found out he was a Lost Boy, you said you couldn't change partners."

"I know. We're not supposed to," I sighed. "I was going to explain the situation and—"

"Let me stop you right there," Meghan interjected. "You want to ask Luca Romano if you can change partners, even though he said you couldn't, because your current partner gets under your skin."

Letting my head drop back against the headrest, I closed my eyes and groaned. "I see what you're saying."

"Akila, like I told you on Monday…and Tuesday…and especially after the dick print incident on Thursday, if you don't admit your attraction, it's going to get the best of you."

I shook my head. I opened my mouth to deny it, but the words didn't come out.

"Think about it," she warned.

I could hear that she was back at her desk and her voice was lower than before.

"Talking about him is making my stomach hurt," I complained.

"And yet, the majority of the conversation this week has been about him."

I was quiet. She was right, and I didn't have an immediate response.

She continued, "You landed your dream job with your role model. You said Luna was great and that she raved about your work. And then you spent fifteen minutes talking about this guy you allegedly don't like."

"I was telling you about him because it was crazy that he is sharing the title of series writer with me." I hesitated uncertainly. "That's all."

"You can lie to yourself, Akila Bishara, but I know the truth. And if you don't admit it to yourself, you're going to drive yourself crazy. I don't want you to lose your job or fail your class because you can't admit that you're attracted to him and it ends up getting the best of you. It's already starting."

"I hear you."

"Now, I have to get back to work so I can send one email off before I take my lunch break. But I have one more question."

"What's that?"

Meghan waited a beat. "Did you see his dick print today?"

I did not expect that question.

"No!" I laughed. "What? No!!"

"I didn't know if it was pressing up against his khakis like it was his sweatpants."

I chuckled hard. "You are ridiculous! And he didn't even have on khakis."

"I bet you know exactly what he was wearing from head-to-toe," she teased.

"Whatever, no I don't."

He had on navy blue dress pants and a crisp, white button-up shirt that made his smug-ass smile even brighter.

"Yes, you do."

I groaned. "Yes, I do." Lowering my voice, I whispered, "What's wrong with me?"

"Once you admit it, you'll feel better."

"He's attractive," I sighed, quickly brushing it off. "There. I admitted it. It's done."

It was indeed, not done.

Chapter Seven

"*W*ith your partner, find a unique location so each of you can capture a photo of a sunrise and a sunset. Post your photos on our online database by Monday at five o'clock. Your next assignment will be posted shortly thereafter," I whispered aloud as I re-read my email after dinner.

Besides the knots in my neck, back, and stomach, the assignment from Luca Romano was yet another reminder that I couldn't escape Carlos Richmond. I considered burning some sage and clearing my space of negative energy but decided what I needed was to clear my body of negative energy.

Meghan had a date, and I had the place to myself for a little while, so I took advantage. Stripping off my clothes and stepping into the hot water of my bath, I slipped under the bubbles and focused on relaxing. With candles lit and the lights low, I concentrated on clearing my mind. The sage would've cleared my home, but smooth R&B, scented candles, and a bubble bath cleared my mind. By the time I felt truly relaxed and the frustration directed at Carlos subsided, my fingers were pruned. I rinsed off the bubbles in the shower and then padded down the hall wrapped in a towel.

I stopped when I thought I heard a noise.

"Meghan?" I called out when I didn't hear any movement in the apartment. I knocked on her door. "Meghan?"

There was no answer, so I pushed the door open and peeked in. She was still out.

I made my way back to my bedroom and quickly dressed in a pair of short shorts and a tank top. I felt better. After being emotionally all over the place, I finally felt like myself again. No fretting over if I would land my dream job. No anxiety about meeting my career role model. No spine-tingling lust mixed with anger-induced frustration courtesy of Carlos Richmond. I was feeling refreshed—until my phone vibrated.

"Speak of the devil," I muttered as I saw the name flashed across my screen for the first time.

My hand shook a little as I opened the text message.

Carlos Richmond: The Riverfront. Tomorrow.

Akila Bishara: For the assignment?

Carlos Richmond: Yes.

He didn't even have the common courtesy to ask. He just told me what to do and expected me to follow suit. I didn't have anything in particular to do on Saturday, but I didn't want to give him the satisfaction of telling me what to do after the stunt he pulled.

Akila Bishara: I have plans. Sunday.

Carlos Richmond: Fine.

Dropping my phone on the bed, I marched out of my room and into the kitchen to grab a bottle of water. I felt the tension in my neck and shoulders, but most notably in my gut.

Deep, deep in my gut.

Although I had the most relaxing bath, just receiving that text message from Carlos aggravated me to my soul.

Why am I letting him get to me like this?

Exhaling loudly, I returned to my room and climbed in the bed. The silky sheets welcomed me and as soon as my head hit the pillow, I gave in. It had been a long week. I was exhausted carrying the enormity of my dreams and expectations mixed with everything else. Since the work week had come to an end, I felt like sleep could do me some good. Closing my eyes tightly, I tried to ward off the unwelcome thoughts. But I was too tired to fight it.

Carlos was sexy—probably the sexiest man I've ever seen in my life. But he was not the kind of man that I would fall for. The day we met was an anomaly. My attraction to him stemmed from that first ninety minutes. His energy, his passion, his wit captured me first. His eyes, his smile, and his determination captured me next. His protectiveness, his intelligence, and his physical attractiveness sealed the deal. But from the moment I learned that he was one of The Lost Boys, everything changed.

Groaning, I rolled over to my side. I felt the anger in the pit of my stomach as I pulled my sheets around me tighter. It wasn't like I wanted to be mad, but something about him triggered me. Maybe it was because I was tricked into thinking there was something between us. Maybe it was because he was part of a podcast that went against everything I believed in. Or maybe it was because the way he called me out in front of Luna was rude, arrogant, and completely uncalled for.

He sucks. His podcast sucks. His friends suck. I kicked my leg out and adjusted the covers again. *Perfect for me, my ass!*

I fell asleep angry and woke up to the sound of the front door closing. My eyes cracked open as I listened to Meghan's heels clicking on the hardwood floor. I barely held on to consciousness as the footsteps moved to the end of the hallway and then the bedroom door closed. Sighing, my eyes fluttered shut and instead of darkness, I saw grey.

But not just any grey.

I saw the grey of sweatpants.

I saw the grey of Carlos's sweatpants.

I saw the grey that covered the biggest imprint I'd ever seen in my life.

I shivered.

As sleep descended upon me, the tingle that ran through me couldn't be denied anymore. The anger that was coiled in my belly gave way to lust, rippling through the apex of my thighs. As my panties dampened, I tried to think about anything else. I couldn't stop remembering it. I couldn't stop imagining it. I couldn't stop wanting it. I couldn't stop fantasizing about it. I couldn't stop. So, I stopped resisting it.

That night, I had a graphic sex dream about Carlos Richmond.

I woke up sweating with my clothes twisted and my headscarf lost in my sheets. I moved through my Saturday morning errands, my mid-day movie with Meghan, and my dinner at Orange Blossom in a conflicted, anxious fog. All throughout the day, I shifted between unabashed irritation and unfiltered lust. Knowing I had to meet Carlos at the Riverfront at five o'clock in the morning was playing with my emotions.

"What is wrong with me?" I complained as I plopped down on the couch beside Meghan.

"Still hot and bothered?" she asked knowingly, frowning a little.

I groaned, covering my face. "I can't think about anything else."

She muted the Stephen King movie marathon she was watching. "His dick was that big?"

Laughing, I uncovered my face and shook my head. "No, I mean, yes. I mean, it appeared to be a good size, but that's not what I'm talking about right now."

She looked genuinely confused. "So, you're telling me that you're not dick-matized?"

I laughed harder as I swatted at my best friend's arm. "I should've never told you about his dick print!"

"You think not talking about it will make you any less dick-matized?"

"If anything, I'm traumatized." When our giggles subsided, I sighed and continued, "It's not about his dick at all. I mean, last night's dream was, but all day today, it's just been about him."

"Hmm."

"I can't get him off my mind."

"Hmm."

I stared at her with pursed lips. "What?"

"Do you think the reason you can't stop thinking about him is because you like him, and you two got into a little spat?"

"No," I answered quickly. "I think it's because I'm meeting him tomorrow for the assignment and then I'm seeing him on Monday for Singles Trivia, and it just hit me that I have so much of my life riding on being able to collaborate with him."

She nodded as she chewed. "I can see that."

"Our last couple of run-ins have been...rocky. I need to prove myself with both Luca and Luna and both require me to work with Carlos Richmond." I leaned forward, letting my head fall into my hands. "What are the odds?"

"It's one of those unrealistic chance occurrences that only happen in TV shows or movies." With a shrug, she added, "If I didn't know you, I wouldn't believe it."

"I know. A couple of weeks ago I'm complaining about The Lost Boys and how they are everything that is wrong with dating. And now my career and my personal goals are tethered to one."

"Sounds like fate."

"Good or bad?"

"That's the thing with fate... it doesn't matter if it's good or bad. If it's fate that thrust you two together, that means you two are supposed to be thrusting together."

"Shut up," I chuckled. "Why does it have to come back to sex with you?"

"Because you decided to take yourself off the market to focus on your work and accomplish your goals, and then here comes Carlos and his dick print giving you hot, sex dreams. Maybe you wanted to take a break from dating, but God sent in the big guns to get you out of the slump—literally and figuratively."

"Who said God sent him? This could be the work of the devil. The devil comes in many forms, right?"

Meghan rolled her eyes. "The way you described that dick print, that could only be the work of God."

"Amen to that," I murmured shaking my head.

"And besides, Carlos is a high school English teacher. He probably can't afford Prada. And we both know the devil only wears Prada."

Laughing, I grabbed a couple of kernels of popcorn and tossed them into my mouth. The knots in my belly loosened. "I'm just frustrated, I guess. And I wish he didn't get under my skin the way he does."

"You know why you're feeling like this, right?"

"Because Carlos is one of The Lost Boys and he represents everything I want to avoid."

Meghan placed the popcorn bowl on the coffee table and put her arm around me. "Yes. But you encounter people you don't agree with all the time. Why is he different?"

"Because." I shifted in my seat.

"Because what?"

I was silently staring at the television, ignoring the uncomfortable truth.

"Because what?" she repeated, shaking my shoulder.

"Because he didn't seem like a bad guy when I met him," I admitted, folding my arms across my chest.

"So, you're mad at him because when you met him you liked him."

"Yes," I grumbled quietly. "But it's more complicated than that."

Tilting her head and giving me a perplexed look. "Is it?"

"Yes," I answered.

"How?"

"Because he aligns himself against everything I've built my career on." I swallowed hard before looking into my best friend's eyes. "And I'm mad at myself for not seeing it sooner."

Meghan gave me a sympathetic smile. "Doesn't it feel better to get it off your chest?" She gave me a final squeeze before leaning over to get her popcorn. She tossed a kernel into her mouth. "Now you'll be able to sleep easy."

Even though I rolled my eyes, I smiled. The unease that hovered over me like a fog seemed to lift slightly. "You're so wise."

She nodded, unmuting the TV. "I am. You're right."

"Thank you. I do feel better." I rose to my feet, scooping a handful of popcorn as I stood. "I have to be up, dressed, and at the Riverfront by five o'clock in the morning, so I'm heading to bed."

"Goodnight! Sleep well. Wake me up when you get back."

Glancing over my shoulder, I gave her a smile. "I'll bring coffee and donuts and hopefully a pleasant story about how Carlos and I didn't get into a fight. Goodnight!"

Her giggle followed me as I closed the door to my bedroom.

Climbing into bed, I double checked my alarm, making sure it was set to wake me up in five hours, and then I forced my eyes closed. Focusing on my breathing, it didn't take long until I was resting peacefully. I felt like the talk I'd had with Meghan was going to help me sleep easier.

I was wrong.

Gasping, I sat up with a start. Beads of sweat gathered at my temple, just below my scarf. My skin was flushed and covered in a thin film of sweat, and my clothes were twisted from tossing and turning. My heart was pounding, but what concerned me more was the pulsating that was happening between my thighs. Maybe it was the self-imposed sex drought I was experiencing, but the dream about Carlos was hot, sexy, and vivid.

Well, damn…

I kicked the covers off me and stared at the ceiling. I put my hand on my chest and tried to slow my heart rate. Each time I blinked, I saw his smile or his eyes or that damned dick print. Taking deep breaths, I ignored the tightening deep in my belly.

I was a whole twenty minutes ahead of my alarm, but I decided to get up and take a shower anyway. Grabbing my vibrator, I put the extra time I had to use. I told myself I wasn't masturbating to Carlos. I'd planned to just take care of myself as I did whenever I was between boyfriends. But the moment the vibrator hit my clit, I thought of how soft his lips looked and how his hands felt when he grabbed me. By the time I imagined what his dick could possibly look like and how it might feel, I was shaking like a leaf in a storm.

After finishing my shower and getting dressed, I felt like myself again.

Maybe I just needed a sexual outlet in order to get my mind right.

I pulled on a pair of black leggings, white tank top, and an off-the-shoulder Hamilton University sweatshirt. It was so early that my sneakers squeaking on the hardwood floor as I left my apartment was the only audible noise. The birds weren't even up yet.

There was a slight chill in the air, but the forecast called for a gorgeous Sunday. Securing my camera in the backseat, I jumped in my car and headed to the Riverfront. I stopped for gas and a bottle of water. I was earlier than I had planned to be, but I wanted to play offense and not defense so I needed to get there before Carlos.

There was only one car in the parking lot besides mine. The white security jeep was in the corner and I let out a little sigh of relief. Grabbing my camera, I exited my car and made a beeline to the makeshift observatory. The elevated structure was where people would go to take aerial shots of their friends in canoes and kayaks on the river. As I eyed the sleeping security guard, I noted that it was also a prime location for a nap.

Clearing my throat, I started humming as I approached. "Hello," I greeted the recently awakened guard.

"Hey, hey, um good morning, ma'am," he stammered, jumping to his feet. "What are you doing up here?"

"I'm going to capture the sunset." Tapping my camera bag, I gave him a look. "What about you?"

"Making my rounds." He gave me a onceover before heading toward the steps. "Uh, this area is secure. If you need anything, I'll be patrolling the area."

"Thanks."

I watched and listened until he was halfway down the stairs, and then I positioned myself on the far edge of the deck. I couldn't see the parking lot, but I had a great view of the river, the trees, and the skyline. Only about ten minutes passed before I heard footsteps climbing the steps. I didn't hear a car, so I assumed it was the security guard.

"Hey."

The short grunt of a greeting made my head snap to the right.

Wearing grey sweatpants, a navy-blue zip-up hoodie, and grey and blue sneakers, Carlos made his way toward me.

Those damn sweatpants!

My eyes jerked up and I felt my cheeks heat. "Hey," I replied, staring at his face and nowhere else.

He silently checked his camera out and leaned against the railing, his back against the wall. I busied myself staring into the darkness, catching the flickering of light as it bounced off the water. On the way there, I'd thought of all the things I wanted to say to him. But as I stood in his presence, all I could do was wonder if he could tell I had a sex dream about him a couple of hours ago. Or that I'd masturbated to him an hour ago.

For fifteen uninterrupted minutes, we stood in complete silence. It was the longest fifteen minutes of my life.

"Everything okay up here?" the security guard asked as he appeared on the deck.

I was concentrating so hard on ignoring Carlos, I didn't even hear the guard walk up the steps.

"Yes," we said in unison.

"I assumed you knew each other since you both had your cameras out and said you wanted to take a picture of the sunrise," the guard continued, ambling over to us with a tired smile. "But whenever there's a young lady around my daughter's age involved, I make a point to make sure she's okay." He gave Carlos a look. "I'm only a call away, just so you know, young lady."

I just nodded. "Thanks, but he's fine. I'm okay with him."

"Okay. I'll be back. I'm going to check around the base, but I'll be back." The security guard gave me a thumb's up before he descended the stairway.

"I'm surprised you didn't tell him I was trash," Carlos muttered as he pushed himself from against the wall and moved toward the railing without looking at me.

I rolled my eyes. "I'm not trying to get you arrested."

He shook his head but didn't say another word.

Sixty agonizing seconds later, I sighed. "Listen, we have to work together for our photography and for Re-Mix. We can't have this tension negatively impacting our work."

"Like I told you at the park, you can think whatever you want." His face was hardened with determination. "But I'm not letting you or anything else interfere with my work."

I swallowed hard. There was something sexy about the way he emphasized his point. "I feel the same way."

"This is business—nothing more, nothing less."

"Well, I'm glad we're on the same page then," I murmured, tearing my eyes away from his.

"Doubt it," he scoffed. "But we'll make do because we have to."

"Doubt it?" My face scrunched up and I frowned. "What's that supposed to mean?" I shook my head after a brief pause. "You know what? Never mind. We'll work together when we have to work together and then when we're not obligated to work on an assignment or a story, we don't have to see or think about each other anymore."

He made a noise but didn't say anything.

"What?" I snapped, jerking my head his way.

"Nothing." He smirked as he lifted his camera to his face and took a test shot.

"What?" My voice came out more forcefully as I put my hand on my hip and glared at him.

"You said we didn't have to think about each other outside of when we work on our photography assignments and our articles." He gave me a taunting look. "Anymore."

Shrugging a little, I furrowed my brows. "Yeah. Exactly."

"So, it sounds like you've been thinking about me."

"What?" I screeched, recoiling. "No, I was—I wasn't...I said we only—"

"Everything okay up there?" the security guy called out from somewhere below us, interrupting my explanation.

My face was flushed, and I was happy for the interruption.

"Yes!" Gathering myself, I took my own test shots. "You're so full of yourself."

"And you're so full of shit."

"What?" My mouth fell open. "You don't know me."

"You don't know me either, but that didn't stop you from calling me trash."

I exhaled, lowering my camera from my face. "I never called you trash."

He turned his head, giving me a withering stare. "Yes. You did."

I shook my head. "I said your podcast is trash and the objectification of women is trash." Lifting my shoulders, I stared up at him. "I stand by that. But I didn't call you trash."

"You said my friends were trash and that if I hung out with them…" He let the sentence trail off like I had, and then he made a face.

"See… I didn't call you trash. I inferred that you were trash adjacent," I continued with a slight smile.

His mouth remained in a hardened line, but his eyes crinkled slightly. I could tell he was amused and that made me smile.

"Hm. Interesting," I coyly murmured as I put my camera to my face again and snapped a photo.

"What?" he asked.

"The trash comment was from when we were at the park?"

"Yeah."

"So, if that comment has been on your mind since I said it…" Tilting my head, I smirked. "Sounds like you've been thinking about me."

The corners of his lips turned upward even as he shook his head. "You are so full of yourself."

"And you are so full of shit."

"Woah, I walked up just in time," the guard interrupted as he strolled onto the deck. "Full of shit, huh? You two don't seem to like each other very much."

"Not particularly," I answered at the same time as Carlos was saying, "No, we don't."

Our eyes locked and something felt different. We both admitted to not liking one another simultaneously. We both verbalized it with the same tone and attitude. But there was no malice or disdain in our admission. As we stared at one another, I couldn't quite put my finger on what was happening. But it felt a little like mutual understanding.

As soon as the security guard left, the first hint of light started to break the night's sky. We stood side-by-side and silently snapped dozens of photos.

"I got my shot," I said hoarsely, finally breaking the silence.

"Good." He continued snapping photos.

"I'm going to head out."

He turned his entire body toward me, fully facing me. "I'll walk you to your car."

Suddenly feeling nervous, I adjusted the strap on my camera bag. "You don't have to."

"I know."

He fell into step with me and we made the short trek to my car. "This is me," I announced, slowing to a stop.

"Ok, cool." With just a solitary nod, he left in the direction from which we just walked.

"I thought you were leaving," I blurted out, shifting from one foot to the other.

Carlos turned around, but continued moving backward, away from me. "I never said I was leaving. I said I would walk you to your car."

Perplexed, my forehead creased. "But you didn't have to—especially if you weren't leaving yet."

"I know." Without another word, he turned around and continued to the deck.

I didn't know how to feel about that.

Chapter Eight

J stared at my reflection and second guessed my outfit again. The olive-green shirt looked excellent against my brown skin. The clingy material and plunging neckline was sexy and paired well with the dark denim jeans. I turned and stared at how the stretch of the jeans flaunted the roundness of my ass and the thickness of my thighs.

"Meghan?" I called out when I heard footsteps at the other end of the hallway.

I hooked my fingertips into the belt loops and pulled them up just as my bedroom door flew open.

"Oh, I like this!" Meghan gave me an appreciative nod. She leaned against the doorjamb in her casual purple dress, matching sneakers, and jet-black wig. "Do you feel more comfortable now?"

"Yeah." I nodded. "I felt too dressed up in everything else."

"Well, you've looked great in everything, so I don't want to assume anything, but... do we have a winner?"

I nodded, staring at my reflection. "Yes. Final decision." I turned to face my best friend. "I just didn't want to look like I was trying too hard."

And I didn't want Carlos to think I was getting dressed up for him.

"That necklace with that shirt is hot." She smiled at me. "And your hair looks so good like that."

My dark, tightly coiled hair was brushed into a high ponytail that sat on top of my head like a crown. My gold hoops and bracelet sparkled in the light. But the highlight was the small, gold chain that formed a T at the base of my neck before dipping between my breasts, almost to my belly button.

I wiped my palms on the thighs of my jeans. "Thanks. And you look amazing—as always."

"This is true," she sang, flipping her hair over her shoulder. "But I understand why you're nervous…"

It wasn't that I was nervous about seeing Carlos. It was just a little awkward thinking about seeing him in a dating environment. The idea of having to mix and mingle with him a few feet away, probably watching me, likely judging me, made me feel out of sorts. But it definitely wasn't because of Carlos himself.

I slipped into my black booties. "Yeah, it's the—"

"…this is your first assignment," she explained.

Hesitating slightly, I nodded profusely. "Yeah, the assignment. Exactly. That's it."

She gave me a bright smile. "You are going to have fun and you might even meet someone. That's why this assignment is so perfect for you. You're getting paid to write about these cool experiences around town that you might have missed out on otherwise. And on top of that, you might meet a man. And the cherry on top is that the man might be Big Dick Carlos."

"Can we just call him Carlos?" I groaned, masking my giggle as I grabbed my black handbag. "Or better yet, can we just forget he exists?"

"Yes, we can," she relented as we walked through the living room and out the front door. "But I have two questions."

"What's the first one?" I asked as I unlocked my car.

"Be honest… you looked at his dick print again, didn't you?"

Laughing, I revved my engine. "It was actually too dark when he arrived, so I wasn't able to see anything—not that I was trying to look, because I wasn't. And he was leaving when I arrived for the sunset photos."

"Mm hmm. Second question…"

My lips still curled into a smile, I pulled out of my parking space. "Yes?"

"If you both admitted you didn't like each other and then you didn't speak to each other for the rest of the morning, why do you think he walked you to your car?"

"I don't know. I haven't given it much thought." My sentence dissolved as Meghan giggled. My own chuckle made it difficult for me to get the whole statement out of my mouth. "Okay, okay, okay… I thought about it and I don't know. I got under his skin with the trash comment. So maybe he was trying to prove he's a gentleman since he thinks I called him trash."

"Well, he probably thinks that because you did."

"Like I told him, I said that he was trash adjacent."

She threw her head back and laughed. "That's hilarious! What did he say when you said that?"

I smiled, remembering the look on his face. "He was amused. He tried not to be, but he was."

"That's too funny."

"Right? There's never an audience when I think of good comebacks." I shook my head as I made my way to the other side of town. "Trash adjacent."

Pulling out her lipstick, Meghan applied the plum color to her full lips. "Even though birds of a feather flock together, we have to admit that there's a slim possibility that he isn't like his friends."

"This is true. But it's just as likely that he's exactly like them."

She lifted her shoulders. "True. But there's only one real way to find out." Grabbing my phone, she scrolled through various podcasts before finding The Lost Boys. "We listened to the latest one?"

"I think so."

"Oh, wait… there was one posted on Friday night. Have you listened to anymore of their podcasts?"

"No, just the ones that helped me come to the conclusion that they are trash."

She hit play.

After twenty seconds, she skipped the intro. We listened to them discuss what women need to bring to the table and the difference between a 'good woman' and a 'bad bitch' and of the two, which is worthy of a date. The podcast was more supporting evidence that The Lost Boys were as bad as their other podcasts painted them to be.

"I can't take much more of this. This episode might be worse than the other ones...and those were bad," I groaned.

It was clear that City Boy was the biggest jackass. Country Boy was a slightly less ridiculous version of City Boy, but he still agreed with most of City Boy's antics. Carlos, better known as Los Cabos, was the voice of reason. Although he still entertained the conversation and laughed at some of the jokes, he never outright said anything that was demeaning. But nevertheless, he silently participated in the degradation.

"Carlos isn't innocent, but I don't think we can lump him with his friends," Meghan stated, leaning to turn the volume down just as we pulled into the parking lot of Pop's Bar.

"Yeah, like I said... trash adjacent." I paused. "Although, I am glad he defended the girlfriend of the one caller who—what?" My mouth was agape, and my sentence came to a dramatic stop.

"*...written by A. Bishara that has been brought to my attention by one of our loyal listeners, KillerMiller1,*" *City Boy started, his voice rising with amusement.*

"Oh, hell no..." Meghan breathed, her hand covering her mouth.

Clenching my jaw, I braced myself.

"*What is this?*" *Country Boy implored, his deep voice full of faux curiosity.*

"*Apparently A. Bishara is blaming our show because she can't get a date,*" *City Boy yelled, causing Country Boy to laugh.* "*We said something that offended her delicate sensibilities, and now she's writing columns about how we are what's wrong with the modern man. KillerMiller1 attached the article, and he wants to know our thoughts on her calling us, and the men who listen to us,* toxic, misguided and communication deficient. Those were her exact words. She said that we feed bad advice to susceptible men!"

"Oh god, here we go," Country Boy muttered as he laughed. "Here we go!"

"Well, A. Bishara, we are not going to apologize that you can't get a date. That's not our issue. Maybe you have a stick up your ass and that's the problem. So, sure… we aren't always the most politically correct, and I already issued an apology for my unfortunate comments. But come on… don't make us the scapegoat for your personal problems, sweetheart."

"So, you think her issue with us is her lack of a man in her life?" Country Boy asked. "Because this doesn't sound like the complaints from last week."

"It's not. Those were complaints of the offended. This is the ramblings of a basic looking spinster chick—probably a three—who is lonely and is looking for someone to blame for her spinster lifestyle!" City Boy roared, riling himself up. "So, KillerMiller1, to answer your question, my response to A. Bishara is for her to get a life. I have more to say, but I'm going to just leave it there. Los Cabos is shaking his head and mouthing for me to stop."

"Los Cabos. Always the diplomat," Country Boy teased.

"What's the problem?" City Boy asked. "We are answering a listener's question about an article that talks about us. It's fair game."

"You already had to issue an apology this week. Let's just let this go," Carlos demanded firmly.

"Well, how about you respond, Los Cabos," City Boy propositioned.

"Yeah, let's let our diplomat speak on behalf of the council."

Carlos cleared his throat. "KillerMiller1, the official Lost Boys response is that A. Bishara is entitled to her opinion—albeit wrong, she's entitled to it." He paused before continuing, "I mean, look, we don't always agree with one another and some of the responses to listeners may toe the line, but we aren't peddling toxic masculinity. This show is for entertainment purposes only. That is our statement."

"Los Cabos has spoken!" City Boy let out a chuckle "That's our official word. But unofficially, A. Bishara still needs to get the stick out of her ass, and that's all I'm going to say about that. That's it! I'm done!"

Country Boy laughed. "Unofficially, her inability to get a man isn't our fault. Officially, no comment."

"Okay that's it for tonight. Tune in next week and we'll answer more of *your emails. We'll have two special guests that you won't want to miss. I'm City Boy——"*

"I'm Country Boy…"

"And I'm Los Cabos."

"And this is Date Night with the Lost Boys," the three of them said in unison.

I turned off the podcast and looked at my best friend. "Wow."

With wide eyes, she just stared at me in disbelief. "Did they really…?"

"They really did. The fact that they dedicated time to me on their show is laughable." I checked the time and then reapplied my lip gloss. Grabbing my keys, I slipped out of my car. "And it lets me know that I was right about them."

"It's no wonder that they keep their faces covered up in all their publicity shots. City Boy is going to get his ass kicked one of these days," Meghan stated, flipping her hair over her shoulder.

"Absolutely." I agreed as we made our way to the front door of the bar. "But you know what this means, right?"

Wiggling her eyebrows, she answered, "That you're getting free publicity and that's going to make you even more successful."

I stopped in my tracks. "I didn't even think about that." Laughing, I started walking again. "I was just thinking about how I know there are people who agree with me who listen to their show. Hopefully they will start holding The Lost Boys accountable as well. And maybe the Date Night listeners who didn't see their toxicity before, will see it now and will be more mindful of the way they talk to and interact with women."

"And also, you're about to get a lot more eyes on your work ahead of your first Re-Mix article!"

I dug my ID out of my bag as we approached the door. "They may have thought they were calling me out, but they were calling attention to my future articles and to the toxicity of their messages."

Moving her shoulders to the music, Meghan nodded. "This is a win, win for you. Screw them. I can only imagine the stuff they would've said if Carlos didn't issue their official response."

I rolled my eyes. "Carlos is a piece of work."

As we entered the moderately crowded bar, she asked, "How do you feel about what Carlos said? It sounds like what he said when you guys were at Re-Mix."

"Exactly." I nodded as I scanned the room. "So, I still feel the same way. Just because he walked me to my car doesn't change anything."

Lowering her voice as we headed to the team tables, she continued, "I don't know how to feel. He didn't talk shit about you like Country Boy and City Boy did, but he didn't defend you either."

"Trash adjacent."

She looked at me. "Are you okay though?"

"Absolutely." I winked at her.

"Cool. I'm going to be at the bar while you work."

"You look hot," I confirmed as she struck a pose.

"As do you." She blew me an air kiss and then strutted away.

I went to the sign-up sheet and found a group that didn't have five people yet. After writing my name, I grabbed a nametag and looked for the Sharks. Turning I nearly collided with the man rushing by.

"Oh, I'm so sorry," he apologized, face twisted in horror. "I didn't get anything on you, did I?"

Glancing down at my outfit and then back to his handsome face, I smiled. "Nope. Nothing got on me."

His eyes quickly swooped up and down my body. "It would've been a shame if I messed anything up. You look incredible."

I smiled. "Thank you."

"I would shake your hand, but…" He held up the three drinks in his hands. "I'm Mark."

Mark had shoulder length dreadlocks that were neatly pulled back into a ponytail. His pearly white teeth flashed brilliantly against his mahogany skin tone. He was a few inches taller than me. And with his slim build, snug fitted button-up shirt, and thick rimmed glasses, he was giving me nerdy vibes. And I liked it.

"I'm Akila." I pointed to his nametag. "You're on the Daily Double team, I see."

"I am. But had I known you were coming, I would've left my friends behind to become a Shark."

I laughed. "Well, now I'm your competition."

"We have five minutes until we start Singles Trivia. If you haven't signed up, there are still a few teams who need players," a woman's voice carried over the hum of the relatively busy bar. "Five minutes!"

"I need to find the Sharks," I mentioned, looking around for people with similar nametags.

"You're actually at the table next to me. My friends and I have a team and then two other guys. Follow me." He leaned over and whispered, "Let me know if you want me to kick one of the guys I don't know off the team and replace them with you."

I giggled. "I don't even know if I want to be on your team." I quirked my perfectly arched eyebrow. "How do I know you aren't dead weight?"

He chuckled. "You're right. But hopefully I can prove to you that I'm an asset and not a liability." Pointing to the table to my right, he continued, "These are the Sharks."

I looked at the table of two men, two women and smiled. "Hi!"

"And this is Daily Double."

I looked to my left and my face froze momentarily.

"Guys, this is Akila. She's a Shark," Mark introduced me to his friends before pointing to a pretty, petite woman with large eyes. "This is Tess." He hesitated when he pointed to the last guy. "And this is… I'm sorry, man. What's your name again?"

"Carlos," I blurted out, my entire body on edge.

"Hello, Akila," Carlos replied, sitting back in his chair.

"You two know each other?" Mark asked.

Staring into the depths of Carlos's eyes, I rolled my shoulders back. "No."

The mostly male Daily Double team reacted with "damn" and "oh shit" as I made my way to the only empty chair at the Shark table.

Unfortunately, it was directly facing Carlos.

I sat down and introduced myself to my team. They added my

name to our answer sheet and we made small talk. After explaining to my team that the Daily Double team was howling because I declined to join them, I happened to look up.

My stomach flipped.

Licking his lips and shifting in his seat, Carlos was staring directly at me.

Oh shit.

When our eyes locked, I felt it deep in the pit of my stomach. Our attraction to one another was undeniable, but I thought since we clearly didn't like each other, it wouldn't be so intense. But even after everything that had happened, there was something about him that my body couldn't deny. Somehow, even after listening to him and his friends, he made jeans and a perfectly fitted white polo shirt look like the sexiest outfit in the room.

But it was more than that.

A buzzing noise grabbed my attention and I focused my energy where it belonged—on the game.

"Welcome to Singles Trivia Night at Pop's Bar! I'm your host, Ellie, and we are going to kick off this fresh new event with a few ground rules. There will be two rounds. Only people playing can answer the questions, so those of you at the bar, keep your answers to yourself. First round, you write your answers down. Second round, the top three teams compete by buzzing in. And if need be, there will be a tie-breaker, and the best and brightest will compete for world domination." She paused. "Just kidding. First place prize is a twenty-five-dollar gift card for each member of your team. Now just be mindful that everyone playing Singles Trivia is single, so make sure you're scoping the scene. It's clear that everyone over here looks good...but who has the brains to match? Are you ready?"

I smiled at my teammates. "I'm ready."

Ellie hit a button that made a loud, buzzing noise. "The first round is a good one... Music from the nineties!"

Everyone cheered.

Regardless of age, everyone seemed to appreciate the music from the nineties.

"Question one," Ellie began. "Smells Like Teen Spirit was by who?"

"Nirvana," the older brunette with the pixie cut answered quickly before writing down the answer. She looked up. "You agree, right?"

Excitedly, we agreed.

"Question two…Who burned her football player boyfriend's house down?"

"Lisa 'Left Eye' Lopez," I answered in unison with the adorable Shark next to me.

"Question three is a little harder," Ellie teased. "A Whole New World was featured in *Aladdin*. But which singer joined Regina Belle in making that song a classic?"

"Peabo Bryson," I whispered excitedly. "My mom loves him."

Ellie continued, "Question four… Which song warned you to sleep with one eye open, gripping your pillow tight?"

"Enter Sandman," I blurted out, hearing the song Alex learned on guitar when we were kids. "Metallica."

The brunette with the pixie cut nodded even though the others looked unconvinced.

"Question five…" Ellie yelled out. "A rap star lost his battle with AIDS in the nineties…"

"Oh, it's the dude from NWA," the adorable teammate whispered, closing his eyes. "Easy E!"

Ellie continued, "…He was known as Easy E. What's his real name?"

The tone and shift in the room was immediate because the questions were definitely getting harder.

Leaning forward, I grinned. "Eric Wright, Easy E."

"Question six…" Ellie's voice boomed over the microphone. "Not many people go from drummer to front man and lead singer, but this nineties artist did it. He happened to be part of two different iconic bands that ruled the nineties."

"It could be a lot of people," the quiet Shark fretted, running his hand through his hair. "I watched this thing about Sheila E the other night. I don't know."

"Is it Travis Barker?" the brunette wondered.

I had no clue.

"Dave Grohl," the brunette gasped. "It has to be."

"Oh! Yes! Yes!" the quiet Shark agreed, nodding profusely.

My team cheered, slapping each other's hands and bumping fists, and we almost missed Ellie dole out the next question.

We answered question after question, feeling confident as we approached the last of twenty. Ellie's scorekeepers came around and collected all the answer sheets and then calculated the winning scores. Even though those who didn't move on to the next round were able to mix and mingle, I was having a good time with my team. Also, my competitive spirit was thriving in the environment.

Music played as we laughed and talked, waiting for the points to be tallied. People moved around to the bars, grabbing drinks and food before returning for round two. The adorable Shark was on his way back to our table with a couple bottles of water when out of the corner of my eye, I saw Mark waving at me. Grinning, I gave him a friendly wave back. I tried to stop myself, but my eyes inadvertently shifted over to Carlos.

I froze.

A dull ache formed in the depths of me as I watched him watching me. He was turning a beer bottle in his hand as his gaze fixed on me. He didn't smile as our eyes met. He wasn't embarrassed to be caught staring. He just continued to look at me as if he were seeing me for the first time.

I swallowed hard.

Ellie cleared her throat in the microphone, startling me. "Time for round two… can we get the Sharks, Daily Double, and Bee-Hive to the front?"

Squealing, I tore my eyes away from the handsome man a few feet away from me and celebrated with my team. We slapped hands and cheered as we made our way to Ellie.

In a lightning round of sorts, we answered questions about history, pop culture, TV shows, sports, and science. We had eight points, Daily Double had eight points, and Bee-Hive had two points. There was only one more question and we needed to answer correctly for the chance to win. All eyes were on us as the entire bar seemed to be invested in the competition.

I happened to notice Carlos smiling at his pretty teammate. She was batting her eyelashes up at him and smiling with her entire face. I looked away and halfway heard something the brunette on my team asked me. Distractedly, I answered her. A high-pitched giggle grabbed my attention and part of me knew what it was, but the other part of me needed confirmation. My eyes darted to Carlos. I saw him smiling as he told her something else that made her toss back her head and laugh.

"What's wrong?" the quiet Shark asked me, his hazel eyes wide.

Jerking my attention away from the flirting over on Daily Double, I lifted my lips into a smile. "Nothing."

"You were frowning."

I shook my head. "Just thinking about what the final question category could be."

He appeared to believe me as he nodded. "I know," he mumbled. "It could be anything, but I'm thinking the category has to be movies. I want to be impressive." Gesturing to the blonde woman who was supportive but hadn't really known any answers, he gave a tight-lipped smile. "If we win, it'll give me a good opening line."

I opened my mouth to reply, but the squeal of the microphone interrupted.

"Final question will determine our winner," Ellie called out, inciting cheers from the ground, nervous rumbles from the contestants. "The category is... literature."

My nerves spiked. I was both irritated and impressed by how many questions Carlos answered correctly. But with him being an English teacher, the final category felt primed for him to win.

I can do all things.

Ellie took a dramatic pause. "The Victorian-era romance novel series starring Misery Chastain was written by which author?"

There was a murmur in the crowd, but we were all silently looking at one another. The rest of the Sharks looked confused and then it hit me.

Unfortunately, Daily Double hit the buzzer first.

"Stephen King," Mark answered confidently.

"I'm sorry," Ellie replied with a pout. "No."

I hit our buzzer without consulting with my group. They looked at me expectantly. All eyes in the entire building felt like they were on me. I quickly found Meghan in the crowd and my smile grew.

Throwing my arms in the air, I yelled, "Paul Sheldon!"

"I'm sorry…" Ellie stretched the word out, finishing with a dramatic pause. "The winners are the Sharks!"

The entire bar erupted in cheers and my adorable teammate spun me around before moving on to the others. We all exchanged pleasantries with the other teams and after receiving our gift cards, we were free to mingle with everyone else.

I was heading to the bar to get a drink and jot down some thoughts about my experience so far with Singles Trivia Night when I felt a hand on my elbow. Yanking it out of the grasp, I turned and looked to see who'd grabbed me.

"Hey, sorry," Mark apologized, holding his hands up in surrender. "I'd called your name five times and I didn't think you heard me. Just wanted to tell you congratulations."

"Thank you." I grinned with pride. "You guys did a good job as well! I guess that was good practice for your Jeopardy-bound friend."

"If I'm keeping it real, your boy Carlos knew most of the answers. Apparently, he's a teacher." He gave me a look. "But I'm sure you knew that."

I nodded, moving closer to the newly open space at the bar.

Mark moved right along with me. "If you don't mind me asking, what's up with you two?"

I shook my head and pretended to be confused. "I don't know what you mean."

"I mean, I caught him staring at you a few times, and the way you said you two didn't know each other seemed deeply personal." He lifted his hand to catch the attention of the bartender before continuing. "So, I'm just curious…"

"Curious as to why he was staring at me or curious about how we know each other or…?" I cocked my head to the side and waited for him to get to his point. "I'm not sure what you're asking."

"Well, it's obvious why he was staring at you… you're gorgeous."

"Thank you."

He placed his order with the bartender and asked for another bottle of water for me. He turned back toward me. "Are you two dating?"

My eyebrows flew up. "No. Oh no, no, no. Not at all."

"Okay." Handing me a bottled water and then sipping his rum and coke, Mark's smile grew. "Okay, well that's good to know. I—"

"Excuse me, Akila." Carlos's deep voice seemed to emerge out of nowhere as he slid up to the bar.

Something about the way his voice wrapped around my name made my insides tighten. Inhaling sharply, I fixed my gaze on him as he asked for a bottle of water from the bartender. Eyeing his profile, I spoke. "Carlos."

"Congratulations." He took the bottled water and then patted Mark on the back. "Even though we technically won, congratulations."

I felt my eyes bulge. "What?"

"Mark here said Stephen King and technically, he's right. Stephen King wrote *Misery*. So…" He lifted his hands and backed away.

I rolled my eyes. "Don't be a sore loser."

"Hey, whatever you have to tell yourself." He smirked. "Enjoy your night."

"I don't have to tell myself anything. Ellie told the entire bar that the Sharks won. But you enjoy your night."

He looked over at Mark and then back at me. "Okay, Akila."

I curled my lip in disgust. "Okay, Carlos."

Carlos looked at Mark. "Good luck."

"Don't 'good luck' him," I hissed indignantly. "What is that even supposed to mean?"

"I'm going to let you two work this out," Mark sighed before turning and walking away.

"Great," I snapped, glaring at his handsome face. "Thanks a lot."

"I didn't do anything." Turning, Carlos put his back against the bar and looked out into the crowd. "Anyway, you're supposed to be reporting."

"Actually, we're supposed to be experiencing and reporting on the experience." I took a sip of water. "And anyway, how do you know I wasn't interviewing him for my article?"

He scoffed. "The way he kept checking you out, there was no way he was just interested in giving an interview."

"Funny, coming from the same man who was grinning in his teammate's face."

He sipped his water. "I was celebrating with my team. But I spent the entire game taking notice of my surroundings, and I saw the way Mark was looking at you."

"I'm surprised you noticed, given the fact that every time I happened to glance at you, you were staring in my face." I pursed my lips to accentuate my point.

His eyes darted around even though his face was stone still. "I wasn't. Not like that anyway."

I let out a short, dry laugh. "Yes, you were."

"I admit, I might have glanced at you a few times. But it's not what you think."

I put my hands on my hips. "Well, then what was it?"

Licking his lips, he silently assessed my face. The longer he looked at me without saying anything, the more of a pull I felt toward him. Staring into my eyes, his voice sounded huskier. "I was staring because you looked different. That's all."

I didn't expect that answer.

My brows furrowed. "Different? How?"

"You were smiling and having a good time. You weren't being serious. You just looked happy. And it was beau…" Ripping his eyes away from me, he continued, "It was different. We have work to do." Pushing off the edge of the bar, he walked away without another word. He didn't even glance back at me.

"Was that Carlos? In the flesh?" Meghan asked moments later as I glared darts into the back of Carlos's head.

Tearing my eyes away from him, I turned to my best friend. "Mm hmm." I rolled my eyes. "I seriously don't think I can work with him."

"I hate to break it to you, but I could see the sparks flying between you two from across the room."

"Those weren't sparks."

Smirking, she gave me a look. "Okay, Kiki."

"Those weren't sparks!" I argued.

"What was it then?" She put her hand on her hip.

I bit my lip. "Um... the glowing embers from the fiery pits of hell from which he arrived."

Meghan and I dissolved in a fit of giggles. We laughed so hard that I was able to push down the sparks, the magic, and all the other feelings that Carlos brought out of me.

Chapter Nine

"As a writer, there's nothing more complex as the feeling you get when you're told by someone you respect how much they love what you've written, and then you look at all the red marks and corrections they've made," I complained with pride as I walked into the kitchen. "It smells so good in here."

"Thanks." Meghan carried breadsticks in one hand and dipping sauce in the other. "Will you grab the lemonade pitcher from the refrigerator?"

"Yeah." I looked around in astonishment as I washed my hands. "You said you were cooking dinner and I'm not going to lie, I expected pizza rolls."

She laughed and gestured to the lasagna, salad, and breadsticks. "I wanted to impress Derrick, so I took a stroll down my grandma's recipe book."

Setting the pitcher on the table, I swung around to the calendar on the wall. "Today is Wednesday, right?"

"Yeah…"

"I thought you said Derrick was coming over on Thursday night."

"He is. But I decided I needed to do a practice run on grandma's recipe. Lasagna is his favorite food, so I wanted to make sure I did a good job."

Sitting across from her, I studied my best friend's face. Without her wigs and makeup, she looked younger than her twenty-five years. But more than that, she looked nervous.

"What's going on? I thought things with Derrick were casual."

"They are. But I think I want to be with him."

I giggled. "Thank you for dinner." I put my head down and blessed our food. "Amen."

"Amen!" She scooped some lasagna onto her plate. "Now what's so funny?"

"I thought you said you wanted to be with David."

"I thought I did, too. But when we had sex, I changed my mind."

My eyebrows flew up. "You had sex with David?! Why didn't you tell me?"

"You were going through a lot last week. Photography class, Re-Mix interview, several run-ins with Carlos… you had a lot on your plate. And then I started talking to Kevin and Derrick more, so I forgot all about it."

"I'm sorry." I shook my head slowly. "I was so caught up in my mess that I wasn't checking in enough. Please, tell me everything. Start at the beginning. What happened with David?"

"His dick was small. I liked him, but his dick was so small that I couldn't feel anything when he put it in."

My mouth fell open. "Nothing?"

"Not a thing."

"Damn." I shook my head. "A huge dick isn't even a require-ment. But if it's small, you have to know how to work it and you have to know what you can and can't do. But if he was so small that you couldn't feel him inside you, that's…yikes."

"I know. And I didn't expect that at all. He was the one that was kind of tall, bigger body build, and big feet so I expected him to at least be of average length and width."

"It's crazy how you just never know what you're going to get. It's like those chocolates that don't have the map to tell you what the filling is. You're hoping it's filled with caramel, but you bite down and it's that weird strawberry nougat filling," I chuckled. "Big feet, a big body, big hands, none of that necessarily means anything anymore. It's all a crapshoot."

"Unless you see a dick print," Meghan said in a sing-song voice.

I took a bite of my food and ignored her comment. "So, after you two had sex, you didn't see him again?"

"Oh, don't think we aren't going to circle back around to that," she giggled. "But no, I didn't see him again. I didn't call him, and he didn't call me. I think he could tell by my body's reaction that I wasn't into the sex. So…" She chewed a mouthful of lasagna. "On to the next one."

"Here, here." I lifted my glass of lemonade. "On to the next one."

She raised her glass. "Here, here."

"Now I need to know about Kevin and Derrick." I chewed the small bite of breadstick that was in my mouth. "And this is delicious by the way."

She grinned and then launched into a story about Kevin and then Derrick.

After dinner, I finished making the corrections to my article and fell asleep at four o'clock in the morning. When I woke up, I had several missed calls and a text from Alex.

"Alexandria Bishara," I greeted my sister when she answered the phone.

"What are you doing?" she responded. "Where have you been?"

I propped myself up against my pillows. "I'm in bed. What's going on?"

"I have a date tonight!"

"Congratulations! With who?"

"Jay. He's the sexy history tutor I had over the summer. I didn't think he was interested, and I hadn't really seen him since summer classes ended. But I ran into him at the library today, and he asked me out."

"That's awesome, Alex!" Pushing the covers off my body, I swung my legs off the side of the bed.

"So, the reason I called is to ask you if I could borrow your yellow dress."

I stopped. "Which one?" My tone was suspicious because I knew she couldn't have meant my favorite yellow dress—the marigold yellow stunner.

"I know what you're thinking."

"Then why would you even ask?" I questioned, my voice riddled in amusement.

"I swear I won't mess it up. Please Kiki. Please."

"You spilled wine on the last thing you borrowed of mine."

"In my defense, I thought it was Meghan's."

Shaking my head, I laughed as I walked over to my closet. "Where are you going?"

"We're going to the history museum in D.C. for dinner and a special exhibit, and then we're going to Kobo Lounge for drinks and dancing. I don't have time to go shopping, and I don't know anything that would be as perfect as that dress. I have an exam tomorrow morning so I don't have time to go shopping and even if I did, I'm not going to find anything as perfect as that dress."

"When is this event?"

"Friday!"

"Tomorrow?"

"Yes! We're leaving after my exam."

I sighed. "Fine."

She screamed.

I moved the phone from my ear and when I put it back, I yelled, "Calm down, calm down… If you borrow this dress—and the key word is borrow—you must bring it back cleaned and steamed by Monday."

"I will, I promise! I promise!"

"I have to go to this singles event tonight and Meghan has a hot date—"

"With David?"

I smiled, remembering Meghan's recount of her unimpressive night with David. "No, not with David."

"Oh! Then with who?"

I laughed. "You'll have to ask her. But in the meantime, if you're picking the dress up tonight, you'll have to do it before I leave at six o'clock."

"I'll be there on time. I'll bring it back in even better condition. I'll have it dry cleaned and steamed at the expensive place you like. Nothing will happen to it."

"Okay, I'll see you in a few hours. Oh, and have you talked to Mom?"

"A couple of days ago."

"Well, she's looking for you. Call her back."

We said our goodbyes, and I trudged my way to the bathroom to get my day started. After showering, cleaning, and running errands, I studied the photography presentation Luca Romano posted online. I scoured my brain and the internet trying to come up with a great location for the self-portrait I was supposed to turn in by Sunday night. I knew I was overthinking the assignment, but it was the first one that didn't involve our partners and I wanted to stand out. I got so caught up in planning and preparing, I lost track of time.

"Hey, I'm home!" Meghan yelled when she walked in our apartment.

My eyes flew to the clock beside my bed. "Oh shit," I mumbled, scrambling to my feet. "Hey, Meghan!"

It was later than I thought, and I needed to be out of the house by six o'clock.

After a shower, I dressed in a pair of black, satin pants with a matching fitted jacket. With no shirt underneath and my push-up bra working its magic, I looked like the quintessential idea of a sexy professional. Posing in the mirror, I didn't have time to wrestle with my thick mass of tightly coiled hair, so I pinned one side up and let the other side be wild and free. Slipping into a pair of metallic spiked heels, I grabbed a metallic clutch to complete the look.

"Come in!" I called out when I heard the knock at my door.

"You look beautiful, Kiki," Alex commented as soon as she walked in my room. "You are an angel who the world has been blessed to bask in your glow. You are fierce. You are Beyoncé. And

I'm not just saying that because you are the best and most generous sister in the world."

I laughed as I walked to my closet and pulled out the dress. "I already said you can borrow it. No need to lay it on that thick."

She giggled as she hugged me. "You do look good though!"

"Thank you." I handed her the dress and looked down at my feet. "I haven't worn these shoes in so long."

"New Year's Eve," she confirmed with a nod as we exited the room.

"Meghan!" Alex yelled.

"Alexandria!" Meghan yelled back.

"Who is your hot date with? Akila wouldn't tell me," Alex pouted as we found her in the kitchen.

"You two can catch up. I have to head out." I looked at Meghan. "I will text you when I'm on the way home, but if things are going well, I don't expect a text back."

"Ow!" Alex exclaimed, gyrating her hips.

Laughing, I waved. "Meghan, have fun! Alex, good luck on your exam tomorrow. Love you both!"

I left the house and found my way to Koi twenty minutes later. I didn't see many cars in the parking lot or many people milling around the entrance. I was a little worried that the night would be a bust, but I tried not to think too long and hard about it.

I hope it's a good time. But good or bad, I'm going to write about my experience for Re-Mix Magazine, and I'm going to get paid to do that.

Entering the elevator to the roof, I caught a glimpse of my reflection.

First thing Saturday morning, my first story in Re-Mix will be published, I thought excitedly as I rode up.

"Wow," I breathed aloud as the doors opened.

The rooftop had people everywhere—some on the dancefloor, some at tables, some at the bar. The music was an up-tempo R&B song that had a great beat. As I made my way to the bar, my eyes swept the room, and I plastered a smile on my face.

"Well, hello," the bartender greeted me as I slipped onto a newly empty stool. "What can I do for you?"

"Hi." I smiled at the good-looking man in front of me. "I'll take a bottle of water and a Koi Kamikaze."

He winked at me. "Coming right up."

"Thank you." Pulling out my cell phone, I checked the time.

"Did you want to put my number in there?"

Slipping my phone back into my bag, I tilted my head to the side. "Depends on how my drink tastes."

He chuckled. "Aw man, the pressure is on now."

I nodded. "It is."

"I'm Tim, by the way."

"I'm thirsty." Unable to keep a straight face, I burst out laughing at my own joke. "No, I'm Akila."

He chuckled, shaking his head. "You're funny. I'll be right back."

Four minutes later, I had an ice-cold bottle of water and a Koi Kamikaze in either hand. Because the bar was busy, Tim didn't have much time for us to talk. We flirted when he'd come by and I wasn't having a conversation with someone, but we never exchanged personal information besides our names.

I'd been there for at least thirty minutes and although I didn't move from my perch at the bar, I was having a good time. The music was the perfect mix for the crowd and the vibe was riddled with pre-weekend excitement. I'd been approached by a few men who held halfway decent conversations but none of any substance. Scanning the room, I slowly sipped the last of my alcoholic beverage.

I froze.

I knew he'd be there, but seeing Carlos Richmond always managed to catch me off guard. I could tell from my vantage point that he was flirting with the cute girl with the braided hair. She was smiling up at him, tossing her hair, and touching him frequently. For about ten minutes, I watched them. I was unable to move, unable to look away. I didn't care what he did or with whom, yet I found myself watching their interaction as if it were a stage play.

My lips pursed as she laughed at something he said. He said

something else and she laughed so hard, she had to hold on to him to keep her upright. I rolled my eyes.

He's not that funny.

She had to be reacting to the fact that he looked good, I reasoned. He was an ass sometimes, but he always looked good. I couldn't deny that fact. Every single time I'd seen him, he had a different look and all of them were on point.

My eyes swept up and down his body taking in his fashion choices. Wearing brown shoes and belt with dark denim jeans and a white shirt, his outfit was unremarkable.

Yet on him, all I wanted to do was remark.

Surprising myself with that thought, I looked away.

Lusting after a man was unlike me. Lusting after a man I didn't even like was unheard of.

"Hi, I'm Brad. Would you like to dance?" a man asked as he slipped onto the barstool next to me, stealing my attention away from Carlos.

Recognizing the voice, I could feel my blood boiling already. "No." Turning to face the man I'd met the last time I'd visited Koi, I crossed my arms over my chest.

"Baby, let me take you out on the dance floor and change your mind. You are way too beautiful to be sitting here alone." His eyes roamed over me. "And your body... mmm girl."

Glaring at him with a mixture of disbelief and repulsion, I was at a loss for words.

He laughed to himself. "You don't have to be shy around me." His eyes were fixated on my cleavage. "Let me get your number."

"Please leave me alone. Like I told you the last time you hit on me, I'm not interested."

Licking his lips, he studied my face. "I would remember a beautiful face like yours. You may have me confused with another guy."

"No, I remember exactly who you are." My lip curled in disgust. "Walk away."

He leaned closer and I could smell the alcohol on his breath. "Don't play hard to get. We both know you are going home with me tonight."

"I'm not. But before I walk away, where do you get these weak ass lines?"

"There's nothing weak about me." He sat back and looked at me again. "And if you play your cards right, you'll get a chance to see that."

My eyebrows flew up. "Are you kidding? This isn't for real."

"I don't kid about handling my business. And this is very real. Every inch of me is real."

I looked around in faux confusion. "This isn't for real. You cannot be for real. Who taught you how to speak to women? I'm seriously curious. You listen to The Lost Boys, don't you?"

"So, what if I do?" He reached over and placed his hand on mine. Snatching my hand from his, I snapped, "Don't fucking touch me!"

The look on his face shifted as if he just realized that I wasn't falling for his charm. "Doesn't matter anyway, you're not even that cute."

I stood. "It's so sad that upon rejection your first instinct is to insult my looks." I let out a dry, mocking laugh. "Two things: you approached me, and I don't give a fuck what you think."

He turned to flag down the bartender and muttered under his breath, "Bitch."

With my clutch in one hand and my half empty bottle of water in the other, I clenched my fists as best I could. "You're the only bitch here."

His head whipped around, and he glared at me. "I remember you now." He stood, looming over me by a few inches before he snarled, "You're the bitch from a few weeks ago. I'll get you put out on your ass!"

I opened my mouth to respond but was interrupted.

"Do we have a problem here?" The deep rumble of Carlos's voice reverberated through me. His hand rested on the small of my back. "Akila, is there a problem?"

"No, I handled it," I replied, staring at Brad's panicky face.

"I had no doubt that you could," Carlos replied. Taking a step toward Brad, he continued, "But I better not ever hear you disrespect her again."

Turning his back on us, Brad stormed away in a silent rage.

I looked up at Carlos and saw his clenched jaw and narrowed eyes burning a hole in the back of Brad's fleeing head. Even though I didn't need protecting, there was something sexy about his protectiveness.

"Carlos." I touched his arm and shocked myself. My hand dropped from his body when his eyes met mine. "Hey."

He swallowed hard. "Hey."

Staring at one another, the air felt thin, and my chest felt tight. It was the most intense thirty seconds of my life.

"I'm going to have to ask you two to leave," a burly security guard commanded, breaking whatever it was that was happening between us.

"What?" I took a step back. "Why?"

"You're disturbing the guests and you've been asked to leave," the security guard's tone was stern, and his face was grim.

"What did we do?" Carlos asked, his tone just as stern.

Without thinking, I put my hand on his back to calm him down. "Who are we disturbing? We didn't do anything to anyone. If anything—oh…" The realization hit me, and my mouth was agape. "This was Brad, wasn't it?"

The security guard looked around and then lowered his voice. "I don't know what happened and I don't care. I just need you two to leave so I can keep my job."

"Unless you can give me a reason why we need to leave, I'm not going anywhere," Carlos responded defiantly.

The guard's face became darker and more menacing. "If I tell you to go, you go. Now."

"Fine!" I stepped in between the two men, one hand gripping Carlos's forearm and the other gesturing to the security guard. "We'll leave, but this won't be the last you'll hear from us. You can tell Brad that he can't hide behind his dad forever."

Grabbing Carlos by the arm, I pulled him toward the elevator. We weren't alone, so we silently rode down to the first floor. We walked through the crowded restaurant, and it wasn't until we were outside that he spoke.

"Fuck!" Carlos's voice boomed, echoing through the parking lot.

I jumped, startled by his outburst. I remained quiet, but I watched him pace five feet away from me.

"They had no right to put us out. That asshole disrespected you, but we get put out?" His angry growl made the knot in my belly tighten.

"The asshole is Brad and his dad owns Koi."

"Fuck Brad and his dad." He shook his head and let out a deep breath. He seemed to be calming himself down and then I saw his body tense all over again. His fiery gaze met mine. "Who is he to you? Why did he disrespect you?"

"He's no one to me," I scoffed. "He's just someone who wouldn't take no for an answer. He hit on me and I wasn't interested. I reminded him that a few weeks ago, he'd tried the same thing and I wasn't interested then either. He got mad and started being disrespectful. And then you came over and I think he was intimidated, so he had us kicked out of Koi."

"This is bullshit. We shouldn't have left. If I was going to be put out, it should've been because I knocked some sense into him." He scrubbed his hands with his face. "Why were you so quick to leave?"

I rubbed my arms before crossing them over my chest. "Because I didn't want them to call the police."

"We had every right to be there."

"I know, but—"

"But nothing, we shouldn't have let that asshole get his way. If he was uncomfortable with us being there, let him be uncomfortable. Fuck him!"

"He felt threatened and wanted to exert his power," I pointed out. "It wasn't about him being uncomfortable, it was about him feeling emasculated. He was mad when I called him on his bullshit, and then when you came over…" I let my sentence trail off as I shook my head.

"Why didn't you just walk away? He was clearly an idiot and you weren't interested."

I balked at his words. "This isn't my fault. He approached me, wouldn't accept that I didn't want him, and disrespected me. I shouldn't have to give up my seat at the bar because he's an ass."

"No, you shouldn't. You shouldn't have had to deal with him at all. If you walked away, we would still be in there and—"

My jaw dropped. I looked at him incredulously. "You're putting this on me?"

"No, I'm—"

"You're the one who escalated the situation!" I threw my hands in the air. "You're the one who came over to me."

He stopped in his tracks, shock radiating off him in waves. "I saw a man disrespecting you. He stood up like he was going to put his hands on you. What was I supposed to do?"

"You could've continued flirting with whoever you were flirting with and left me to handle my own business." I put my hands on my hips. "I don't need to be saved."

"I never said you needed to be saved! God dammit, Akila!" He scrubbed his face with his hands again and let out a growl in frustration. "I'm not doing this with you."

Swallowing hard, my chest was getting tighter as each second ticked by. "Well, you shouldn't have insinuated it was my fault that we were kicked out."

"I didn't! It was that asshole's fault we were kicked out. All I'm saying is that you shouldn't have entertained his conversation for as long as you did."

"So now you're telling me who—"

"I'm not doing this with you!" he burst out, clearly annoyed with me.

"I'm not doing this with you," I returned petulantly, taking a step toward him. "You swooped in to 'rescue me' from a man who said he got his dating advice from The Lost Boys."

The information seemed to catch him off guard. "What?"

"Yeah." I nodded. "So, before you try to say that I should remove myself from situations so I won't get disrespected, let's acknowledge the fact that he felt emboldened to disrespect me because he listens to your show."

He shook his head. "We've never told anybody to call women bitches. I don't know what happened before I started with the podcast, but there's never been a situation when we'd tell anyone to do what he did."

"But you do call them basic looking spinster chicks?"

He seemed momentarily caught off-guard, so I continued.

"Disrespecting a woman and belittling her appearance because she calls you out. Hmm... sounds exactly like what Brad did."

"I would never disrespect..." His voice lowered and there was a turbulence in his eyes I'd never seen in anyone before. "I would never do that. To you or anyone else."

The sharpness of his tone took my breath away. My mouth was dry. He looked more than offended. He looked hurt. Licking my lips, I didn't know what to say. I was at a loss for words.

Seconds ticked by before I weakly muttered, "Okay."

He just stared at me, not speaking. His handsome face was stony and expressionless.

"I believe you," I whispered faintly.

He remained silent.

The air between us was thick and I felt like I was suffocating. His eyes said so much—none of which I could decipher. I didn't know why it affected me the way it did, but his gaze hurt.

Clearing my throat, I looked away. "We can report him and Koi to the business bureau. We can leave reviews online. It's okay—"

He took a step toward me. "No, it's not okay, Akila," he interrupted me, his tone gruff. "Fuck him and Koi. We had an assignment. This wasn't just a social outing, we were here for work."

His words hit me like a punch in the gut. I didn't even think about that. It hadn't occurred to me that Brad's temper tantrum negatively impacted our work. My mouth was agape. "Shit," I cursed, hands on my hips.

He laced his fingers together and rested his intertwined hands on his head. "Whatever this is, isn't going to work," he sighed, his voice riddled with resignation. "Not like this."

My stomach twisted. "What do you mean?"

A car slowly approached, loudly blasting a pop song I'd never heard before. He dropped his hands and took another step toward me, moving out of the way of the empty parking spot he was standing in. The car continued to another spot, but Carlos remained in his new position, a foot away from me.

I stared at his profile as he looked around at our surroundings. My eyes traced the sharp edges of his face, the perfection of his nose, the precision of his haircut, the sexiness of his beard.

Without warning, his head turned, and his eyes landed on me. There wasn't a hint of amusement in his expression as he took me in. The tightening between my thighs, I expected. The way my heart fluttered was unexpected.

Even though we were closer than before, his voice was low, almost vulnerable. "Having a byline in Re-Mix will make it easier to get my book reviewed. I need the free promo, free publicity, free marketing. This job opportunity will open doors like nothing else I've ever done. I need this."

He was open and exposed as he explained the importance of his work with Re-Mix. Because he was being transparent, I felt like I should do the same.

"Same here. This is my livelihood. This job isn't just a stepping stone or an opportunity to me. This is my dream job." Taking a measured breath, I continued in a hushed tone. "I need this to go well. I can't lose this job. It means too much to me."

"Then we're going to have to work together and not against each other. Between photography class and then this co-series writer assignment, we can't win if we keep doing this. Not like this. Not successfully."

I squeezed my eyes shut. "I know." I let my eyelashes flutter open. "I know. Something has to change. We need to have a civil conversation."

"Then let's talk it out."

I looked him in his eyes and kept my voice as even as possible. "Every time I think about Date Night with The Lost Boys…" I shook my head. "I get angry."

"You know my voice. You know I'm not saying those things," he pointed out softly, stepping forward. "The show has three different points of view so that there's something for everybody."

"But you are associated with them," I explained as calmly as possible. When he sighed, I stepped a little closer. I wanted to reach out and touch him but resisted the urge. "I understand your point, Carlos. I know you're not saying the words. But City Boy sets the tone of Date Night and he represents everything that I'm against. I know he's your friend, but he's the worst. So, when I think of The Lost Boys, I think of the tone that's set. And unfortunately, City Boy is setting that tone."

"And when you see me, you associate me with what City Boy has said."

"Yes."

"Is that fair to me? We have so much on the line and you're judging me based on someone else's thoughts and opinions."

"If you sit in the car knowing your friend is robbing a bank, when the police come, and the car is pulled over, you're going to jail too. You may not get as many years because you didn't do the actual crime, but you're guilty by association." I lifted my shoulders in an apologetic shrug. "Same rules apply."

The corners of his lips turned upward slightly as he tried not to be amused. "Akila, you drive me crazy."

"And you get under my skin."

"You're judgmental," he pointed out.

Bristling, I jutted my chin to make myself a little taller. "Well, you're complicit."

"You're argumentative."

"You're hypocritical."

He licked his lips. "You're frustrating."

The pull deep in my gut twisted at the sight of his tongue passing over his full lips. I shifted my weight from one foot to the other and it unintentionally rocked me a little closer to him. "You're defensive."

"You're difficult."

"You're delusional."

His eyes flicked down to my lips while he licked his own again, slower. In a hoarse whisper, he admitted, "Working with you is hard."

My heart pounded in my chest. "The feeling is mutual."

We weren't touching yet, but my entire body hummed with the anticipation of his lips on mine. It was clear that the energy between us was as toxic as it was magnetic. I knew it was in my best interest to walk away. Even as we were listing the qualities we didn't like in one another, there was something pulling us together. We went from a car length apart to mere inches. And as much as I told myself I didn't like him, I couldn't explain why every square inch of me yearned to be touched by him.

I have to walk away, I told myself as I held his gaze.

I told my feet to move, but they didn't listen. Instead, they remained firmly planted in place. We were either going to continue taking shots at one another or he was going to put those beautiful lips against mine. Either way, I knew I needed to leave.

"When we asked you to leave, we meant the premises!" the security guard roared, startling us apart. "Don't make me have to call the police."

"Have a goodnight," I called over my shoulder as I jumped in my car.

Shit. Shit. Shit. Shit. Shit. What just happened?

Chapter Ten

I couldn't sleep.

And not because I ran away from Carlos and barely said goodbye when the security guard yelled at us. And not because I stopped at a diner for dinner and the ice cream float I ate was messing with my stomach. And not because Meghan had her sex playlist blasting from her room. And not because I wrote a scathing review of Koi and posted it online. Although any one of those reasons could've kept me awake any other night, I couldn't stop thinking about what that almost-kiss with Carlos meant.

As I laid in bed, I tried to think about what I was going to tell Luna Daniels, but I kept thinking about how badly I wanted Carlos to kiss me. I forced my thoughts to the fact that I didn't get to experience the full singles happy hour to give it an authentic review, but every time I blinked, all I saw was Carlos Richmond.

Do I like him? It doesn't make any sense. Yes, I'm attracted to him, but we had a moment, and that's ridiculous because he's a Lost Boy! He doesn't see anything wrong with that so I can't like him… can I? Do I? Oh my god… do I?

There was something about him that was unlike any other man I'd ever dealt with. He treated me as his equal. He didn't like me, but he respected me. He didn't sexualize me, but it was clear he was attracted to me. He didn't agree with me, but he didn't shy away from debating me. He was associated with a group that I hated on principle alone. But his interactions with me were respectful, kind, and protective. Except when we were at each other's throats. And even then, those exchanges were sexually-charged and raw.

Raw.

Giving in, I imagined what it would be like to have him kiss me. I fantasized about what his hands might have felt like on my body. I considered how big his dick could be. My body stirred, my nipples hardened, and my panties dampened.

As my hands slipped under my t-shirt, I let my fingertips skate along my smooth skin. Closing my eyes, I imagined my hands were Carlos's hands. I made my way to the apex of my thighs. With visions of his hands, mouth, and dick pressed against me, I was just about to touch myself.

"Oh!" I gasped, eyes flying open.

My phone vibrated loudly against the wooden nightstand for the second time. Grabbing it, I sat up in bed and then gasped again.

Sorry for the late notice, but it just occurred to me that you are not on the staff email. Bring your notes and your unfinished drafts to Re-Mix tomorrow at six o'clock. We're having a staff meeting and I want to see what you have so far. Because it's short notice, I won't hold you to the fact that these meetings are mandatory. But I do hope you can make it. Luna.

"Oh my God," I breathed as I reread the short email from Luna Daniels twice.

I went through a range of emotions. I was excited. *I'm going to be meeting with other staff members of Re-Mix.* I was nervous. *I'm going to be meeting with other staff members of Re-Mix.* I was panicked. *I'm going to be meeting with other staff members of Re-Mix…and I don't have any notes from tonight!*

I spent ten minutes trying to think of excuses I could tell Luna that wouldn't get me fired or make me look incompetent. I had my integrity and I didn't want to lie. I planned to just tell her the truth and hope for the best.

And then it occurred to me.

The truth.

Guided by moonlight, I hopped out of bed and turned on my laptop. While it started up, I grabbed my phone and scrolled down my contact list. Taking a deep breath, I drafted and sent a late-night text message.

Akila Bishara: Hey, sorry, I know it's late. But did you get the email from Luna?

Carlos Richmond: Yeah, I just got it. I might not go to the meeting. I need to buy some time.

Akila Bishara: This job is important to us both and I think we should go. I have an idea for our articles. Can I give you a call?

Carlos Richmond: Yeah, that's fine.

Fiddling with the edge of my shirt, I listened to the phone ring. Something shifted between us with the conversation in the parking lot. But after the security guard yelled at us, I barely said goodbye before I hopped in my car and left. I groaned. He hadn't even picked up the phone yet and I'd already started freaking out.

"Hello?" Carlos's deep raspy voice curled my toes.

"Hi-hey," I stammered, shaking off the lingering effects of his voice and our almost-kiss. "Sorry. I didn't know you were sleeping. I know you have to wake up early."

"Thanks." He cleared his throat, but his voice still sounded like he was sleeping. "What's your idea?"

"We tell the truth," I announced, the wheels turning in my head.

There was a distinct pause. "We tell Luna Daniels that we were kicked out early so we have no idea how the singles happy hour ended?"

"Yes."

"You want us to tell her that even though her email said for us to be there the whole time, we were only at the four-hour event for an hour?"

"Yes."

"Okay." He let out a short, amused laugh. "You can do what you want, but I'm not doing that. I need this job."

I smiled, sitting back against the chair. The sound of his laugh was unexpected and felt good to my soul. "I'm not trying to tell you what to do. But hear me out... I'm going to write about my experience. Everything that happened from the moment I arrived to the moment security asked us to leave. You should write about your experience from arriving to the interaction with the woman with the braids to being asked to leave."

He was quiet for a second. "My interaction with the woman with the braids," he repeated slowly. "I don't even remember what we talked about."

"Well, you must have talked about something because she thought you were so funny," I blurted out without thinking. My eyes widened as I held my phone to my ear. "I mean, I happened to look and...um, she seemed to be laughing."

I could hear him shifting on the other end of the line. "So, you were watching me?"

"No, no." Nervously, I shook my head even though he couldn't see me. "I mean, I saw you. I wasn't watching you or anything. But I did see you talking to a woman with braids, right? That was you? I was pretty sure...no, I wasn't watching."

I was mortified that I couldn't stop talking, but the silence on the other end was deafening.

"Akila, it's cool," Carlos laughed sleepily. "It's good to know you had an eye on me."

I rolled my eyes, but his laughter eased the nervous tremble in my chest. "My point was just that you have an experience to write about, so you can write about that: how you two were able to engage, the music, the atmosphere, all that."

"I was only talking to her for like five minutes, but I guess... yeah, I could write about that."

It was ten minutes. I pursed my lips. *Yeah, I was watching.*

"I didn't finish my conversation because I saw you arguing with that asshole at the bar," he continued.

Grinning, I crossed my arm over my chest. "Wait…so, if you saw me arguing with Brad, that means you were watching me."

He let out an amused grunt. "Okay, you got me."

"It's cool, Carlos. It's good to know you had an eye on me," I teased, causing him to chuckle.

"I'm tired. I don't know what I'm saying," he explained with a yawn.

Reflecting on the events of the night, something nagged at me. "Was the altercation with Brad loud? Did you notice me and what was going on because it was louder than the music?"

"Are you serious?" he asked with a sexy rasp.

"Well… yeah." I got up from my desk and climbed back in bed. "My adrenaline was pumping so all I was focused on was telling him off. I didn't know if people were staring or not. And it just occurred to me that we probably caused a scene."

"I wouldn't worry about that."

"I'm not worried. Just curious. When did you see me?"

He let out a combination of a yawn and a short laugh. "When did I see you and when did I notice what was going on with you at the bar are two different questions. I made my way over to you when I saw people at the bar looking at you. But I noticed you the moment you walked in the door."

Caught off guard, my breathing hitched. "Oh…"

"In my defense—"

"You don't need a defense," I interrupted quickly.

He was quiet.

I shifted my body in bed, fidgeting from nerves. "What's your day looking like tomorrow?"

"He yawned again. "I have an early morning."

"Oh, I should let you go!"

"No, I have a few minutes… I want to know something personal."

"Like my social security number?"

He chuckled quietly. "And your banking information."

"Hell to the no."

"Tell me something."

"I don't know. How personal are you talking?"

"How long have you been single?"

"Almost three years now."

"Really?"

I narrowed my eyes even though he couldn't see me. "Yes," I answered slowly. "Why?"

"Just surprised, that's all."

"Why? Because I'm too pretty to be single?" I rolled my eyes at the common line men used.

"No…with your conceited ass." He let out a tired laugh causing me to laugh along with him. "You just carry yourself with… I don't know. You have a lot of fight in you."

"Which is probably why I'm single," I joked with a giggle. "There are a lot of men who seem scared of a woman with fight."

"Boys fear a woman with fight in them. Men respect it."

My lips curled upward. "I agree with that. I've met a number of boys."

"Well, you're not talking to one now."

My heart thumped, but I tried to ignore it. "How long have you been single?"

"My last real relationship ended two years ago."

"And since then…?"

"Since then I've been working on my book."

"Why did the relationship end?"

"She cheated."

"Oh…" I didn't see that coming.

"You sound surprised."

"I am."

"Why? Because women don't cheat?" His tone was playfully mocking.

"No," I giggled. "Because of your energy."

"And what's my energy like?"

Soul stirring.

"Like a stand-up guy." I paused. "For the most part."

His deep rumbling laugh sounded like a warm blanket covering me. "For the most part," he repeated.

We traded stories about past relationships and before I knew it, another hour had passed.

He yawned. "It's getting late. I have to wake up in three hours."

I looked at the clock. "I didn't even realize we were on the phone this long."

"You're pretty easy to talk to when you want to be."

I smiled. "And you're not as bad as the company you keep would indicate."

"And we're back here," he sighed dramatically.

I bit my lip. "Oh, we never left."

There was a contented pause before he spoke again.

"It was nice getting to know you tonight, Akila."

"You too, Carlos."

"I'll see you at Re-Mix."

Burrowing under the covers, the warmth I felt outside my body matched what I felt inside. "Okay, yeah, of course. See you tomorrow."

"Goodnight."

"Goodnight."

My skin was warm, and I didn't realize how hard I was smiling until I leaned over to connect my phone to the charger. Falling back against the pillow, I stared at the ceiling.

There were a lot of reasons to like Carlos. But his association with Date Night, the fact that he was a Lost Boy, and the fact that he silently condoned his friend's bullshit were huge red flags. He made me feel magic, but he also got under my skin like no other had before him. While the way he looked at me heated me to my core, we seemed to be unable to have a normal face-to-face interaction with one another.

"I can't cross that line again," I whispered aloud, anxiety and panic working its way through me.

We brought out the worst in one another. We stood on the

observatory at the river and when we were trading shots, we ignored each other. We argued at Empire Park and in the parking lot of Koi. We were snippy with each other at Re-Mix in front of Luna Daniels. We tried to have a civil conversation and that resulted in us being intensely drawn to one another. It was as if our automatic response to one another was passionate. We were either defending our beliefs passionately or fighting our passion driven attraction.

In the beginning, before I knew he was part of The Lost Boys, I was attracted to him. It was the way he carried himself, the way he spoke to me, the way he looked at me, the way he respected me. I was attracted to his drive and his intelligence. I was attracted to his energy. And then I found out who he was and that he was affiliated with Date Night, and I didn't like him anymore. And when he recognized that I didn't put up with the vile bullshit his show spews, he didn't like me anymore.

We had an honest conversation and established a temporary cease-fire so that we could move forward with our career goals. Any attraction is just lingering from when we first met and is fueled from our hostility.

"It's fine," I murmured as I closed my eyes. "It's going to be fine."

It wasn't fine.

I woke up sexually frustrated and two hours late.

After realizing the time, I jumped out of bed and scrambled to get my day started. I sat in front of my laptop and got to work. And while I complimented the DJ, the bartender, the drinks, and the atmosphere, my opinion piece took a quick turn. I fleshed out what happened and my experience as a single woman at Koi's singles happy hour was not pretty.

As the article came together, in the back of my mind, I knew it was going to rile up The Lost Boys. I thought about my truce with Carlos, but I pushed that thought aside and continued putting together my article. I wasn't attacking him or the garbage they called a show. I was being completely honest about what happened and tying it to the facts. As I worked through what happened in my mind and for my article, I couldn't help but think about the parallels between the podcast I listened to with Meghan earlier in the week and the experience I had with Brad. And by four o'clock, I had a rough draft ready for the staff meeting.

"It's rough…really rough," I told Meghan in lieu of a greeting as I answered the phone an hour later.

"It's so good, Kiki!" she exclaimed.

Her excitement fueled mine. "Ah! Seriously? You don't think it's too much?"

"It's well over the word count, but besides that, it's perfect. You manage to capture what it's like to be out by yourself as a single woman and the retaliation some men use when they don't get their way. Oh, and you cleverly shamed both the owner's son and Date Night with The Lost Boys all at the same time. This is basically your opus."

I laughed. "Okay, it definitely needs work, but I thank you for your support. You are the best cheerleader."

"That's what Derrick said," she joked.

Giggling and catcalling, I tucked in my grey Super Casanova band t-shirt into my high-waisted black pencil skirt. I slipped into black ballet slippers and grabbed my black leather jacket. I was going for cool, yet professional writer, and I felt like I was pulling it off. Listening to my best friend detail her sexual exploits, I was reminded of how long it had been since I'd had sex myself.

"So, what's the update with Derrick? How do you feel about him?" I asked as I grabbed my notebook, laptop, and printed copy of the article.

As my best friend filled me in on everything she wasn't able to tell me earlier while I was writing, I locked up our apartment and made my way to the Empire Building for my first official staff meeting at Re-Mix.

"Are you there yet?" Meghan asked.

"Yeah…" I dragged out the word as I backed into the parking spot. "Just parked."

"What are you wearing?"

"My black pencil skirt—"

"The one that makes your ass look amazing?"

"Of course."

"Nice pick! What top?"

Climbing out of the car, I grabbed my belongings. "I dressed it down with the Super Casanova t-shirt."

"Okay, I love that together! And it's perfect for your meeting—it's cool, low-key, sexy, smart. Not too dressy, but not too casual. You'll be relaxed enough for the staff meeting, but sexy enough to catch Carlos's attention. Did you wear the spiked heels?"

"No, the flats."

"Oh."

I stopped in my tracks. My eyes widened as I looked down at my feet. "What's wrong with the flats?"

"Nothing if you were just going to a staff meeting. But you're going to a staff meeting with Carlos."

"Oh my god," I groaned with a giggle.

"If you want Carlos to start mixing business with pleasure, you need to wear the shoes that give you the sex walk. The flats sound cute, but the heels would've said pleasure."

"I'm not trying to mix business with pleasure!"

"That's not what your sex dreams were saying," she countered in a sing song voice.

"It's not like that! We're…cordial, at best."

"You two agreed not to embarrass each other on the job and then you almost pounced on each other. That's not cordial. That's two people in denial."

Grinning, I switched the phone to my other hand and repositioned my bag. "I should've waited until after the meeting to tell you about that."

"And you should've told me before the meeting that you were opting out of the fuck-me heels. I mean, let's not pretend you didn't wear that skirt that makes your ass pop for Luna Daniels."

Approaching the door, I snickered. "I'm not dressing up for him."

"If you are choosing to believe that lie, the flats are fine."

Looking down at my feet, I tried to keep the amusement out of my voice. "It's the truth! I'm not dressing up for Carlos."

"You're not dressing up for me?" he inquired from behind me.

Startled, the deep rumble of Carlos's voice stopped me in my tracks.

I swallowed hard. "Let me call you back," I mumbled into the phone.

Reaching around me, he grabbed the handle of the door and opened it.

Clearing my throat and holding my head up high, I walked through the door. "Thank you."

"You're welcome." He saddled up beside me as we eased our way through the lobby. After a few moments of silence, he continued, "So, are you going to pretend I didn't hear you talking about me?"

My heart pounded in my chest, but I rolled my eyes. "You act like you're the only person named Carlos in the world."

"Are you implying that you weren't talking about me?" He hit the elevator button.

Refusing to look at him at first, I prayed my face wasn't flushed. "I'm implying you need to stop eavesdropping on private calls." Once we were in the elevator, I gave him an unaffected glare as I hit the button to the second floor. "So, mind… your… business."

He chuckled under his breath while holding his hands up in surrender. "Duly noted." He checked me out. Stroking his beard, he gave me an appreciative smirk. "I know it's specifically not for me, but you do look nice, though."

I bit my lip to keep from laughing. "It's not at all for you and thank you."

"In all seriousness, thanks for hitting me up last night." He tapped the notebook in his hand. "Once I started writing some thoughts down, I have a few ideas and can pull something together by Monday. What about you?"

Seeing his soulful eyes light up, I was reminded of our truce. Not that I was doing anything wrong, but a part of me felt like I should warn him about the direction of my article. As each second passed, my bag felt heavier. I didn't owe him anything, but not telling him in advance had created a lead ball in the pit of my stomach.

The elevator dinged as he looked at me expectantly.

"I actually got a first draft completed."

He put his hand out, gesturing for me to walk out of the elevator before him. "Oh wow, nice!"

"Yeah, thanks." I held up my badge for the receptionist to see. Casting a wayward glance at Carlos, I forced the words out of my mouth. "Um, but before we go in, I just wanted to let you know that I referenced The Lost Boys."

He stopped.

I didn't know what to do so I kept moving.

"Akila?" His tone was questioning as he fell into step with me.

"Yes?"

"What do you mean you referenced us? I thought we had a truce."

I stopped, my eyebrows furrowed. "Yes. You and I have a truce. And that still stands. I listened to some more podcasts today as I wrote, and I didn't text you and question your moral compass. I didn't call you and tell you that I know you're better than that. But as I wrote the truth of what happened to me, I had to mention the impact of Date Night."

He ran his hand down his face. "Okay."

I stared at his strong profile. His chiseled jawline clenched as we made our way down the hall to the conference room.

"Are we cool?"

He looked me square in my eyes and I saw conflict. His handsome features lacked any emotion, but his eyes told me he was warring with his answer to my question.

"We're cool, but…" He shook his head as his sentence trailed off. Licking his lips, he repeated, "We're cool."

My stomach dropped. Even though there wasn't a coldness in the way he said it, there was a definite shift.

"I wrote what I had to write," I explained, searching his eyes for the gleam I'd seen in the elevator. It was gone. Swallowing the disappointment, I held on to what mattered. "It was my story, my truth."

"You don't have to explain anything to me."

"I know." I wanted to reach out to him, but I didn't. "I just wanted you to know before we got inside."

"Thanks for the heads up." He opened the door to the conference room for me. As I walked by him, he leaned down and whispered, "And this is why I don't mix business with pleasure."

The feeling of his breath on my neck sent a shiver down my spine. With a sharp intake of air, I ignored the familiar ache between my thighs. I looked up into his eyes and saw he knew exactly what he was doing.

"Welcome!" Ann greeted us. "I'm so sorry I hadn't included you two on the staff email group yet. But I'm happy you were able to make it. Take a seat at any of the seats over there." She gestured around the room.

Smiling, I took the first empty seat against the wall. Most of the seats at the table were taken by what appeared to be seasoned staff members. I expected Carlos to take the seat next to me, but he continued walking, sitting directly across the room.

I stared him down until he looked at me, which didn't take long. Quirking my brow, I gave him a single nod.

Noted.

"Hello," Luna Daniels greeted us as she glided into the room. She looked flawless and comfortable in jeans and a t-shirt.

I made a mental note to let Meghan know that if ballet flats were good enough for Luna, they were good enough for me.

The meeting was a typical staff meeting, but I was riveted. She went over story ideas, traction with last week's edition, last minute changes to the October edition, and so many other things that my head spun. I took notes about everything and hung on to every word. Those of us along the wall were mostly spectators as Luna and the staff at the table loudly discussed issues regarding content.

"Speaking of new," Luna began, extending one arm in my direction and one in Carlos's. "We have a special series running for the next few weeks. Akila and Carlos are co-series writers for the He Said, She Said opinion piece that'll debut in tomorrow's online edition."

As everyone clapped and cheered, pride and excitement filled me. I grinned and couldn't help but look over at Carlos who was smiling as well.

"They are taking on the Richland dating scene and hitting the recurring singles events—the trivia night at Pops, the happy hour at Koi, the artist showcase at Rich Gallery, and Sunday Expressions. They are giving us accounts of their experiences. The hope is to grab men and women from eighteen to forty-nine and give them two different perspectives."

"I like what I read," a redhead at the table commented. He flashed me a smile before continuing. "Both articles were engaging, and they paired well together."

"Thank you," Carlos and I said in unison.

"But will it translate to the print copies of Re-Mix?" the redhead man continued.

My heart sped up as I watched Luna pondering over my future with Re-Mix.

"We haven't gotten that far yet. We need to see how it goes before we think about adding it to print," Luna declared, rising to her feet. "Meeting adjourned."

As everyone started talking and began exiting the conference room, Luna called Carlos and I over to her.

"How was last night?" Luna asked, folding her arms across her chest.

I shifted my eyes to Carlos before responding. "Last night was unique…"

"Yeah, there was an incident at Koi," he added.

"Oh, I know. I read Akila's rough draft and wow…" She turned to me. "It's really good. It has multiple layers with the dating dynamics, power plays, and socialized behavior. But I don't know how we can get it down to five hundred words and adequately tell that story. I'm considering it for a separate piece in the print version. I'll let you know."

"Oh my God," I breathed. Shaking my head in disbelief, I put my hand over my mouth. "I mean, thank you. Oh my—thank you…so much. Oh my god."

"In the meantime, you'll need to write something for next week's online edition. I want you to focus on the parallels you created between Date Night with The Lost Boys and this loser at the bar." Luna looked at Carlos and smiled. "I want you to focus on your experience, and without naming Akila, feel free to detail how and why you came to her defense."

"I can do that," Carlos replied.

Luna flashed him a wide smile. "I have no doubt in my mind. The two articles will reflect the differences between the way a real man handles a night out and how a loser spirals out of control upon rejection." She winked at him. "Have you read Akila's article yet?"

He took a quick look at me before returning his sights on Luna. "I haven't read it yet, but I'm sure it's great."

"As yours will be," I returned with sincerity.

She looked between us and her smile slowly grew. "You two get out of here and enjoy the rest of your night. I need your articles by Monday."

With that, she turned on her heel and walked out.

Hoisting my bag on my shoulder, I tentatively peeked at Carlos —who was staring at me.

"What?" I asked softly.

He hesitated. "Did you do the homework for Romano's course?"

"The relaxation picture?"

He nodded, opening the conference room door open for me. "Yeah."

"I've already submitted it. I did mine here actually. Well, Empire Park." Studying his face, I kept the conversation going. "What about you?"

"The Riverfront."

"Have you taken yours yet?"

"Yeah. I did it Wednesday."

"Oh, okay."

We continued down the hall in silence.

With each step we took, the awkwardness between us grew. It was a tension like no other and every time I looked at him, he seemed unbothered.

Is this cordial? Is this how it's going to be between us?

I didn't know what I expected, but stiff conversation about assignments wasn't it.

"I'm going to run to the restroom before I get on the road," Carlos announced before checking his phone. "You take it easy."

As I watched him walk away, my stomach sank. "Bye," I called out to him.

He didn't turn around.

Chapter Eleven

"So, I see you're wearing the fuck me heels this time around," Meghan observed from the doorway of my bedroom. "Would this have anything to do with the weird way things ended with you and Carlos on Friday?"

The weekend flew by. Saturday was spent printing out and framing my very first Re-Mix byline. Tears and celebratory carbs filled my day. I was happy, and my belly was full of laughter and sweet treats. But as I stood in a sexy black dress Sunday night, the knot in my stomach grew. Even though I knew I had nothing to feel bad about, I thought about Carlos all weekend.

"These were the shoes that looked best with this dress," I replied as I eyed the gold spikes that covered my heels in the mirror.

"Yes, they do," she acknowledged, taking a seat on the edge of my bed. "But you're looking pretty sexy for a work event."

I shifted my gaze from my reflection to my best friend. "You think it's too much?"

"No, it's just the right amount of sexy for a gallery event. It's not too short, but it's showing off your legs. It's not too low cut, but it's showing off your cleavage. And with your back out like that, it's showing off your ass."

That was the hope.

"Okay, good." I readjusted the gold pins in my updo and took a step back. "I'm ready."

"So, what are you going to say when you see him? Are you going to tell him about the article you're turning in tomorrow?"

The knot in my belly tightened. "If we cross paths, I'll tell him."

She scoffed. "If we cross paths," she mimicked me, rolling her eyes. "If these last two singles events are any indication, you two will find your way to each other. Trust and believe."

I shook my arms at my sides. *I can do all things.*

We said our goodbyes and twenty minutes later, I was standing outside of Rich Gallery. Gathering myself and gripping my gold clutch with all the strength I could muster, I walked inside with a group of women I didn't know.

"Welcome to Sapphire's showcase," a woman in a sparkly dress welcomed us. "If you're single, I need you to wear this."

After checking my jacket, I got in line behind the four women with whom I'd walked in. I watched as they held out their wrists and received black sparkly wristbands so when it was my turn, I followed suit.

"I think you have an admirer," the woman in the sparkly dress whispered. Once she attached my wristband, she signaled with her eyes.

Following her line of vision, the knot in my belly grew as I anticipated laying eyes on Carlos.

"Oh," I mumbled aloud, locking eyes with a good-looking man I'd never seen before. "Thanks."

She held on to my wrist a little longer than necessary. "If you don't want him, send him my way," she giggled causing me to toss my head back and laugh.

The nerves I'd felt initially dissipated as I moved into the gallery space. The mid-sized gallery in the heart of downtown Richland featured the art of new and upcoming artists for a two-week period. Sundays of the opening weekend were designated singles events and as I looked around, I was impressed with the turnout for Sapphire.

"Hi, I'm Michael," a deep voice met me at the first painting.

Reaching out, I met his outstretched hand. "Hi, Michael, I'm Akila."

"You look familiar." He checked me out. "But I know I would've remembered you if I met you."

"What do you think of this piece?" I inquired, shifting the focus to the dark colored painting in front of us. I felt him gawking at me, but I continued to look at the fluid lines in front of me. "What does it say to you?"

"It's cool." He paused until I looked over at him. "Can I get you a drink or something?"

"No, thank you." I looked back at the painting. "What do you think it means?"

"I don't know. This isn't really my scene."

"Oh? So, what made you come?"

"To meet women like you."

I gave him a look. "Women like me?"

"Beautiful women who could tell me about art." He let out a sheepish chuckle. "I know nothing about art."

"Art is subjective. It's just about what you see and what you feel. I don't know much about painting or Sapphire's work, but I know what I see and what I feel when I look at it…" I gestured to the darkest areas of the portrait. "It's all about your experience with the work."

"You are so beautiful," he commented.

I twisted to face him. "Thanks. Did you hear what I was saying?"

"I was distracted by your beauty," he flirted.

I blinked.

His smile widened.

I looked at him blankly.

"I'm going to go get a drink."

"Yeah, that'd be good."

He spun around and had only gotten three steps before I heard his voice. "You are absolutely beautiful," he greeted an unsuspecting woman who giggled.

Shaking my head, a smile played on my lips. *Men.*

I met a couple of other men as I moved from painting to painting. There were questions placed around the gallery to stimulate conversation about the art. For singles, there were additional get-to-know-you questions. The entire format promoted discussion while simultaneously honoring the art.

I was in a discussion with a small group of people about the painting of the faceless woman on the red canvas.

"I think it represents a woman on her cycle," one woman observed.

"Yeah, because of the red," a man chimed in, nodding. "I think she feels powerless to the pain of her cramps."

"Yeah, because it's a heavy flow. It's pooling around her. This could be representative of the most emotional time of our month," she elaborated before tapping my arm. "What do you think?"

I stared at the painting. "I think she's living a vibrant life and she wants to be heard by a world that doesn't want to hear her," I stated, eyes transfixed on the work.

They were quiet as they considered what I'd said, nodding in agreement without adding any additional commentary. Even as they moved on to the next painting, I remained in place, studying it.

"If you were on time, you would've gotten a personal escort around the gallery," Carlos informed me as he positioned himself next to me. "Perks of living three blocks away."

The sound of his voice curled my toes.

I gripped my clutch tighter as my entire lower body clenched. "I was only fifteen minutes late," I whispered, still staring forward.

"And you would only know that if you were looking for me."

"You aren't hard to miss, Akila."

It wasn't the words so much as the way his voice wrapped around my name that did me in.

Drawing in a shaky breath, I looked over at him. The sheer sight of him gave me butterflies. He wore black pants and a black button up shirt, tucked in with a black belt and shoes. He oozed sexiness and all he was doing was standing there, staring at the painting.

"What do you see?" I asked, praying he didn't hear the wispiness of my voice.

"A lot of red," he answered as I stared at his profile. "I see a woman who drinks red wine to deal with her invisibility."

My lips turned upward as he took a sip of brown liquor from his tumbler. "Interesting," I responded.

"And you?"

"I think the absence of blue means that she's probably not sad. I think red is vibrant and sexy. I think she is living this full life and she wants to be heard, she wants to shout it from the rooftops."

"You probably know her social security number, too, huh?" he joked, amusement dripping from his voice.

Stifling a giggle that threatened to bubble through me, I moved toward the next exhibit. I stayed a step ahead of him and didn't stop until I was standing directly in front of the monochromatic depiction of intertwined limbs.

"Hm," I murmured, eyeing the suggestive painting. "What do you see?"

He didn't answer for a while. I didn't push him to rush his answer. Giving him a sidelong glance, I noticed the way he took in the large canvas. I focused my attention back on the image and tried to figure out what the art was saying to me.

Carlos cleared his throat. "It looks like…ecstasy."

"Yes," I agreed. As I stared at the image, I tilted my head to the side. "It's pleasure. It's desire. It's…" I couldn't come up with a strong enough word to describe the lust displayed, but I felt it within me.

"It's what?" His deep voice ricocheted in my head and then shot down to the apex of my thighs.

Peering at him, my lips parted, but I still had no words. Turned on and standing next to the man who had frequented my fantasies, my body understood the painting better than my mind could comprehend.

When he looked over at me and our eyes met, my heart stopped. Just for a second, it stopped. And then it pounded. We stared at one another and the seconds ticked by.

Breaking the trance, I took a step back, almost bumping into someone. "I should—we should, um…mingle." Tearing my eyes away from him, I strode across the room as if I wasn't affected by him.

I was glad I broke away from him when I did.

While I had great conversation with a number of people attending the event, I was getting hotter and more bothered. The art became darker and sexier as the exhibit continued, so the conversations around me did, too. But neither intellectually stimulating conversation nor art held my attention for long. Even when I wanted to engage in conversation with someone about the art, I found myself looking for him subconsciously. Every ten minutes, my eyes would locate Carlos in the crowd. And every time, my eyes found him, his eyes were already on me. And we'd both instantly look away.

I tried to get him out of my head. But with two glasses of champagne swimming through my system and a very phallic painting in front of me, I couldn't stop thinking about him. I couldn't stop thinking about it. At one point I just kept picturing his hands on me, his mouth tasting me, and his dick in me. I tried to focus on the art in front of me, but my mind kept wandering to him. He had officially consumed my thoughts.

"You should go for it," a man's voice interrupted the fantasies brewing in my head.

I glanced over my shoulder and it was a cute couple having a private conversation.

"I think you're right. I'm going to ask the gallery owner about signing up for my own show," the woman squealed. "Thank you for supporting me, boo."

I smiled at them even though they weren't paying me any mind, and I turned my attention back toward the painting. Even though I wasn't facing them, I heard the man repeat his advice to his girlfriend.

"You should go for it," he said.

His words mixed with the champagne as I studied the painting in front of me. The heavy usage of red and black were so sexual and primal to me.

I should go for it.

It was right in that moment that I decided that I was going to have to fuck Carlos to get him out my head and off my mind.

Slowly spinning on my heels, I saw him sipping his drink and discussing something with a woman who looked like she was hanging on to his every word. While he was distracted, I allowed myself the pleasure of taking him in from a distance. My gaze traveled down and then back up his body to that stunningly handsome face of his.

Shit.

I was caught.

But unlike all the other times when we quickly averted our eyes, our looks lingered, and something shifted. The room felt hotter, the air felt thicker, and my body felt tingly. The energy between us was calling the shots and the atmosphere in the entire gallery had changed. I felt it instantly.

Licking my lips, I strutted across the floor, more mindful than ever that his eyes were searing into my skin. As I walked across the room to the painting we'd last looked at together, I lifted my eyebrows, hoping he'd understand my signal to follow me.

It worked.

"It's captivating," Carlos commented. His voice low and husky.

"I can't take my eyes off it." My stomach fluttered, and my voice came out breathier than normal.

"I don't understand it."

"Neither do I."

"But I know I want it."

"So do I." Taking a deep breath, I gazed up at him. "I keep thinking about it."

He stepped a little closer to me. "I haven't been able to stop thinking about it."

The way he looked at me mixed with the sound of his voice to cause a quiver in my belly. "I don't think it's going to stop until we do something about it."

"What would you like to do about it, Akila?"

"We should go somewhere quiet and discuss it."

His tongue ran from one corner of his mouth to the other.

"When? I would suggest tonight, but I have to be up early, and I don't want to rush it. I want to make sure there's enough time to discuss everything that needs to be covered."

"I appreciate that." I bit my lip and moved a little closer. "But I don't think this conversation can wait."

"There's a twenty-four-hour coffee shop a couple of blocks away."

My head moved up and down sluggishly, in a trance. "That's cool." I swallowed hard. "But I was thinking some place a little quieter."

His chest rose and then fell. The tension between us was building. With each word, each look, and each minute that passed by, I was being seduced by him. The magic was happening.

"I'll take you anywhere you want to go." He paused. "Just tell me where."

"You live three blocks away." I stepped closer to him, so close that we were almost touching. "I want to go to your place."

His brown eyes bore into mine and for the first time, I could see how bad he wanted me. He lifted his hand and touched my shoulder, running his fingertips down my arm until his fingers intertwined with mine. "Let's get your coat."

After helping me into my jacket, we walked to where I'd parked. His hand was firmly placed on the small of my back, under my jacket. His fingers danced against my skin as we approached my car. His touch felt so good I was unable to speak.

"This is me," I murmured, pulling my keys out of my bag with shaky fingers.

They dropped to the pavement with a jingly thud and without missing a beat, Carlos stooped down to pick them up. As he was crouched down before me, I flashed back to that day in the park.

And those sweatpants. And that dick.

He worked his gaze up my body before making eye contact again. Leisurely, he stood, pinning me between his body and the car. His eyes lingered on my lips and when I licked them, his eyes darkened. I waited for him to make a move, but he didn't. He left me in a dizzying state of wanton need as he pressed his body against mine.

Finally, I couldn't take it anymore. "Kiss me," I whispered.

He responded by kissing me with enough passion to take my breath away.

Wrapping my arms around him, I moaned into his mouth. The electricity crackled between us. Butterflies started at the base of my stomach and fanned out. I felt them in my chest as he deepened the kiss. It wasn't just sparks and fireworks, the kiss was magic and soul stirring. Fire burned through my entire body

Impulsively, we moaned together, loudly, when our tongues touched. Shivers traveled up and down my spine. I found myself clutching his shirt in an effort to help me climb him. I wanted to keep our bodies connected and feeling him hardening beneath his pants only intensified my urges. My heart thudded in my chest and because we were so close, I could feel his doing the same.

A deep growl from the base of his throat soaked my already wet panties.

He was rock hard and although he pulled out of the kiss and only our foreheads touched, I could still feel the heat of his hardness against my belly.

"We should stop," he said. His hands were running up and down my arms before cupping my face again. His eyes were shut tightly. "

I lifted my right leg and pulled him closer. "We really should," I replied, pushing my lips up against his. My heart was drumming in my chest, and something deep in my gut tightened.

His sweet lips moved against mine sensually, allowing me to relish in the taste of him. I nipped and sucked at his bottom lip. As his hands moved down to my hips, he turned slightly so he could grab the thigh of my raised leg. My body responded to his, curving toward him, into him. I could feel how hard he was and it took everything in me to not snake my hand down his torso just to see if he was as big as he appeared at the park.

"Carlos," I murmured between kisses.

Groaning, he dug his fingers into my skin a little harder before resting his forehead against mine. "You have no idea what you do to me."

"Will you show me when we get to your place?"

"For as long as you'll let me."

He opened my door for me and as he walked around to the passenger side, I felt a chill roll through me. The excitement and anticipation was so intense that I had to squeeze my thighs together to calm the ache.

"Do you know where Liberty Lofts is?" he asked as he got in, filling my car with his scent.

Sandalwood.

I inhaled deeply before nodding. "Yes."

"That's where I live."

I started the car. "I can't wait to see it."

He stared at me until I looked over at him. "I can't wait to show it to you."

Good Lord. I swallowed hard.

It was a three-minute drive from the gallery to Liberty Lofts.

I got there in ninety seconds.

Chapter Twelve

*H*is hand rested on the small of my back and I felt like I could feel the heat of his touch through my jacket. As he opened the door to his loft, he gestured for me to walk ahead of him. Moonlight poured into the room, cascading light through the glass windows. Not knowing my way around, I waited for him to flip the light switch on before moving any further into the loft. As light flooded the room, he moved behind me. He was so close that I could feel the heat radiating from his body.

"Can I take your jacket?" he asked.

"Yes." As he took my jacket and hung it on the coatrack by the door, my eyes swept over his spacious concrete home. The black leather couch and oversized chairs were poised near a seventy-inch television. The other side of the space was a kitchen and dining room area. Two doors were straight back—a bathroom and a bedroom. "Your place is so cool."

"Thank you." He made his way over to me. "You want something to drink?"

"A bottle of water, please."

"I got you." I watched him as he strolled over to the kitchen area. "You want to have a seat?"

I didn't answer, instead I gravitated toward a collection of pictures that were above a fake fireplace on a mantle. "You were so cute."

I felt the heat of him behind me. A puff of air escaped my lungs as the soft material of his shirt gently brushed against my bare back. I shivered.

"Were?" The amusement was evident in his question.

"Were," I corrected, equally amused.

The cold bottle connected with the exposed skin of my back and caused me to yelp. "Carlos! You ass!" Giggling, I twisted so my back was safely against the wall and swatted at him.

"What did I do?"

"You know what you did!" I tried to playfully smack his arm again, but he blocked it. I laughed harder. "You're lucky I'm in heels."

"Why is that?"

"Because if I wasn't, I'd have to bring the guns out."

Holding my wrist, he pulled me closer. "Oh really?"

Our bodies were close and looking into his eyes, all amusement fell away, and it was just us. The silence that engulfed us was so absolute that all I could hear was my heart racing. His eyes focused on my mouth and he licked his lips. I noticed his throat moving as he swallowed before he returned his eyes to mine. We held each other's gaze for what felt like a solid minute as the sexual tension between us became palpable.

He moved his hands up my arms, giving me chills. "Tell me why you wanted to come here."

I licked my lips. "Because..." My truth coming out as a rush of air, "I can't stop thinking about you."

His brown eyes burned into mine. "I haven't stopped thinking about you since the day we met."

"There's something between us."

"What do you think it is?"

"I don't know. But I think maybe if we get it out of our system, we'll get along better."

Cupping my face, he brought my mouth within an inch of his. "You think so?"

Fisting his shirt, I pulled his body closer. "It's worth a try."

He shifted so I could feel his hardness pressing against me. "You think us crossing the line will change anything?"

The breath left my body before I fully registered the sparks. I swallowed hard. "I think it'll change everything."

Silence filled the room, sucking out every other word except for the magic that had existed between us from the beginning. As much as we tried to deny it, in that moment it was undeniable. With each quiet moment, I felt myself giving in to the feelings he brought out of me, and my heart still raced because of him. The intensity of his gaze pinned me to the wall as I just stared at him wide-eyed, not knowing what else to say.

"So, what is it that you want to do?"

My stomach knotted as I stared at him. "Everything."

His breathing changed, and his tongue ran across his lips seductively. "Everything," he repeated faintly.

My heart thumped loudly against my chest. I moved my hand slowly down his body. "If we're doing this just once, I want to make it count." As I moved over his zipper, I felt how thick and hard he was through his pants. I exhaled shakily as I felt the size of him.

Good Lord.

His lips came down so close to mine that if I moved fractionally, we'd kiss. "Tell me exactly what you want."

The air instantly became thick. With him so close and my hand pressing against his erection, I could feel how badly he wanted me. My body responded in turn. Although he couldn't see how wet he made me, my hardening nipples made it clear.

"What do you want, Akila?" The need in his voice, in his question turned me on.

"I want you inside me—"

Before I could finish, he crashed his lips into mine. I gasped as he pushed me against the wall, kissing me hard. His soft lips moved over mine, overpowering me, overwhelming me. When his tongue grazed mine, I moaned into his mouth. I lost myself in that kiss, in that moment. It was magic in its purest form and my panties were soaked with it.

He pulled away, leaving me breathless. He pressed his forehead against mine. "I want to take my time with you," he murmured before covering my mouth with his again.

I moved my fingers, squeezing and gripping as best I could through his pants. It was a rush feeling how hard he was and when he groaned into my mouth, I quivered. That sound was music and shot fire through my body, straight to my core.

Sliding his hands down my neck and chest, he grabbed my breasts. He kissed me harder as he kneaded my flesh. Using his thumbs, he rubbed my hard nipples gently. As my body reacted, he repeated the action until they were so hard they hurt. His hands were cupping and kneading my breasts, my nipples begging for more attention.

Breaking the kiss and resting his forehead on mine, he moved his hands back to my shoulders. His eyes bore into mine as he slid the dress off my shoulders, slowly exposing one breast and then the other.

He took a step back and gave me a look saturated in desire and want. He licked his lips and then placed them on my collarbone. Trailing downward, his mouth brushed against the inflamed skin of my chest. He paused only when he reached the first nipple and my breathing became erratic. Without warning, his warm, wet mouth covered one and then the other nipple, alternating after sucking hard and tight. His tongue swirled around and then he gently scraped his teeth over them. The heat spread from deep within my belly throughout my entire body. Kneading the meaty flesh, he didn't let up until I was under his complete control.

"Is this to get along better or is this because you like me?" Carlos asked between licking and sucking.

My head fell back as his teeth gently nibbled on me. I cried out as everything below my waist clenched. His mouth felt so good I didn't even realize my dress had pooled down at my feet. But when I did, I stepped out of it automatically.

"You like me, don't you, Akila?" The low growl in his voice made me ache.

"Yes," I moaned as I tried to grip the wall behind me.

"I want to hear you say it," he challenged. His left hand still had a tight grip on my breast while his right hand moved down my belly. His fingertips lightly touched my skin, leaving a scorching path to my last piece of clothing, my lace G-string. "Say it."

I murmured incoherently as I tried to get ahold of myself. But as soon as his long fingers reached my panty line, I was in no condition to speak.

"Your panties are soaked," he whispered as he stroked me through the damp material. "You want me to take them off of you?"

I couldn't do anything but nod as his stroking became more insistent.

"Then tell me what I want to know."

I closed my eyes and relished the feeling of him playing with my body. My wet panties were sticking to me, causing extra friction that would surely do me in sooner rather than later.

"How do you feel, baby?" His whispered words mixed with his skilled fingers and I moaned louder.

"I feel good." My breathing was erratic and my hips started gyrating into his hand. "So good."

"And how do you feel about me?"

Both sexually and emotionally, I felt myself approaching the point of no return. "I want you. I need you."

He stopped.

My eyes fluttered open to find him watching me.

THE LOOK in his eyes made me have to hold on to his arm to keep my balance.

"Why'd you stop?" I panted.

"Because the first time you cum won't be wasted on my fingers." Staring deep into my eyes, he unbuttoned his shirt. "You will cum on my lips as I taste your pussy." His shirt fell to the ground. "Or you will cum as I'm buried deep inside you." He unzipped his pants and pushed down his boxer briefs with them. "The very first time I make you cum will be me tasting you or filling you."

I couldn't breathe. Swallowing hard, my mind was spinning from his words and my eyes were mesmerized by his body. I exhaled audibly.

I stared at the length and girth of what was tenting his pants. It was everything I thought it would be and more.

"Wow," I breathed in appreciation. I couldn't help reaching out and touching it. He was hot and heavy in my hand. Wrapping my fingers around him, I ran my hand up and down the length while maintaining eye contact.

He groaned. I started to stroke him harder. I watched his face for a second and then my eyes went back down to the biggest dick I'd ever had the pleasure of knowing.

"Can you handle it?"

Gazing up at him, I licked my lips and nodded.

He pulled my G-string down enough so that he could slide his finger over my wet slit. With his lips hovering above mine, he asked, "Can I lick your pussy until you cum?"

"God, yes," I moaned.

As soon as the words were out of my mouth, Carlos's mouth was on me. He parted my lips with his tongue and kissed me hard and deep. My hands slid up his torso to his chest and then back down so I could continue stroking him. I squeezed him in my hand, marveling at the thickness. He groaned into my mouth in response.

Pulling away from me, he turned me around and placed my hands flat on the wall. "Don't move," he demanded as he slowly removed my panties the rest of the way down my legs. I trembled with desire as the anticipation of what he might do kept building.

Standing behind me, I felt his dick pressing against my ass as he trailed kisses down my back. "Do you like that?"

"Yes." My voice was soft and breathy.

"You sure?" he asked, rubbing himself against my wet opening. His touch was electrifying as he slid across the most sensitive part of me.

I moaned and pushed back against him in an attempt to feel

more of him. Gripping my hips, he held me steady. "I told you not to move."

Without warning, I felt the shock of his hand firmly making contact with my ass. The spanking wasn't hard, but the mixture of pleasure and pain had me dripping. I pushed back against him and again, he held me steady, preventing himself from entering me.

"How do you feel about me, Akila?" Carlos inquired once more. "I don't think you're telling me the truth."

Before I could get myself together to reply, his fingers played in my wetness. "Because I see the way you look at me."

Plunging his fingers into me, I could no longer speak. Desperately grinding on his hand, my orgasm was building to something massive. The deep ache that overwhelmed me was reaching the point of no return as he skillfully worked his fingers in and out of me. I panted wantonly and unabashedly.

"Oh, not yet, baby," he whispered, pulling his fingers out of me and causing me to whimper involuntary. "I told you how I want to get you off. There's just something I need to hear before I can do it."

"What's that?" I murmured, my fingers pressing hard into the wall.

"The truth."

I moaned as he rubbed the pads of his fingers against my wetness.

"Say it," he demanded as he slipped a finger inside me, massaging my g-spot.

"I like you," I panted as he instinctively knew how to touch me. "I have feelings for you. I have fantasized about you. I—oh god, oh my god…"

Before I had a chance to finish my admission, I felt the heat of Carlos's mouth as he buried his face in me from behind. His tongue felt like it was everywhere, causing my mind to go blank. Moving systematically over me until finally, he started to suck on my clit.

"Oh shit!" Arching my back violent, I gave him better access to all of me.

The new angle made him groan into my wetness. I moaned his name repeatedly until I bucked against his tongue.

My legs felt wobbly and he had to help me turn around.

"Can you stand?" he asked me.

"Barely," I panted.

As soon as I was facing him, our mouths crashed together. As we kissed, I felt him stroking himself. He pulled out of the kiss momentarily to run his fingers over my sensitive flesh. Using my wetness, he went back to stroking himself, and I couldn't look away. The highly erotic sight of him, slick with my excitement, pleasuring himself was almost too much for me to take.

Taking a couple of steps to the couch, I bent over the back of it and spread my legs wide. Turning my head, I looked over my shoulder at him, and he eyed me with pure lust.

"Please."

That one little word was all it took.

Lining up behind me, I felt the head of Carlos's dick moving up and down my slit. "I'm going to take my time." He exhaled roughly. "I don't want to hurt you."

"Mm hmm," I whimpered.

"Are you okay?"

"Yes," I groaned as he leisurely pushed against me and then withdrew, never truly penetrating me.

A chill ran through me as I anticipated being stretched by him.

"So, you've been fantasizing about me?" His voice was strained.

"Ummm," I stalled.

His hand came down solidly on my ass cheek as pleasure radiated from the point of contact.

"Tell me." With each word, he applied a little more pressure, and the head of his dick was opening me up. He exhaled. "What was the fantasy?"

"It was more than one," I admitted faintly.

"Shit… did you play with yourself as you fantasized about me?" His voice was just above a whisper.

"Yes…oh, yes." My body was giving in to him as he gently

pushed just the head inside me. It hurt in the best way possible. "Oh my god."

"And what did I do in these fantasies?"

"You filled—" My voice tapered off into a deep, guttural moan as he slowly sank into me. He paused, holding himself still, making me beg for him to continue.

"Please," I begged. "Please, don't stop."

"You feel so fucking good," Carlos whispered.

"Yes, yes, yes, yes, give it to me," I pleaded with him, my voice wavering as he continued stretching me out.

"Shit," he cursed before we moaned in unison.

With each inch, he filled me, and the pure pleasure my body felt weakened me. Once he was completely in, he held himself still.

"I thought about you, too,"

I clenched my muscles, letting the wet heat clamp down around him. He sucked in a sharp breath between his teeth. "You feel even better than I imagined," he said hoarsely.

Knowing that he imagined being inside me caused me to tremble. Grabbing my hair from the root, he started moving, slowly at first. I was so wet that it didn't take long for me to adjust and his thrust had a little more power. He'd pull almost all the way out, before crashing into me again. His hands were everywhere as his dick kept a steady pace. My body adjusted to his size and milked him for everything he had. The ache deep inside of me became unbearable as his strokes became less controlled. The sound of skin slapping together reverberated through the air as he increased his pace.

My breathing became more labored and ragged as he lost control.

"Akila," he groaned as he gripped my hips.

The sound of my name mixing with the pleasure he was giving me was everything. I stiffened against him, my back arching, my muscles tensing, and my body shaking. He climaxed immediately after I did. And as I lay over the back of the couch like a ragdoll, I struggled to catch my breath from the most intense orgasm I'd ever had.

Wrapping his arms around me, he helped me up and carried me to his dimly lit bedroom. The room had the faint smell of sandalwood and vanilla—my new favorite smell.

"Are you okay?" he asked, helping me onto the bed. He climbed in after me and pulled me close. "You looked unsteady on your legs."

"Because my body is still recovering from what you did to it," I murmured, twisting until I was comfortably resting my head on his chest. "I should probably go as soon as I can walk again."

"You don't have to." He was quiet for a moment. "You can stay."

Listening to his racing heart, I smiled. "Don't tempt me." Running my hand over the firmness of his body, I tried to commit every ridge and muscle to memory. "I've never actually felt weak in the knees before. I thought that was just a saying."

His fingertips skated over my back and his lips brushed my forehead. "I don't think this is going to help me not think about you."

My smile grew. "You thought of me often?"

"Every day since we met."

"All good things, I hope."

He chuckled to himself. "For the most part."

"What?" I yelped playfully.

Laughing harder, he countered, "Was everything you thought about me all good?"

"Touché," I giggled. "But mostly it was good."

"Honestly, the things that frustrate me about you are the same things that I find incredibly sexy about you. Except the fact that you're judgmental."

I swatted at him and tried to pull away, but he held me tight. "Hey! I think everything about you is amazing except for the fact that you are complicit." Giving up the half-hearted attempt to get out of his arms, I returned my head to his chest.

"I'm not complicit."

"I'm not judgmental."

"I don't agree with what City Boy says most of the time."

"I'm not judgmental. I'm discerning."

We were quietly holding each other as our words hung in the air between us.

"What does your family think about what you do?" I asked, breaking the silence.

For three hours, we talked and discussed things beyond writing and photography. For three hours, we cuddled and got to know each other better. And when we both began yawning, we kissed good-night. But that kiss deepened and before I knew it, I was sitting on his dick.

Chapter Thirteen

"How exciting! Your assignment for the week is to capture a photo of a beautiful man. That shouldn't be hard, right? You could ask whoever has been taking you on all these dates recently," my mother pried. I could hear her motherly nosiness clearly through the phone call.

My brows furrowed. "I haven't been going on a bunch of dates recently."

"And that's part of the problem," she joked, giggling hysterically.

"Why are you like this?" I laughed. "You're a crazy person, you know that?"

"Yes. And it's where you get it from, my child."

I smiled. "I love you, Mom."

"I love you, too, sweetheart." She paused. "But I do worry that you work so much and don't have much of a social life..."

My mind flashed to the night before and my body stirred. Just thinking about the ways in which Carlos had satisfied me was almost too much to handle.

"...Once this photography class is over and you get into more of a flow at Re-Mix, maybe you'll have time for a date. You know who has been asking about you? Nancy's son, Eddie."

"Mom, I'm fine."

"I know you're fine. I just don't want you to be lonely."

Rolling my eyes, I sighed. "I'm not lonely, Mom. And I'm not interested in Eddie."

"Why? Because he's a little lanky?"

"No, I don't—"

"Because your high school boyfriend was a little lanky, too."

"Good Lord, Mom," I snickered. "Calm down."

"I'm just saying, maybe Eddie—"

"Mom, it has nothing to do with what he looks like. I'm more concerned about who he is as a person. And Eddie isn't the great kid you think he is."

"He isn't a kid. He's a man now. He's twenty-two."

I rolled my eyes. "That's not the issue either."

"Is it because of that time he teased you and said you had a big butt when you were in elementary school?"

I laughed. "No. But I still remember you telling me that having a big butt was something to be proud of and that I'll grow to appreciate it." I paused. "You were right."

Mom giggled. "Well, let me be right about you and Eddie."

"You know he posted a status update on social media about how the only thing a woman can offer a man is sex and a sandwich."

"Oh!" The surprise in her voice was evident. "I didn't know."

"Yeah. I don't know what he had going on in his life, but he's posted a lot of questionable things about women."

"Hm." I could hear my mom's lips pursing. "Well, then he's out. I know you don't play about stuff like that, so I won't bring that up again."

"Thank you."

"But you still need a date to our recommitment ceremony next month..."

"I don't need a date. You want me to have a date."

"True. Your dad and I just want to make sure you're getting out there. We don't want you sitting around, cooped up in your room with your laptop. If Meghan didn't live there, I'd be worried you didn't have any social interactions at all."

"I have plenty of social interactions."

"But are any of them romantic?"

"I can be happily single, Mom."

"You can be. But are you? That's all we want, honey. And single people socialize." She sighed. "You don't need a man to make you happy. Just make sure you're doing something more than writing. Go out and have some fun."

I had some fun last night.

"Mom, I'm happy. I swear. And as a gift to you and Dad, I'm coming with a date to your ceremony."

"Yes!" She was giddy. "And will you go on a date soon? Maybe someone in your photography class will catch your eye."

Carlos.

I cleared my throat, blinking away the vivid images of the night before. "I'll see what I can do. But in the meantime, I have an article to write and a good-looking man to photograph."

"I'm so proud of you."

I grinned, warmth and happiness filling my soul. "Thanks, Mom."

"I'll let you get back to work. Have a good day, Kiki."

"You, too. Love you!"

"Love you, too."

I ended the call and then did a double take when I looked at the screen.

A text message from Carlos.

Carlos Richmond: Did you see the email from Re-Mix about He Said, She Said?

Akila Bishara: No, not yet.

I clicked my email icon on my phone and clicked on the first Re-Mix email I saw. As I read the short email and reviewed the chart, tears pricked my eyes. We not only were one of the most viewed articles, but we had the most clicks and shares online.

Akila Bishara: I just read it!!! Oh my GOD!!!!!!!!!!!!
Carlos Richmond: Congratulations A. Bishara!
Akila Bishara: Congratulations Carlos Richmond!
Carlos Richmond: I'm leaving the school now. Are you free to talk?

I stared at the phone for a few seconds and then I hit the button to place the call.

"Hey," Carlos greeted me.

Hearing his voice put a smile on my face, but I kept my tone even. "Hey, how are you?"

"I'm good. How are you?"

"I'm good. Just working on my stuff about Rich Gallery."

"I finished my first draft during my planning period. I need to take another pass over it. I was a little distracted."

"Oh?" I blinked, trying to clear my mind from our night together. "Distracted?"

"Yeah…"

I licked my lips. The small flutter in my belly became even more noticeable as the idea of me being on his mind settled upon me.

"…the kids were wild today and didn't want to listen."

Wait, what?

"Oh." Covering my eyes with my hands, I squeezed my eyes together. "Yeah, of course. It's Monday. They were probably still riled up from the weekend."

"Do you think you're going to have your work done today?" he inquired, seemingly unaware that I was slightly embarrassed.

Get your shit together. It was a one-time thing.

"Yeah, I spent the morning trying to find my subject for Luca's assignment, I reworked my article about the happy hour at Koi, and then I started my prewriting process before talking to my mom for over an hour."

"Oh, that's cool. Your mom lives far away, right?"

"Not too far away. My parents live in Virginia. Maybe an hour and a half away. With traffic, four and a half hours."

He chuckled. "Yeah, the DC traffic is crazy. I was thinking they were in Georgia for some reason."

I shivered. The sound of his laugh always managed to infiltrate my soul. "That's where my mom is from, but my parents live in Virginia now. Your family is from Philadelphia, right?"

"Most of my family is in Philly, but my parents live right outside of Richland. We moved here when I was in fifth grade and they moved to the suburbs after I graduated high school."

"If I'm understanding this correctly, she's close enough that if you wanted to, you could call your mom and ask her to make you that cake you swore would change my life?"

His laugh cracked the air like thunder. "Yeah, pretty much."

My toes curled. "Interesting. So, I would imagine I'd have a slice within the week."

"You're killing me."

"Let me eat cake!"

His amusement was still evident in his voice as he spoke. "I can't believe you're not a spoiled only child. Are you older or younger than your sister?"

"She's a few years younger."

"That's cool. I had to join a frat to get brothers."

"She's one of my best friends so I get that."

Speaking of best friends…

"Um," I started slowly. "Speaking of your fraternity… Luna wanted me to focus on the parallels between Date Night and Brad."

"Yeah, I remember."

"And that's what I did."

"I had no doubt."

"I just wanted to be sure you knew…"

He chuckled under his breath. "You wanted to make sure I knew that last night didn't change anything?"

I took a breath. "Work wise, no."

"Work wise, no," he repeated. "And what about otherwise?"

I tugged at the edge of my shirt. "What do you mean? It was a one-time thing."

"So, it helped… it took your mind off of me?"

I hesitated, not willing to let myself be embarrassed again in the conversation. "Mm hmm."

"So, you've been able to get through the day and not think about last night?"

I swallowed hard. "Mm hmm."

"Because I have to tell you, I haven't been able to stop thinking about last night."

"I mean… it may have crossed my mind once or twice," I lied playfully.

The sexy rumble of his laugh sent a jolt through me. "Once or twice, huh?"

Grinning, I switched the phone to my other ear. "Mm hmm."

"It was a one-time thing."

It didn't sound like a question. It sounded like a reminder. I wasn't sure if he was trying to remind me or remind himself.

"It was a one-time thing," I agreed. "But it was a hell of a truce though."

"Yes, it was," he agreed with a groan. "Allegedly to help with the sexual tension."

I bit my lip. "Allegedly."

"Maybe it'll start helping after a good night's sleep," he joked softly.

"After a good night's sleep, we won't be starring in each other's thoughts."

"I've been starring in your thoughts, huh? That sounds like I was on your mind more than once or twice," he pointed out, causing me to laugh.

"And on that note, I need to get some work done," I snickered. "I'll talk to you later—about the article."

"Akila?"

"Yes?"

"You can hit me up about more than just the article or photography class. I know a truce doesn't mean we're…I know the truce doesn't change anything. I just wanted you to know."

My voice faltered a bit. "Okay."

"It was nice talking to you."

"You, too."

After we said our goodbyes, I found myself sitting and smiling for a solid minute.

"What is this? A school girl crush? You're a grown ass woman with work to do," I muttered to myself, massaging the smile from my cheeks.

Newly focused, I immediately opened my laptop and continued writing my He Said, She Said article. Because I wanted to focus without any distractions, I put my phone on silent. I was in the zone and didn't realize how much time had gone by until I heard the front door opening.

"Akila!" Meghan shouted.

"In my room! I thought you were going to the gym after work," I replied, still typing. I glanced at the time.

Wow, it's late.

"I did!" She burst in my room, sweaty and wigless. "Why haven't you been answering the phone?"

"It's on silent." I turned back toward the laptop. "I'm almost done and then I'll cook dinner. I chopped a bunch of veggies while I was talking to my mom earlier."

"Have you talked to Alex?"

Grabbing my phone, I checked my missed calls and messages. I turned to face Meghan. "No. She called once, but I missed it."

"She called me, but my phone was in the car while I was in the gym. I called her back on my way here, but she didn't answer."

The sound of the front door opening made us both look at each other quizzically.

"Alex?" I called out, standing up, following Meghan toward the living room.

"Yeah, it's me," Alex answered.

My brows furrowed at the dejected sound of her voice. As soon as I came around the corner, I searched her face. "What's wrong?"

"I need to talk and neither of you picked up the phone and... I'm so fucking mad!"

"What's wrong?" I repeated.

Alex started pacing across the living room. "Date Night with The Lost Boys," she grumbled.

Meghan and I looked at each other.

"What about them?" Meghan asked slowly.

I hadn't told Alex about the sex dreams about Carlos. I also didn't tell her about the actual sex with Carlos. I didn't know what she was about to say, but I knew that it was going to make telling her about him that much more difficult.

"You know how people email them questions and stuff?" She closed her eyes and shook her head. "Well apparently, people email them stories and pictures, too."

"For what? It's a podcast." I wondered, folding my arms across my chest.

"Apparently for their newsletter." Alex's tone was bitter.

"They have a newsletter?"

"They do now. And guess who was featured in the debut newsletter." She dropped her head into her hands.

"What?" Meghan screeched.

My blood was boiling. "I need more information."

She unlocked her cell phone and opened her email. After a shaky breath, she began to read. "Date Night Announcement: In honor of a certain 'journalist' who can't keep our name out of her mouth—"

"They're talking about you," Meghan gasped.

I nodded, fuming.

Alex's jaw dropped. "Really?"

"They got wind of the article I wrote for the Times and weren't happy about it. I said they objectified women so I'm assuming it has to be me they're talking about. Keep reading."

"Wow," Alex muttered before reading again. "And since the colder weather is coming, we are bringing you something special. With fall here, there are only a few more days remaining for unobstructed fun bag sightings. Send us your favorite photos and stories about big, beautiful breasts that need to be celebrated before it's officially fall. We want to see the cleavage! Show us the fun bags. To get us started, here's a few we've received."

"What is wrong with these people?" Meghan burst out as photo after photo of women in low-cut tops were displayed on screen.

When Alex paused, I nervously waited for what was coming next.

"HistoryBuff says he was distracted by his date's fun bags all night. Here's his story and why his date gets Fun Bags of the day." She lingered on that spot before she read the story aloud. "My date for this weekend is hot and I couldn't stop staring at her tits. It was the first thing I noticed about her, but after getting to know her, I thought she was cool, too. But this weekend, in this yellow dress I'd never seen her in before, I couldn't think about anything else but fucking her. When I tried to make a move, she said she wasn't ready. I said okay and didn't try again, but I'm confused. She was flirting with me. She went out of town to this important event with me. She was wearing this dress, for God's sake. Am I wrong for just wanting to fuck her or was she sending mixed signals?"

"That tutor did not submit your picture to Date Night with The Lost Boys," Meghan fumed.

She scrolled down, and a picture of Alexandria filled the screen. Although the photo was cropped to only show from her mouth down to her waist, it was clear it was her.

"So, not only is he a Date Night subscriber, but he submitted your photo to them?" I asked in horror. "Who does this?

"Someone with no friends and no game." Alex continued looking at her phone. "HistoryBuff, you're not wrong. She's wrong. She wouldn't have had that dress on if she didn't want it. So, stare all you want, fantasize all you want, and when she gives you the green light, motorboat those puppies. Women like that piss me off. She's hot, but she loses points for dressing like a slut and then not acting like one. Attention, fellas, if you see these tits, know that she's a little cock tease. The honor of fun bags of the day goes to History-Buff's tease because damn!" Alex let out a growl and stood up. "How is this okay?"

"It's not okay. Not only were you and the other four women objectified, this whole thing is just gross," I commented.

"This should be illegal," Alex stated, hands on her hips.

"Was this picture taken without your knowledge?" I asked, pulling out my phone to research.

"Well, no." She stopped walking. "I posed for the picture."

"You're not doing anything wrong. You are wearing a dress that looks damn good on you. The fact that it's being twisted into something different by The Lost Boys is wrong on their part."

"Yeah. That tutor guy, Jay, is lame and completely wrong for sending it in, and for seeking advice from those assholes, but The Lost Boys are the real villains of this story," Meghan pointed out.

"Definitely," I agreed. "Jay could've told a friend that he was disappointed that you didn't want to sleep with him. He shouldn't have reached out to Date Night. But what Date Night did is disgusting."

"And it's not even on a website that can be taken down. It's part of a newsletter that went straight to their subscribers' inboxes," Alex wailed. "Do you know how many people asked me if it was me?"

"How many?"

"Five people! And two of the people asking weren't even subscribers. They were just forwarded the email by someone else." Alex shook her arms at her sides. "And because my face is cropped out and it doesn't use my name and it's a picture taken in a public venue, it's not illegal. But all these skeevy guys are sitting around looking at my breasts, calling me a slut."

"I'm sorry, Alex." I wrapped my arms around her and gave her a squeeze. "They thought I was giving them shit before, but they have no idea what's coming their way now. What can we do to make you feel better?"

Meghan went to the other side and hugged her from behind. "Whatever you need, we have your back."

As we stood in our three-person hug, we waited for Alex to tell us what she wanted us to do. But my mind was racing. It was one thing when they verbally attacked me. But they elevated their objectification of women by using pictures to shame and disrespect women.

"Can I stay for dinner?" Alex asked.

"Of course."

"Akila's cooking vegetables," Meghan added with a hint of sarcasm.

"I have another question," Alex announced, lifting her head from my shoulder.

"What's that?"

"Can Meghan cook?" she joked, untangling from our hug.

We laughed, breaking the revenge fueled thoughts that flooded my brain.

"Thanks for making me feel better, guys," Alex sighed when her giggles subsided. "I know I can't do anything about the situation, but I feel better."

"Good. And I will make sure I add this to my article," I informed them as I headed into the kitchen.

"No!" Alex's reaction took me by surprise.

I turned around and looked at my sister. "Why not?"

"It's only going to make things worse. Once word is out that there's daily photos of breasts being sent out, they will have even more subscribers and even more listeners," she argued.

I considered what she said for a minute. "You're right. But we can't let them get away with this. They basically called me out and then used a picture of my sister. That can't be a coincidence."

"Maybe there's another way to call them out about this. Because Alex is right. Giving the newsletter attention will only make things worse," Meghan pointed out.

I walked into the kitchen and they followed me. Washing my hands, I considered a few different things, but my mind kept coming back to one. "I'm going to confront them face-to-face."

"What?" Alex screeched.

"How?" Meghan inquired.

I smiled.

Drying my hands, I walked over to the kitchen table where they were seated. "I'm going to call them out on their own show."

"How are you going to get on there? From the looks of things, they don't like you too much." Alex stopped. "Your photography partner! I know he's one of them, but you liked him! You said he wasn't that bad. Maybe you can find out something."

I swallowed hard. "Yeah. Maybe."

Meghan tilted her head. "Why do you look like that? You don't think he's involved, do you?"

They both stared at me, waiting.

I couldn't tell them I slept with Carlos—not yet, anyway.

I shook my head. "I-I don't think so. I mean, I know he couldn't have done it last night because we were together—for an assignment… for Re-Mix," I stammered. My eyes shifted between the two of them.

As the people who knew me best gave me critical looks, I felt embarrassed and ashamed. I busied myself pulling out the ingredients to make stir-fry.

I slept with someone who willingly and knowingly associates with the type of people who send out newsletters of breasts. And calls them fun bags, of all things. I slept with someone who condones the disrespect that Date Night encompasses. What have I done?

"Um, Akila? Hello?" Meghan summoned.

"Huh?"

"I was asking if you thought Carlos seemed different last night? Like he knew?"

Different? You mean before or after he fucked my brains out?

"No. Not that I could tell," I answered, pouring extra virgin olive oil into the pan. "He seemed… he seemed different in a good —positive way. He seemed okay."

"Hm. Do you think he was just being nice because he knew?" Alex wondered aloud.

Was he just being nice because he knew the shitstorm was coming?

"I don't think so." My words were slow, measured.

"Did something happen?" Meghan eyed me suspiciously. "You're being weird."

With my focus on sautéing the veggies, I replied, "I'll ask Carlos if he can get me on the show and I'll settle this once and for all."

When I glanced up, Alex was staring at her phone, but Meghan was watching me. She quirked an eyebrow when our eyes met, and I looked back down at the pan.

"Do you want rice?"

Chapter Fourteen

"'ll pose for you anytime. Let me know if you ever need anything else and I'd be happy to oblige. Good luck with your assignment. Cheers, Niles," Meghan read the card aloud before tucking it back within the bouquet of flowers. "What kind of flowers are these?"

"What am I? A botanist?" I joked, throwing my hands up in the air. "The only flower I know is a rose."

She tossed her head back and laughed. Her curly red wig swaying with each bout of laughter. "Well, looks like Niles is still thinking about that date you two had almost a month ago now."

"Or he's just being a sweetheart since he posed for my photos. The subject was supposed to be a good-looking man, and Niles is a good-looking man so…" I shrugged. "I really didn't have anyone reliable I could use. I wanted to capture someone who has inner and outer beauty. And men like that aren't ringing my phone."

She pursed her lips but remained quiet.

"I know what you're thinking." I narrowed my eyes at her.

She plopped down on the couch next to me. "What am I thinking?"

"You know what you're thinking."

She laughed. "I didn't even say anything! I was just minding my business."

"Cut the shit, Meghan! You were going to ask me about Carlos."

Tucking a leg underneath her, she turned her entire body to face me. "Well, now that you mention it, you fucked him on Sunday night and then had the audacity to wait until Tuesday to tell me—"

"I didn't get home until after midnight so technically, it was already Monday at that point. But I was going to tell you when you got home from work, and then Alex came over with the Date Night newsletter bombshell. And after hearing about what happened with Alex, I didn't think that was the time to say, 'hey, by the way... you know how you guys have been teasing me about my lack of sex? Well, guess who got fucked by one of the men who posted pictures of my sister in the newsletter?'"

Meghan snickered. "Yeah, that probably wouldn't have been the best timing, but still... we don't keep secrets. I feel like there's been this huge rift in our relationship all week because of it."

"Stop it!" I exclaimed with a laugh. "It's Wednesday. I told you on Tuesday, and it happened late Sunday night. Basically Monday. So technically, you knew the next day."

"Still... I told you the day I had sex with Derrick."

"I heard you the day you had sex with Derrick!"

We giggled.

"And in my defense..." I looked down at the ground. "I was a little embarrassed."

"Why?"

My head snapped up. "Because he's a Lost Boy. He represents everything I'm against. His friends are trash, and he's—"

"Trash adjacent," she interrupted, rolling her eyes. "I know, I know. But you don't really think Carlos had anything to do with the newsletter, do you?"

I sighed. "I don't think so, but I don't know."

"What does your gut say? And have you asked him?"

Wordlessly, I shrugged.

My gut said he didn't have anything to do with it. But part of me was scared to find out that he really was associated with it and I had sex with him. The fact that he was part of the show was evidence enough that he didn't make the best decisions. If I found out he wasn't who he presented himself to be, it would be evidence that I didn't make the best decisions. Either way, I'd been stressed about it for two whole days.

She reached out and squeezed my hand. "Have you talked to him?"

"Not really. I mean, we talked on Monday for a little bit. He called Tuesday, but I didn't answer. We texted a little today, but that was to confirm we submitted our photos. I texted him earlier asking him about Date Night."

"Speaking of that... what's the update?"

"Update on which thing?"

"On getting on Date Night?"

"When I sent my article in, I contacted Luna and told her I was thinking of doing it. She said it was a fantastic idea." I made a face. "I figure if I go through Carlos, I can get on the podcast sooner than if I were to send an email."

She nodded. "So, what's the update on the other thing?"

"What's the other thing?"

"You climbing on Carlos's dick again."

"Meghan!" Caught off guard, I covered my face and hoped she didn't see that I was starting to blush. Not because I was ashamed of the sex talk; I was ashamed that after everything, I still thought about it.

"It's not happening again. It was a one-time thing and in lieu of the newsletter, a lapse in judgement."

"I could tell by the way you told me the story that the sex was good. No one gets starry-eyed over mediocre dick."

Unable to contain myself, I burst out laughing. My entire body was shaking, and I didn't hear my cell phone vibrating on the couch beside me.

Seeing Carlos's name, I looked to see if Meghan saw the name on the screen.

"Yeah, I saw it." She folded her arms over her chest. "Are you going to answer it?" Making her voice higher in pitch and comically sexual, she imitated how she thought I'd sound. "Oh, Carlos! I've been thinking about that big dick since you wore those sweatpants in the park!"

Swatting at her, I was barely holding it together when I answered my vibrating phone. "Hello?"

"Akila?" Carlos sounded confused.

Getting off the couch and heading to my room, I left a giggling Meghan in the living room.

"Yeah, it's me. My best friend lost her mind and was making me laugh. What's going on?"

"Just getting home. I got your text earlier and wanted to talk to you about it."

I closed the bedroom door behind me. "Okay…?"

"I thought you said you hated Date Night."

"Oh, I do."

"Why do you want to do the show?"

"Because I was personally attacked, and I deserve the opportunity to defend myself."

And because I'm about call The Lost Boys out about their toxic masculinity and their bullshit advice.

He hesitated. "Personally attacked?"

"Yes. I believe it was City Boy who said there was no validity to what I was saying and that I was just a spinster looking chick who was just looking for someone to blame for my spinster lifestyle."

"You don't care about that."

"You're right. I don't care what they think of me. But I care that their toxicity is being passed off as advice especially after what happened with Brad. And also, our articles on Koi come out on Saturday, and it'll be good to hear what City Boy has to say in response to real life application of his advice."

Carlos was quiet.

"And Luna thinks it's a good idea, too."

Carlos let out a heavy breath. "I don't know, Akila."

"What's the problem?"

"I just don't know if it's a good idea."

My eyebrows furrowed. "What's really going on?"

"They've made you public enemy number one and I just don't know what's going to happen if you're on the show." He spoke slowly as if choosing his words carefully.

"I'm not worried about those two trash ass friends you call City Boy and Country Boy. I want to be a guest on the show. Preferably this weekend."

He sighed, taking a few seconds to think about it. "Okay, I'll see what I can do."

"Great, thanks."

"We record on Friday." He hesitated. "Let me reach out to them and then let you know."

"Okay. Thanks, Carlos."

"Don't thank me just yet. I'll get back with you."

"Okay." I smiled. "Thank you."

"Bye, Akila."

"Bye, Carlos."

One hour and forty-seven minutes later, I received a text message.

Carlos Richmond: Are you sure you want to do this?

Akila Bishara: Yes.

Carlos Richmond: I told them to, but I don't think they're going to take it easy on you.

Akila Bishara: I don't plan to take it easy on them either.

Carlos Richmond: I have no doubt. Empire Building. Studio B. Eight o'clock.

Akila Bishara: See you Friday!

Because I had completed my assignment for Luca Romano's

class early and I was up to date on all of my articles for Re-Mix, I spent the next thirty-six hours brainstorming and planning my attack on Date Night's bullshit podcast and mentality. I listened to as many recent podcasts as I could stomach. I looked up statistics and sources to emphasize my point. I was ready for an intellectual debate that would hopefully change the mindsets of their listeners. It didn't matter if The Lost Boys were a lost cause, I wanted to reach the masses and let them know that their behavior had real life consequences.

But just in case The Lost Boys decided to play dirty, I researched City Boy B, or Bryant as his mother named him, and Country Boy Q, or Quentin as is written on his birth certificate. I had a harder time locating their personal social media accounts, but once I found Carlos Richmond's personal social media page, it didn't take many clicks to find out a good deal of information about all three of their lives. I didn't plan to use the information unless they got personal in their attack of me. But it was interesting to see how close they were to their mothers, sisters, female cousins, and friends.

By Friday evening, I was a mixture of nerves and excitement.

"I wish I could be there to see the look on their faces when you call them on their shit." Meghan's laugh was so loud and boisterous that I had to pull my cell phone from my ear.

Smiling, I found a parking spot close to the Empire Building. "I feel like I've been waiting for this moment my whole life."

"Well you left out of here dressed to kill and ridiculously early, so I know you're ready for it."

I left twenty minutes before seven o'clock dressed in a navy blue mini dress with a high neckline, over-the-knee grey boots, and a grey sweater with blue dots. My hair was big and wild, in sharp contrast to the refined sexiness of my wardrobe. I was early, and I looked good.

"I just don't know what to expect, so I'm preparing for anything and everything." I gasped. "Oh, I see Carlos. I'm going to try to catch up with him. I'll text you afterward. Enjoy your date with Derrick!"

"See if Carlos can help you fill this extra hour you have."

I chuckled as I said goodbye to my silly best friend.

Before I could put my phone away, I noticed a text message from Alex. I looked up and Carlos was gone. Looking back down, I read the message.

Alexandria Bishara: You really are the best sister. Thank you for going toe-to-toe with those assholes and standing up for me and the other women in the newsletter. As of this morning, twenty-five of us have been put on display. It's demoralizing, you know? Makes me question if I should wear the tops that I like that happen to be low cut. Thank you, Kiki.

Akila Bishara: I love you and I will always have your back.

Tossing my phone in my bag, I eased out of my car and made a beeline for the Empire Building. I wanted to find Carlos and talk to him for a minute, so I could get the butterflies and heart palpitations out of the way. It made sense why thinking about him turned me on and lit my body on fire. But I didn't understand why just the thought of him caused my heart to race. I could admit that I liked him a little, but that was in constant war with the fact that he was part of The Lost Boys. And I didn't have time to be distracted by Carlos's handsome face, witty commentary, or the flurry of feelings he inspired within me.

I opened the main door and froze.

Dick print.

Carlos was standing there as if he was waiting for me—in grey sweatpants. I could feel his gaze sweeping over my body. Heat rose from beneath the surface of my skin. I shifted my weight from one foot to the other as every inch of me reacted without my consent.

"Hey," he greeted me, pushing off the wall and walking toward me.

"Hey," I responded, unable to move.

He licked his lips. "You look nice."

"You look…" My eyes zeroed in on the noticeable bulge in his pants, and I swallowed hard. Jerking my head and my gaze back to his face, I continued, "Comfortable."

He smiled, shaking his head. "I had to break up a fight in the student parking lot and my pants got fucked up." He made a face. "But the kids are mostly unharmed and safely at home, suspended for ten days."

"Oh, I'm sorry to hear that. Are you okay?"

"I'm fine. Thanks though." He paused, stopping about a foot away from me. "You're here early."

"Yeah…"

"Did you want to go to the studio this early?"

"Where else would I go?" I asked slowly.

"There's a little break area."

I cocked my head to the side and narrowed my eyes. "Why do I feel like you're trying to keep me from the studio? You were standing here waiting for me and now you're trying to take me to a break area. What's really going on?"

"I saw you getting out of your car and I waited for you."

I tried my hardest not to smile. "So, you were watching me?"

"Yes."

My heart thundered in my chest. I asked him the question jokingly and between his answer and the way he was looking at me, it felt like so much more.

"Oh," I breathed in reply.

He glanced behind me. "Let's go to the break area for a minute."

His closeness was intoxicating. All I could do was nod.

With his hand on the small of my back, I allowed him to escort me to the communal break area. I heard people entering the building, but I didn't even bother to turn around. We walked into a cute, clean space. There were tables, vending machines, and not much else. But the view was phenomenal.

"Oh wow," I remarked as I moved toward the floor to ceiling glass pane that showcased the beauty of Empire Park.

"We can see out, but they can't see in."

"It's a gorgeous view."

"It sure is."

My heart rate spiked. From a few feet behind me, I felt him staring at me. I turned to face him and watched his eyes dart away and then back to my face.

"What are we doing here?" I asked, hoping he didn't hear the way my voice shook.

He strode over to me. "I just wanted to talk to you for a minute."

I exhaled. "About?"

"Are you sure you want to do this?"

"Are you trying to talk me out of this?"

"No, I—"

"Because I can handle myself."

"I know."

"I don't need your concern or protection."

"I know."

"I'm not the one that should be worried."

Licking his lips, he took another step forward. "I know."

Instinctively, I took a step back. The cool glass of the window was against my back. My chest rose and fell in anticipation as he stood less than a foot away from me. Wordlessly, taking me in. The longer we stood there like that, I felt nothing but the intensity of his gaze. His eyes pierced me as if he could see into my soul. The energy between us was undeniable, but I wanted nothing more than to deny it.

"What are you doing?" I whispered as his face seemed to hover above mine.

"You've been on my mind all week," he murmured.

Hearing those words were too much. I had to rip my eyes away from him in order to keep myself from getting too caught up in the feelings he brought out of me. It was a dangerous mix of desire, lust, and familiarity.

"Carlos."

"Akila."

The butterflies in my belly were forceful as his deep voice wrapped around my name. As he closed the gap between us, I could feel how hard he was pressed against me.

"What are you doing to me?" I wondered aloud.

"Anything you want me to."

I gasped. "Carlos…"

"We have forty-five minutes until we should be in the studio. I wanted to talk to you before going on air. And I wanted to kiss you." Moving the hair off my shoulder, he leaned down so that his lips were against the shell of my ear. "I still want to kiss you."

Ignoring the desire that churned between my legs, I opened my mouth to tell him that our last time was our last time. I looked into his eyes, ready to emphasize my point. But when he wet his lips and I caught a glimpse of his tongue, that yearning deep within me caused me to have a temporary lapse in speaking ability.

Putting my hands on his chest, I planned to push him and create distance between us. I wanted to give myself the space to breath freely. He was too close, too intoxicating, and I couldn't think straight. But feeling the way his heart raced didn't help. Letting my hands move down his defined chest to his hard abs to the waistband of his sweatpants, I started throbbing.

I looked down and could see the prominently displayed bulge in his pants, no longer at rest. My eyes flew up to his and all I saw was want and need etched into his handsome features.

Pulling him a little closer, I slipped my hand inside his sweatpants and wrapped my hand around his hard cock.

Sucking in a sharp breath, his eyes closed. "Akila…"

I responded by lightly running my hand from the base to the tip of his dick.

He groaned, bringing his forehead to mine. "Don't start something you don't want to finish."

"I've already started," I murmured wantonly before pushing my lips to meet his. "Take me somewhere. Now."

The kiss was explosive.

"Come here," he demanded, pulling me into one of the single-stall restrooms within the break area.

I walked in first, and he was right behind me. As soon as the door locked, we were all over each other. The desire I felt for him was too much and I couldn't stop myself.

"We don't have much time," I breathed as he cupped my face with both hands.

My eyes were fixated on his lips as he slid his hands down my neck and over my shoulders, taking my sweater off with them. He reached over and hung the sweater on the hook behind the door.

"Akila," he uttered before covering his mouth with mine. Feeling the sweet heat of his lips, my body curved into his. As he deepened the kiss, his tongue grazed mine, and I felt my resolve break.

"Do you know how sexy it is when you say my name like that?" I peered up at him through my lashes as the palm of my hand applied pressure against his dick. I rubbed him over his sweatpants.

He closed his eyes and let his head drop back momentarily as I pushed his sweats down.

"Mmm." My fingertips had a full, unobstructed access, and I took advantage of it.

"I spent every night this week thinking about your touch." He grabbed my face and kissed me softly. "I've wanted to touch you, kiss you, be inside you." He pulled away from my lips and started trailing kisses across my jawline, down my neck, and over my shoulder.

"I thought about you, too," I answered breathily.

His fingers gripped my hips as he kissed his way to my breasts. He nuzzled my hardened nipples with his face before biting them through my dress.

I moaned.

He continued kissing down my belly until he was squatting in front of me, his hands on the back of my knees. "Do we have time for me to taste you?" he asked as he stared at the apex of my thighs. He licked his lips and leisurely moved his hands up the back of my thighs.

I could see the desire in his eyes as his chest heaved, looking up at me.

I swallowed hard. "I don't think there's time."

With his fingers hooked into my G-string, he pulled the lace strip of material down over my boots.

"Lift," he commanded, helping me step out of my panties. "Lift."

As I lifted my right leg, he shifted his body, maneuvering his shoulder under my knee. With the new position, he was able to open me up and run his tongue over my slit.

My legs buckled. "Oh, my God," I called out, leaning against the wall for support. My moans only encouraged him as his tongue strategically toyed with me. I placed my hands on the back of his head and rocked into his mouth. He hit a spot that caused my legs to shake. I almost tipped over in my boots.

"I got you," he whispered. He kissed my thighs before standing. "Spread your legs."

My heart skipped a beat.

The anticipation to have him fill me up was like nothing I'd ever experienced. My heart pounded in my throat as he lifted my skirt. Using his middle finger, he massaged his way into me. Sliding in and out of me, he curled his finger into my g-spot. I moaned loudly. Smothering my moans with his mouth, he kissed me like he missed me.

"The things I would do to you if we had time," he growled, pulling his finger out of me and rubbing my clit. "You have no idea what you're doing to me."

"Carlos," I panted as he kissed me harder, caressing his tongue against mine.

Leaning down so that my lips brushed against the shell of my ear, he whispered my name as he applied pressure as he rubbed me. My fingernails dug into his shoulders and my breathing changed when I felt myself approaching the edge.

"Listen to how wet you are," he growled as I gyrated against his hand. "Have you been thinking about me?"

"Yes."

He groaned as he kissed me. His fingers moved in and out of me until I felt the tension tighten my entire lower body.

"Do you want me?"

"Yes."

"Tell me what you want from me."

"I want you inside me," I murmured.

"Say it again."

"I want you to fuck me."

Moving his lips over mine, we kissed with reckless abandon. I wanted him so bad that I was starting to lose control. I wasn't thinking clearly.

Spinning me around, he pushed me against the wall and pinned me with his body. Caught off guard, my breathing hitched at the force of the movement, and I trembled in response.

Gripping my hair at the root, he gently tugged. "Is this what you want?"

"Oh god yes. I want you—all of you."

He placed his hand in the center of my back, bending me over. He lifted the skirt of my dress, grabbing my exposed hips tightly and pressed his dick against me.

"You ready for me?"

"Yes, yes, god yes…" I moaned as he pushed himself into me.

"Shit," he swore, digging his fingers into my skin as he restrained himself.

I was so wet that the pressure of him stretching me was a delicious pain. Even though I was wet enough to accommodate him, he was so big that he had to work his way inside slowly. After every inch he pushed into me, he paused to let me adjust. The deeper he got, the closer I felt to him. He wasn't just stroking my body, he was stroking my soul.

I shuddered as I gave into the feelings we shared. Grinding my hips against him, I worked myself up and down his shaft. The rapid bursts of air from his ragged breathing coupled with the sound of my wetness, intensifying the moment for me.

"You feel so fucking good." His voice was hoarse and needy. "Damnit, Akila. Shit."

With my hands against the wall, I let my head dangle languidly. "Yes, Carlos. Please fuck me."

"Oh shit," he groaned softly, flexing his fingers against my hips and picking up the pace.

"Carlos, please don't stop," I begged in the throaty purr that seemed to do something to him.

"Shiiiiiiiiiiiiiiiit." His strokes were longer, deeper, faster.

"Yes, yes, yes, yes."

Keeping one hand firmly planted on my hip and the other twisted in the soft curls of my hair, he switched to long strokes. Pulling almost all the way out and then slamming back in, his balls slapped against my ass loudly.

He sucked in a sharp breath between his teeth. "Akila," he swore.

"Please. Don't. Stop," I panted.

Untangling his fingers from my hair, he grabbed my other hip and let loose, ramming into me.

As he continued to thrust his hips, I threw my ass back to meet him. Each swear, each groan, each grunt added to my building orgasm, and I let out a series of moans. We were getting louder, but it didn't matter. It wasn't long before I was crying out in ecstasy. Quivering, I shut my eyes tightly and rode the wave.

Pulling my hair, making my head lift to the ceiling, his dick touched my soul. My muscles clenched, and I started clamping down around him. My back arched, and my body shook, and he stiffened. The ache deep inside me exploded as I felt his throbbing dick and heard the raspy need in his voice.

As our bodies came down from the high we were riding, all I could hear was our heavy, satiated breathing.

"Stay right there," Carlos instructed. Grabbing paper towels, he cleaned me up and then himself. "Turn around."

I turned, still propped up by the wall, and he assisted me in stepping into my panties. As he rose, he pulled them up and then straightened the skirt of my dress.

"That was…" I bit my lip. Pulling his face toward mine by his beard, I pressed my lips against his. "That felt so good."

"I don't know what got into me." He shook his head before whispering, "It's like I can't resist you."

"It's like there's something drawing us together, even though we shouldn't."

A look crossed his face and he swallowed hard. "Are you sure you want to do this?"

Smoothing down my dress, I walked to my sweater then turned to face him. I watched him watching me as I put it on. "What's going on?"

He licked his lips. I'd never seen him look nervous before. "I just…"

As I waited for him to finish his sentence, I felt exposed. He was able to do things to my body that blew my mind, but it was the emotional connection I felt when he was in me that made me feel vulnerable. "What's going on?" I repeated, feeling anxious.

He closed the gap between us and cupped my face. "I like you."

My mouth opened and then closed, conflicted. "It-it's the sex." I blinked rapidly, hoping he didn't see the truth in my expression. "We have a show to do."

"It's more than the sex." He kissed me. "You feel it, too."

"Whatever I feel doesn't change the facts," I reminded him softly, my arms falling by my sides.

Holding me firmly around my waist, he searched my eyes. "I want to hear you say it."

We were face-to-face, and I let out a breath I didn't realize I was holding. My heart pounded in my chest and I felt dizzy. I wanted to grab on to something. My mind told me to grab the wall; my body told me to grab him. But I just stood there, hoping I didn't pass out. I opened my mouth to put an end to whatever it was that was happening, but my mouth felt dry.

"Say it." His tone was steady, but his eyes pleaded with me.

My chest rattled as I inhaled. "Why?"

"Say it."

I hesitated for a while before I admitted the truth. "I like you."

The moment the words were out of my mouth, his lips were against mine. The passion that emanated from the kiss set me ablaze. I wrapped my arms around his neck and pulled him even closer.

"Why did you make me say it?" I murmured against his lips. "It makes it real."

He pulled away fractionally. "Because… I needed it to be real."

"Is someone in there?" a voice asked, knocking on the door and jiggling the handle.

Carlos and I stared at each other wide-eyed.

What am I doing? I work here now! I stared at the door, willing the person to stop knocking and to go away.

"The bathroom around the corner has stalls," a second voice said. "Come on, we'll try that one."

Thirty seconds later, silence.

"We have to go," I whispered, turning my head to face him. "We…"

My voice wavered at the way he was staring at me.

With one final chaste kiss against my lips and then my forehead, he took a step back. "You go first. I'll meet you at the studio."

I gave him a questioning look. "Okay." I paused. "Is everything okay?"

He nodded, kissing me again. "I'll see you in a minute."

I started to leave, but he grabbed my hand and kissed it. "I have to tell you something. Before you go on air. The guys will kill me if they knew I told you but…"

I froze. "What is it?"

"There's a newsletter that started going out this week. It's… listeners submitted photos and Bry—City Boy compiled them and picked the women to showcase."

I watched his face for any tells. "When did you find out about this?"

"When I checked my email on Tuesday."

I closed my eyes as I struggled with the new information. "So, you've known most of the week that women were being objectified and disrespected?"

That my sister was being objectified and disrespected!

"Yes. But I didn't put it together. I didn't know anything about it until it was already put together," he assured me, before his phone started ringing.

I stared at him with a blank expression as he used his free hand to pull his phone out of his pocket and answer the call.

"What's up?" He never took his eyes off me as he listened to the male voice loudly talking on the other end. "I was handling something important. I'm always ready. You're the one that needs to be on your A-game." He paused, running his thumb across the back of my hand. "Yeah, she's going to show up. I told her to be here at eight. She still has ten minutes…"

Removing my hand from his, I exited the bathroom.

Chapter Fifteen

I stared between City Boy and Country Boy as they did the Date Night with The Lost Boys introduction. They barely said hello when I entered the studio. Carlos arrived two minutes after I did, and he was the one who set me up at the microphone and tested my headphone. He was on the other side of the glass, but I could see him clearly. Everything seemed simple enough, but my head was spinning. I eyed City Boy, the baby-faced asshole with curly, reddish-brown hair and Country Boy, the tall, lanky jerk with dimples, as they sat across the table. While the two men looked like they'd be harmless, the reality was that they were toxic.

"…and without further ado, we have Date Night adversary, A. Bishara, in the building," City Boy announced leaning into the microphone. "Welcome!"

"Adversary is right. And thank you," I returned staring daggers into him.

"Oh, you want to get right to it, I see," Country Boy chuckled, looking at me with amusement. "But before we give you a chance to tell us what your problem is with us, we need to take some calls and emails."

"Let's give our listeners a little back story on A. Bishara." City

Boy grinned. "She wrote an article attacking us, folks. She said that we were toxic and that we gave out bad advice. When that wasn't enough, she did it again in another article. It's like she's obsessed with us."

"Stage-five clinger," Country Boy added.

"Definitely," City Boy laughed. "So, now that you're caught up on who our guest is and what her jaded perspective is, let's get started with your emails and calls."

"We're ready to show her that we're not who she says we are," Country Boy cheered.

I shook my head. "I've listened to enough——"

"Sorry, sweetheart, your mic isn't on," City Boy interrupted me with a smug grin. "We'll turn it on when it's time for you to do more than just sit here and look pretty."

"I didn't want to be the one to break it up, but now that City Boy has opened the door: A. Bishara… not bad." He stood so he could see more of me. "Not bad at all."

"Fellas, come on," Carlos spoke up, his jaw clenched. "Let's show the lady some respect."

"Los Cabos, the diplomat," Country Boy groaned. "We're paying her a compliment."

He looked from me to them. "Let's just get to the emails."

"Someone is in a mood tonight," Country Boy joked, looking at City Boy for backup.

City Boy was staring at me. "I think I know why Los Cabos is getting bent out of shape." He paused for a beat too long. "You know he likes to keep us on time."

"That's the truth," Country Boy agreed.

"So, let's get to it." He looked down at a piece of paper. "First up, we have GreatestShowman27. His email says: What's the best advice you can give me to meet women and score a date? I'm a pretty good-looking guy. I have a good job. I dress well. But I've never been good with striking up conversations with women. I get nervous and I end up going home early—and alone. What are some ways I can score a date? Or even some regular ass? It's been so long, I'm okay with either at this point."

I looked around the room as I braced myself for ignorance.

"Well," City Boy started. "This right here is a common issue with lots of men, so this is a perfect place to start." He winked at me. "Give our guest a taste."

I rolled my eyes. Country Boy stifled a laugh, avoiding eye contact with me. Carlos sat back, expressionless.

"GreatestShowman27, you're a good-looking dude with no game. Sounds like you feel intimidated by women. You have put pussy and women on a pedestal, and that's why you're having such a hard time. You need to remember that women are just people. If you see a woman and you think she's out of your league, level the playing field. If you're nervous, make her nervous. If you're feeling like a seven, make her feel like a six. You have to feel like you have the upper hand. Once you feel like you have the power in the situation, all your nerves and anxiety will disappear." City Boy looked around. "Let's see what the boys think. Los? Country?"

"I have to say I agree with City Boy," Country Boy stated, nodding aggressively. "You have to level the playing field. If you think she's better than you or too good for you, you'll never be comfortable enough to make a move. Even if it's just in the beginning."

I sighed loudly to convey my displeasure.

"GreatestShowman27, you should work on your self-esteem, man," Carlos chimed in. "Your focus shouldn't even be on getting a date or a one-night stand. Your focus should be on you. Women like a confident man, so until you figure out how to channel your confidence, you won't have the success in meeting women that you're seeking."

"The man is trying to get some ass, Los! You're always trying to mentor somebody! If the man wants ass, let him have ass," Country Boy joked, causing City Boy to laugh.

Carlos chuckled to himself. "You know I'm right though."

"I know working on himself is important, but you can't tell me it's better than pussy," City Boy responded before looking at me. "Oh, excuse me, vagina."

I knew he was hoping for a reaction out of me and I refused to give it to him. I just stared at him, expressionless, taking in all his bullshit.

"City Boy, chill," Carlos cautioned.

"I'm speaking the truth! Back me up, Country." City Boy looked to his left.

"Like I said, if the man wants ass, let him have ass." Country Boy shrugged. "Maybe you need to get some ass, Los. Maybe that's why you think this man should write daily affirmations or some shit instead of running game and fucking. When was the last time Los got some?"

My eyes darted to Carlos. *Ummmmm…*

"Good point!" City Boy exclaimed, hyping the situation up. "Let's talk about it! When was the last time you got some? I don't mind answering. For me, it was last night."

"For me, it was this morning," Country Boy interjected.

City Boy howled. "So, Los, let's talk about it. How long has it been? Your dry spell could help somebody out. Even good-looking, confident dudes go through dry spells, and the world needs to know about it!"

"Maybe Los Cabos is really GreatestShowman27," Country Boy clowned before succumbing to raucous laughter. Everyone joined in while I sat silently holding on to the truth about Carlos's dry spell. Country Boy shook his head once he caught his breath. "I'm kidding, I'm kidding. It's funny because nothing intimidates Los. I know it doesn't sound like it, but Los has game."

"When you're confident in yourself, you don't need game," Carlos countered, redirecting the conversation. "So, like I was telling our listeners—focus on being confident in yourself and then you don't have to run game on anyone."

City Boy chuckled. "Since Los doesn't want to admit to his dry spell, we'll move on to our next email…"

Three more painstaking conversations took place that I had to listen to, and I considered leaving after each one. It was like the longer I sat there, the angrier I'd become. Because I'd already been announced, I didn't want to give them the satisfaction of telling their listeners that I left. So, I sat there, stone-faced, taking mental notes.

"And for our last email, we have Cole," City Boy started. "His email says: I want to convince my girlfriend to have a threesome. She's not into it. How do I get her to change her mind?"

Country Boy whistled. "That's a tough one. But I don't think there's a way around that. If she's not into it, she's not going to do it."

"Unless you can finesse her," City Boy replied with a laugh. "Here's what you do, Cole. If you want a chance to score a threesome, you'll have to make it seem like it's her idea. Don't bring it up again unless she specifically asks you what your fantasy is or what you would want if you could have anything in the world. Instead, every few weeks, watch a movie with a threesome in it. If you two are into watching porn together, watch threesome porn. Think of all the ways she'd get pleasure from it and when she asks you why you want a threesome, tell her all the ways she'd be pleased. Make it about her, and you'll convince her that this is something that she wants, something that she's into."

I couldn't take it anymore. "So, basically gaslight her?" I muttered, crossing my arms and leaning back in my chair.

"Do you have something to say?" City Boy directed his question at me.

I narrowed my eyes at him. "Are you going to turn my mic on?"

"First…" He turned to Carlos. "Los Cabos, what do you think?"

"I think you have to hang up the dream, Cole. I agree with Country Boy. If she says she's not into it, leave it alone. Decide what's more important: your girlfriend or your fantasy. Because if you go for one, you'll lose the other."

"I've never known Country Boy and Los Cabos to give up so quickly." City Boy laughed and then directed his attention to me. "We haven't made it to the guest portion of the show, but it's good to see A. Bishara already has some thoughts."

Country Boy laughed.

I shifted my eyes to him and curled my lip in disgust. City Boy was the worst of the worst, but Country Boy's willingness to normalize and cosign on City Boy's bullshit was astounding.

And then there's Carlos.

He was there to gently admonish and to keep the other two in line, but much like what I'd heard in the four months' worth of podcasts I'd listened to, he never blatantly called City Boy out.

"We're now turning on A. Bishara's microphone," City Boy announced. He hit a button and then sighed dramatically. "Here it comes."

"What you're calling advice is really just manipulation, predatory behavior, and ignorance. Just sitting here listening to the complete bullshit coming out of your mouth has really just proved all my points for me."

"Woah!" City Boy held his hands up as he laughed. "She's just as aggressively annoying in person as she is in print. That's crazy."

"What's crazy is that you don't see how destructive your advice is."

Country Boy whistled. "I have to say I didn't see this coming."

"I did," Carlos spoke up.

"When you said you wanted to come on the show, I thought you would give it a chance. But it's clear you were never trying to give us a chance," City Boy baited me. "Sounds a little judgmental to me."

"You told one of the callers to not take no for an answer when pursuing a woman." I leaned forward. "You actually said that women play hard to get and no doesn't mean no except for in the bedroom. While I'm glad you had the common sense to add that caveat, what message are you trying to convey by telling people to not respect a woman's no."

"It's called being persistent," City Boy argued.

"It's called being a predator," I countered, narrowing my eyes.

Country Boy's eyes bulged as he watched us. Carlos silently observed the scene, his face emotionless.

City Boy's jaw dropped. "Predator? Are you serious? Come on… you're taking it too far now."

"Taking it too far? If someone tells you no and you keep pursuing her, you're taking it too far."

"I don't like how you're trying to twist this so chill out," he barked at me. "I'm serious."

"I'm serious, too. You told someone to disregard a woman's no and keep going after her. What kind of shit is that? If a woman says no—leave her alone."

"Women like the chase."

"Women like to be pursued, not chased. If you pursue a woman, she's an active participant. If you chase her, she's running from you."

"Bullshit. You seem focused on just me. The Lost Boys include Country and Los. You haven't directed your anger at them. Why are you so focused on me? You have a thing for me?"

"I'm focused on you because you're the primary problem. The other two are complicit. And I have issues with that as well. But you are the one who says the outlandish bullshit. And no, I don't have a thing for you. I actually don't like men who promote toxic masculinity."

City Boy chuckled. "Let me ask you something… are you single?"

I made a face. "What does that have to do with anything?"

City Boy laughed. "I guess that explains everything, fellas." He grinned. "Your advice comes from your perspective as a single woman with no prospects. Now I'll admit, you're not bad looking, but your overbearing attitude is a real turn off."

"I don't exist to turn you on," I snapped. "And don't try to deflect from the topic at hand. All of the advice that you've given has been disgusting and sad."

"What's sad is the fact that you can't get dick because of your ugly ass personality and—"

"City, chill," Carlos cut in roughly.

City Boy glared at him. "No, she wanted to step into the ring. She asked for this." He took a breath and then his lips turned upward, but the smile didn't reach his eyes "But I'll chill. You just have to stop slandering me."

"How am I slandering your name?" I shrugged my shoulders, purposely ignoring the fact that he called me crazy. "You advocate for disrespect. My issue is that you're trying to normalize emotional manipulation and the objectification of women. That's not me slandering you. That's me calling you on your shit. And I get why you're so mad right now… there's nothing a man like you hates more than a woman who calls you on your shit."

"You must not have had dick in a while, huh?"

"That's enough," Carlos growled. "Show her some respect."

I didn't look his way, but I could hear the warning in his voice.

City Boy's eyes darted to Carlos before making a face. "Are you going to be like this all night because a lady is present? I mean, I'll give it to her. She's not a four. But you're acting like—hey! I have an idea." His face brightened with apparent amusement. "Since Los Cabos hasn't gotten any in a while and A. Bishara needs some dick in her life, so she can get the stick out of her ass, maybe they should do each other."

Country Boy stifled a laugh.

I didn't know what to do or say so I just sat there, eyes narrowed, and mouth set in a straight line.

"I'm getting tired of telling you to chill, City," Carlos warned. "This is supposed to be a conversation. So, converse and stop with the other shit."

City Boy stared at Carlos for a tense thirty seconds. "For those of you who don't know, Los Cabos collaborated on a little project for Re-Mix magazine with A. Bishara. So, if you're wondering why all of a sudden Los is a little more vocal tonight, that's why. But fine..." Turning his attention to me, he smirked. "Let's switch gears. I don't want to get your panties twisted."

I scowled. Opening my mouth to respond, I was interrupted.

"Bishara, can I ask you a question?" Country Boy inquired, speaking up for the first time in a while.

"Yes."

"What is your main issue with Date Night?"

"Like I said, the disrespect, the use of emotional manipulation, and the objectification of women," I answered.

"How do we objectify women?" City Boy asked.

Is he serious? My eyebrows furrowed.

"You talk about women as sex objects as opposed to people. You sexualize women in your advice and even in the conversation that we're having, you've put more emphasis on my looks and my sex life than on the things I'm saying."

"Women objectify men, too," City Boy argued.

"Not to the degree that men objectify women. Not to the degree that you and this show objectifies women," I countered, adding several examples from the podcasts I'd listened to and from the show. "And if we did, men wouldn't know how to handle it."

"Okay, okay, okay, okay, okay," City Boy cut me off with a laugh. "But you're telling me that women don't sit around and compare muscles and dick sizes of the men they're sleeping with?"

"What I'm saying is that you give advice as if women aren't human beings with the right to decide what they want to do with their lives. For instance, we have the right to turn down dates from people we don't want to date We have the right to say no. We have the right to not participate in threesomes. We have the right to do whatever the hell we want. When you give advice that aims to not only take away that right but treat us as if we are here for your pleasure, you're treating us like objects."

City Boy made a skeptical face. "So, you've never checked out a man's package before?"

My thoughts immediately went to Carlos in his sweatpants. Heat crept up my neck as the thought of how we spent our time prior to the interview.

I cleared my throat. "I check out the whole package—starting with the things that he says, the way he thinks."

"City has a point," Country Boy interjected. "Have you seen the way women react at strip clubs?"

"I'm not talking about in strip clubs. I'm talking about the way you objectify every day women who are going about their lives. Just because they have breasts doesn't give you the right to ogle them, to sexualize them, to..." I exhaled, trying to keep cool and choose my words carefully. "You know what you did and it's wrong."

"And what did we do?" City Boy asked, a slow smile spreading on his face.

I narrowed my eyes. "You already know."

"Well we're almost out of time, but for those listening, I think she's talking about the special shout out we gave her in the newsletter."

I looked at Carlos to see his brows furrowed.

"All of this because of a little shout out in our newsletter?" Country Boy exclaimed with a laugh.

Staring pointedly at City Boy, I repeated myself. "You know what you did and it's wrong."

Licking his lips, City Boy smiled cunningly. "But seeing the look on your face is worth it." He winked. "Okay, that's it for tonight. Tune in next week and we'll answer more of your emails. We'll have the Date Night O.G. that you won't want to miss. I'm City Boy—"

"I'm Country Boy…"

"And I'm Los Cabos."

"And this is Date Night with The Lost Boys," the three of them said in unison.

"We're off air," Carlos announced, standing up. "What the fuck is going on, Bryant?"

City Boy laughed, sliding his headphones off. He stretched his arms above his head. "I should be asking you the same thing, Carlos." He pointed at me. "She got in your head? We're supposed to have a difference of opinion, but goddamn, you acted like your job was to protect her honor."

"You were being disrespectful," Carlos informed him with a clenched jaw.

"She got the same treatment anyone else would get. You were the one acting different." City Boy looked at Country Boy. "Back me up, Quentin."

"Come on," Country boy sighed. "You two have been getting into it over bullshit ever since we took over this show. It's always something. We only have three more months left and then it's done."

City Boy raised his hands in surrender. "It's Los acting like he's in his feelings. I was just doing an interview and providing quality entertainment."

Carlos ran his hand down his face. "You were being an asshole and disrespecting Akila. You—"

"Oh, it's Akila, now," City Boy taunted, egging him on.

"B, Los is always keeping you in check. And Los, B's an asshole to everybody." Country Boy glanced at me. "But it's not like she didn't shit on us in her article."

"That's my whole point," City Boy grumbled, rising to his feet. "And when I told you about the article, you were mad about it, too. And now you're up here defending her. You stand with your bros at all times. You don't switch up because a chick comes in here with a short ass skirt on."

Carlos rubbed his hands together. "I didn't switch up. I thought her article was an unfair portrayal of who we are. But I'm not going to let you disrespect her."

City Boy walked around the table. "Let me?"

"Yeah, that's what I said."

"What are you going to do?"

"Yo, come on now," Country Boy yelled. "Over some chick? Really?"

City Boy shrugged. "Date Night has been on for almost ten years and in the final few months of our year, we're getting scrutinized thanks to her. Come on, man."

"You're getting scrutinized because what I'm saying is valid." I stood, smoothing down the front of my dress. "I'll see myself out."

"Thanks for being a guest today. It was a pleasure." Sarcasm dripped from City Boy's words.

I rolled my eyes. Turning on my heels, I stormed toward the door.

"Akila, wait. I'll walk you out."

I looked over my shoulder. "It's cool. Sounds like you guys have a lot to talk about." Without another word, I walked out the door.

"Akila!"

Even though I heard Carlos call out to me, I didn't look back. I hesitated for a second, but the click of the door behind me made my decision for me

"Let her go, man." City Boy's voice traveled as he screamed. "We need to get this prepped and uploaded."

"And I'll take care of it in a minute," Carlos barked back before I heard his footsteps down the hall. "Akila!"

I slowed and waited for him to catch up.

"You held your own in there," he informed me as he fell into step with me. "Did you get what you wanted to get out of it?"

"I did. I hope people will realize that the whole show is trash." I smirked. "Maybe with one exception."

"Oh, just maybe?" His hand grazed mine and my stomach flipped.

"Maybe. The jury is still out."

He was quiet for a moment. "Are we still cool?"

"Yeah." I snuck a glance at him. "Why? Aren't we?"

"I didn't know how you were going to feel after doing the show. I know you hate Date Night and The Lost Boys so I thought you would... I don't know."

He knew. And I knew, too.

"Wait... is that what the sex was about this afternoon?" I hissed, looking around to make sure I wasn't overheard.

"No." He paused, slipping his hands into his pockets "But—"

"But it was why I told you how I felt. In case the interview changed how we saw each other."

"And did it?"

His gaze was penetrating as he said, "No." He swallowed hard. "What about you?"

"It's complicated."

"What is?"

"My feelings."

He was quiet.

We eyed each other, and a chill ran through me.

Clearing my throat, I shifted my gaze. "You don't have to walk me to my car."

"I'm not going to let you walk to your car alone."

"You are such a mystery to me," I mumbled as he held the door open for me.

We walked out of the building and as soon as the cold air hit me, I pulled my sweater around me tighter. He placed a hand on my back.

"What do you mean?" he asked.

"Hm?" I was completely distracted by his touch.

"You said I was a mystery."

"You're the kind of guy who is on Date Night, and you're also the kind of guy who makes sure I get to my car safely. You're the kind of guy who relentlessly defends The Lost Boys but also gets into a fight with your frat brother to defend me. You just…" I eyed him as I unlocked my car. "I struggle with that."

"I have a newsflash for you…" He leaned around me and opened my car door. Taking his finger, he stroked it down my cheek. "You don't agree with what City says, but you were also on Date Night."

I shook my head and tried not to smile. "Goodnight."

"Goodnight."

Before I knew what happened, his lips brushed mine, and then he was already headed back to the building.

I sat in my car for a minute, smiling. Carlos Richmond was completely unexpected. I was conflicted, but there was something about him. Sighing, I put my key in the ignition and started my car.

"Shit!" I hit the steering wheel.

I didn't want to go back in there, but there was no way I could leave without my notebook.

Summer is officially over, I thought as I shuffled to the front door of the Empire Building.

I was still shaking off the chill when I headed to Studio B. I stopped when I heard yelling through the partially closed door.

"…kept this going for ten years and because some pissed off girls complained, we might get shut down. All thanks to her!" City Boy yelled.

"Well, now Los is pissed," Country Boy responded.

"He'll get over it. He always does. I cross the line, he smooths it over so we can stay on air. It is what it is. I didn't say anything worse than I ordinarily say, so I don't know why he's tripping over this."

"Do you think you helped your case or helped hers by acting like an asshole? If she wrote about us before, you didn't help," Country Boy snapped.

"Look, she held her own. It's not like I steamrolled her," City Boy barked in frustration.

"What was she talking about at the end? When she said you know what you did?" Country Boy asked.

"I don't know," City Boy lied.

Bullshit.

"Don't bullshit a bullshitter, B. Carlos will be back any minute and he's already pissed, so I don't think you want me to ask again in front of him. What was she talking about? She looked right at you when she said it."

"It was the newsletter thing," City Boy blurted out, lowering his voice.

I crept closer to hear more.

"Oh, okay. I can see why she'd be mad about that——"

"Her sister might've been featured in the newsletter this week."

So, he knew... he knew it was Alex. I felt like I'd been punched in the gut. *He knew and to get back at me, he went after my sister.*

"Wow," Country Boy whistled. "That's low, Bryant. Even for you."

"She said that we were sexualizing and objectifying women. So, I decided to show what it would look like if we were really sexualizing and objectifying. Come on... stop looking at me like that. In my defense, I thought it was her. I didn't know it was her sister until I did a little research."

"What the fuck, man?"

"It's not like the faces were in the newsletter. And the dude wrote the email! Is it my fault that he mentioned the event he was at and used their names? I saw Alex Bishara and figured she was A. Bishara. It was an honest mistake." City Boy let out a rough laugh.

I felt sick. I had to get out of there.

Fuck the notebook.

Chapter Sixteen

I couldn't stop thinking about it. I spent my entire weekend in my room brooding and guilt-ridden. I couldn't even bring myself to tell Meghan and I told her everything. I felt so responsible for what happened to Alex and all those other women. I didn't break out of my angsty, anguished mindset until I received the information about the final photography project on Sunday evening.

"Something that makes a statement," I repeated to myself as I sat on the edge of my bed.

I looked up at the door as it slowly creaked open.

"You've been in a funk since you did the podcast. What's going on?" Meghan asked from the doorway.

Groaning, I let my head fall into my hands and shook my head.

Crossing the room, she took a seat next to me. "I listened to the show yesterday and you were excellent. You gave City Boy the business! You were all like that's cute that you don't think you're an insecure, disrespectful, objectifying predator, so don't try to change the subject on me." She giggled. "You were awesome!"

"Thanks."

"So, it's not about the show. Does it have something to do with Carlos?"

I shook my head.

"Have you talked to him since you had sex? I mean, really talked to him?"

I picked my head up and looked at her. "Talked about it? Not really. Did it again? Yes."

"What?!"

I nodded.

"You had sex with him again?" Meghan shrieked.

I nodded.

"When? How? You didn't leave at all this weekend. Unless it happened at the studio..." She gasped. "Did you sleep with him at the studio?"

"I got to the Empire Building early. I was originally going to chill in the park, but I saw him, so I went inside. I don't know what happened. But he was wearing those damn grey sweatpants."

"Oh, he knew wat the hell he was doing. When dudes with big dicks wear grey sweatpants, they know exactly what they're doing. Showing off his dick print was basically his way of reminding you of what you two had a few days prior."

"Well, I remembered. And it resulted in us locking ourselves in the break room bathroom on the other side of the building."

"Oh, my god! That sounds hot!" She searched my face. "Were you okay with it happening?"

"Oh, yes. Absolutely." A flutter in my belly occurred at the thought of it. "The sex was...magic. Pure magic. I thought the first time was a fluke, but it happened again. It's just something about when we connect like that..."

She stared at me. "Look at yourself in the mirror. Look at your face right now."

I turned toward my wall mirror and I saw myself—face flushed, eyes bright.

"You like him so much," Meghan pointed out. "It is written all over your face."

"I can't like him."

"Have you talked to him?"

"He called yesterday to tell me he would bring my notebook to the thing we have to go to tonight. I said okay and then made an excuse to get off the phone."

"Why? You obviously like him."

"I can't like him."

"That's not a denial."

"I can't like him," I repeated, closing my eyes. "Especially after finding out what I found out."

My eyes started watering and the bright, lovestruck look on my face was replaced with guilt.

"What happened, Kiki? Talk to me."

I sighed. "The newsletter was all my fault. They—well, City Boy —put the newsletter together to spite me."

"Yeah, we knew that. They gave a shout out to the journalist who wouldn't stop talking about them." She rolled her eyes. "We knew they were talking about you from the beginning."

I blinked back tears. "Yeah, well I overhead them talking and City Boy said that he put Alex in the newsletter on purpose. He saw the last name and assumed it was me when he got the email from Alex's date. But even after her found out it was about my sister and not me, he still put her out there like that. He did that to her in order to get to me. It's all my fault."

"First of all, no, it's not your fault. And second, how did he find out?"

I shrugged. "I didn't hear that part. I just heard him say that it was basically his 'fuck you' to me."

"Wow…" She put her hand on my back. "I'm sorry."

"I've been sick thinking about it. I just keep hearing him saying it and every time I replay it, over and over again. I'm the reason this happened to her."

"You know this is his fault and not yours, right?"

"I know."

"Kiki…" She pulled me into a hug. "City Boy is an asshole. He wanted to get back at you because he couldn't dispute the facts in your articles, so he decided to try to come after someone you love. It's not your fault."

I squeezed her tightly. "I know he saw an opportunity and capitalized on it, but that doesn't stop me from feeling so guilty."

Pulling out of the hug, she eyed me. "Are you going to be okay tonight?"

"Yeah. I don't have a choice."

"You have nothing to feel guilty about. This is on City Boy. He did this. You did nothing wrong."

"Thanks."

She stood up and walked to the dress I had hanging on the closet door. "Is this what you're wearing?"

"Yeah."

She smirked. "You're wearing this for Sunday Expressions or you're wearing this for Carlos?"

"I told you I can't—"

"But do you?"

"Yes," I pouted, letting my head fall into my hands again. "I do, but I couldn't really be with one of The Lost Boys. It goes against everything I stand for. My brand and my career are tied to who I am and what I believe. And he represents the opposite of that. How can I fight for what's right while being tied to someone who supports what's wrong?" I lifted my head. "He's so confusing, Meghan. On one hand, he's part of this trio and on the other hand, he's passionate and intelligent. I'm drawn to him and I don't know how to stop it. It's not going to work between us."

"Maybe. Maybe not. Have you talked to him about it?"

"No. When we talked yesterday, it was seriously just about the notebook, and that's it. It seemed like he was in as big of a rush to get off the phone with me as I was him."

"Well, talk to him tonight."

I nodded. "Maybe."

She gave me a look.

Smiling, I sighed, "I said maybe."

Two hours later I walked into Café Nervosa where they host Sunday Expressions. The dimly lit café was perfect for creating the intimate vibe for spoken word performances. Even from a quick look around, many people were there on a date, and there were far more women than men in the building.

Hmm. This is a great date spot... But for a single, heterosexual woman, I don't know...

I got a drink from the bar and saw a small high-top table in the far corner. I made a beeline for it. Slipping off the black jacket, I could feel the eyes of the man at the next table on me. I knew I looked good—it was my favorite dress. I always felt confident in the way the sweetheart neckline was both sexy and sweet, and the fitted material showcased the width of my hips and the roundness of my ass. I wore my tightly coiled hair brushed into a high ponytail that sat on top of my head like a crown. The plan was to look good, but also because I wanted to make a point.

"You look beautiful," the man at the next table said.

"Thank you," I replied, taking a seat.

"Can I get your number?"

I pretended I didn't hear him.

"Are you here alone?" he asked a little louder.

I looked at him with a healthy dose of suspicion as I zipped up my jacket. "No."

The squeal of the microphone echoed through the speakers and pulled my attention. I was listening to a woman with amazing hair welcome us to Sunday Expressions, but I was distracted. I felt him before I actually laid eyes on him. Scanning the room, I stopped once I zeroed in on Carlos who was staring at me.

Without breaking eye contact, the corner of his mouth turned up in a half smile. We continued to just watch each other. He started walking over to me. It seemed as though time slowed down, and the world quieted so we could focus on each other. When he reached me, I didn't know if I should shake his hand or hug him. Deciding to play it safe, I stood, reaching out to shake his hand. He broke our eye contact for a moment to look at my outstretch hand as if it were some foreign object. I watched the confusion quickly play out on his face before his face was again, emotionless.

"Akila," he murmured, slipping his hand over mine.

As soon as our skin connected, my hand tingled, and I felt a powerful surge of energy course through my body.

I gasped.

All the guilt, anxiety, and anger I'd felt all weekend temporarily dissipated as I breathed him in. He was like a breath of fresh air and I forgot everything that was wrong prior to that moment.

"Carlos," I whispered.

"Is our truce still intact?"

"For now."

"May I sit with you for a minute?"

"Sure."

After he helped me into my seat and was no longer touching me, all of the feelings from before gradually seeped back into my mind. Unfortunately, it didn't do anything to quell the rush of dopamine that he filled me with. The conflicting feelings did nothing but confuse my system.

"It's mostly couples and single women in here." He smirked. "I'm sure that'll come up in your article."

"Of course." I tilted my head to the side. "And I'm sure you'll enjoy yourself for the same reason."

"Of course."

I struggled not to give in to the smile he pulled out of me. "Are we going to be treated to a poem by you tonight?"

"You would like that, wouldn't you?"

"I actually would. It would be good to see you sweat."

With a straight face, he replied, "You've seen me sweat."

I tossed my head back and laughed hard. "That's not what I meant!"

"Oh, sorry. No, I'm not a poet. I could probably do better than you up there."

My jaw dropped. "How dare you? You don't know what skills I have." I laughed at the way his eyebrows quirked. "What I meant is that I could be a hell of a poet!"

"Well, let me hear something."

"Um... let's see." I rubbed my hands together. "I met a man

named Carlos in my photography class / We have one more assignment until we pass / I think he's cool, but his friend's an ass."

The sound of Carlos chuckling brought a smile to my face.

"That was pretty good," he complimented me before sipping his drink.

"And accurate."

"And accurate."

"Now, it's your turn. You can either do a spontaneous poem or answer a series of questions."

"I'll take the questions." He squinted while pointing at me. "But I reserve the right to make up a poem to get me out of answering a question that will incriminate myself."

I let out a short laugh. "Sure."

"Let's do it."

"Okay, question one… When's your birthday?"

"November eleventh."

"Ahh… you're a Scorpio." I bit my lip. "That explains so much."

"What is that supposed to mean?"

"Scorpios are sexual and passionate. All about seduction."

"By that description, that could be you, too."

I shook my head. "You seduced me on Friday. You were in the lobby waiting for me wearing those sweatpants. You know damn well what you were doing."

He laughed. "What?"

"Question two… you know those sweatpants you had on showed off your big ass dick with that big ass dick print, right?"

Carlos laughed hard and loud.

"I'll take your laugh to mean you knew what you were doing," I giggled.

"Let me ask you a question."

I made a face. "I did a poem. I get to ask the questions here."

He lifted his hands in surrender. "Okay, okay. I'll give you one more and then it's my turn."

"Well, then I have to make this one good…" I tapped my chin.

"What's your book about? I know it's a book of essays, but what are the essay topics?"

The way he looked at me made my stomach flutter.

His eyes lit up. "It's about a bunch of different stories from my life. It's pretty funny. Some stuff is more serious. But overall, it's just an entertaining read. It's going through a second round of editing now, and I'm hoping that the stuff I've been learning from Luca is going to give a little hint of what each essay is about."

"That's a really good idea. What made you decide to write essays instead of fleshing out each of the essays into a whole book?"

"Time." He shrugged. "Honestly, I want to write a novel one day. But with my teaching schedule and my other commitments to my fraternity, I don't have the time to commit to it. But with an essay, I can write it and when I'm done, I'm done. It doesn't have to be a certain length. It just has to tell the full story of what happened."

"I look forward to buying it when it comes out."

He took a sip of his drink before offering, "I'll send it to you when it gets through this round of edits."

I smiled at him. "I'd like that."

"Now, can I ask you a question?"

"Yes."

"Reading some of your work, I'm interested in knowing how your dating life is going—off the record."

"Off the record." I looked beyond him momentarily. "I don't get out to date much."

His eyes moved over my face as if he were studying me, studying my features, studying my words. "Why not? When was your last date?"

"I'm busy. My full-time job is a freelancer, so I don't have the security of a steady paycheck. I have to grind for every opportunity, every check, every byline I get. I love that because it's all me— everything I have is because I worked my ass off for it."

He lifted his glass to me. "Respect."

I clinked my glass against his. "Respect."

"But you didn't really answer my question. Why don't you get out to date much? And 'busy' isn't an answer."

I opened my mouth in faux disbelief. "What do you mean? Yes, it is!"

"Yeah, okay," he responded. "You still didn't answer the other part of the question though."

I cocked my head to the side. "And what was that?"

He chuckled to himself. "When was your last date?"

"About a month ago. And before then, three months ago."

"That's what I want to know about. Why aren't you dating, Akila Bishara?"

I lifted my shoulders. "When was your last date, Carlos Richmond?"

"I've been on a few dates over the summer, but once the school year started, my focus has just been elsewhere."

"See? Busy!"

He shook his head. "I'm busy, but that's not the reason I'm not dating." He licked his lips. "For the right one, I'd make time."

My stomach flipped.

"Oh, I love this song!" The sexy new single by Super Casanova moved through my body and I swayed to the music.

"Would you like to dance?" he asked, amusement dripping from his words.

"There's no dance floor!"

"We'll create our own."

I laughed. "No!"

"You sure?" he asked, making me laugh harder.

"I'm sure, I'm sure." Wiping the corners of my eyes, I let out a contented sigh. "Do you like to dance?"

"I would've done it if you wanted to."

"Oh, okay." I took another sip of my drink to hide my smile.

"So, you're a Super Casanova fan, huh?"

"Yes. Are you?"

"I am. I like their sound. I listen to almost anything that has a good beat. But my go-to is hip hop."

"What's your favorite song?"

"You can't ask a music head a question like that!"

I wiggled my eyebrows playfully. "I just did."

"Let me think about it."

"Okay, but if you're thinking about it, here's a better question: who's your favorite artist?"

"Damn, Akila..." He chuckled under his breath. "That's another hard one. I'm thinking it might be easier to write you a poem."

I laughed. "Yeah, it is hard. I agree with what you said before. If it has a good beat, I like it. If it has lyrics that affect me, I love it." I leaned forward and lowered my voice. "Music is important, so if you didn't have quality taste in music, I would've had to ask you to leave my table."

"You would've kicked me from the table? That's cold."

"It's a cold world," I quipped playfully.

He chuckled. "I guess that's better than being escorted out by security."

I groaned. "Don't remind me. That was ridiculous. It was something out of a movie."

"Yeah, it was crazy."

"So, what else do you like?"

He smiled sexily before pouring the remaining contents of his drink into his mouth. "You're going to have to be a little more specific."

Biting my lip, I tried my best to not grin. "What do you like to do when you're not working?"

Ordering drinks and appetizers, we went back and forth talking about movies, television, current events, family, friends, and the future. The conversation flowed effortlessly, and time was flying by. He was interesting, insightful, and a great listener. For what felt like the twelfth time, I got caught up in a fit of giggles courtesy of something he'd said.

"Watching you laugh is something special," he uttered, a hint of awe in his voice.

My heart raced at his words, but I rolled my eyes. "Save your lines for one of these unsuspecting women in here."

"I don't have lines. I don't run game." He paused. "I just say what it is…and I think this could be something."

I swallowed hard. "I don't…know what to say." I took a shaky breath.

"You don't have to say anything. I just… I just wanted you to know. This isn't game. This isn't a line. This is how I feel."

"We don't work. We couldn't date."

"What do you think this is?" He gestured to us and the food between us. "This is basically a date."

It wasn't just a date. It was the best date I'd ever had.

I stared at him, lost. "I can't date you."

"But you want to."

"Do you understand how being part of Date Night and one of The Lost Boys goes against everything I'm about?"

"Yes."

"So, there's really nothing to talk about." I sat back in my chair, inhaling deeply.

The way he assessed me made me hyperaware of my body language. I sat up a little straighter.

He stroked his beard. "You knew I was part of Date Night, you knew I was one of The Lost Boys from the beginning, so what changed?"

"Nothing changed." I threw up my arms. "Nothing! And I've said it since the beginning. You may not be a bad guy, but when you silently condone the problem, you become the problem by proxy, and Friday night—"

"I was wondering how long it would be before you brought something up from the interview. I'm sorry that B—City Boy—was an asshole. He's like that, but he was over the top with you. I checked him for that. Believe me, you didn't see the worst of it."

"It's not just the interview. It's everything Date Night with The Lost Boys represents. It's…" I shook my head. "Do you believe in Date Night and what it promotes?"

"It promotes conversation and it's for entertainment purposes. The money raised is used for service work with the fraternity. It has its issues—mostly City Boy's point of view—but this year we've increased streams and raised more money than any other year."

I felt like I was being punched in the chest. "So, you believe in Date Night and what it promotes?" My voice was a little more emotional, a little more raw. "Yes or no?"

"I believe in what we do with the money raised." His eyes pleaded with me to understand.

"Yes or no?"

"It's complicated."

I shook my head. The only thing that was complicated was my feelings for him. "No, it's not." My lips parted, quivering slightly. "Yes or no?"

He hesitated. "Yes."

I felt like the wind was knocked out of me. Nodding, I replied, "Okay, then. I guess that's the end of that."

"Akila."

Instead of replying, I held his gaze and unzipped my jacket, letting it slip off my shoulders.

I caught Carlos's eyes raking my body. My skin flushed under his gaze. But when our eyes met again, I froze.

He wasn't looking at me with lust. He wasn't even looking at me with attraction and appreciation. I didn't know what was in his eyes, but it wasn't sexual at all. Even though my plan was to wear that dress on purpose, I didn't expect to feel the way I did when realization hit him.

I wanted to make a point, but I didn't expect this—whatever this is.

He swallowed hard. "I have to talk to you about something."

"…so please put your hands together for Meta Day!" The woman with the amazing hair clapped, prompting everyone in the packed café to clap. Once Meta Day stepped on stage, the place was silent.

The poem started, but I didn't hear a word of it. Carlos's eyes were glued to me.

My breathing hitched.

"Can I talk to you?" He mouthed the words to me.

Nodding, I slipped out of my chair and pulled my jacket closed.

Grabbing my hand, Carlos led me out of Café Nervosa. Just feeling his fingers intertwined with mine sent butterflies ricocheting through my entire body. They traveled through each of my extremities and gathered in my chest. My heart was beating so fast, I couldn't handle it. When we were outside, I removed my hand from his and crossed my arms just under my breasts.

"What else is there to say?" I asked, looking around the active downtown area.

He handed me my notebook. "Before you left on Friday, you told City Boy that he knew what he did... what were you talking about?"

"Why didn't you ask him?"

"I'm asking you."

"The newsletter objectifying unsuspecting women."

"You already knew about the newsletter. I told you about the newsletter." His eyes flicked down to my dress and then back up. "What did you mean?"

I unfolded my arms, opening my jacket wide. "You keep looking at my dress, so I think you know."

He scrubbed his face with his hands. "Was that you in the news-letter? That first one that went out had someone in a yellow dress—that yellow dress. It didn't look like you, but..." His voice was a low, rumbling growl. "Was that you?"

"No."

His eyes cast over me and I could see a mixture of relief and confusion.

Blinking back tears of anger and frustration, I yelled, "It was my sister!"

Carlos took a step back. "What?"

"City Boy used a picture of my sister to get back at me for speaking the truth about Date Night and the trash advice that he gives. He objectified my sister because he thought it was me. He saw the name Alexandria Bishara and figured she was A. Bishara. So, while he hurt my sister, he originally thought he was hurting me."

Carlos shook his head. "Bryant wouldn't do that."

"Bryant did that."

"I know you don't like him and I can't say I blame you, but…" He stared at the dress. "Someone sent that email in. B wouldn't do some shit like that—especially knowing that we work together at Re-Mix. He wouldn't."

"Are you telling me I didn't recognize my dress on my sister's body in the newsletter?"

"I'm saying that it had to be a coincidence."

I rolled my eyes. "You don't really believe that."

"I've known Bryant since we pledged freshman year. That man has been a brother to me for eight years, and he wouldn't jeopardize it by doing some dumb shit."

I took a step back. "So, you're calling me a liar?"

"No, not at all. I'm sorry. If that's your sister, I'm sorry and I will cuss him the fuck out. All I'm saying is that I know Bryant a lot better than you. He's not perfect, but he's not what you're saying. He wouldn't have done this on purpose."

"Are you kidding me? He's exactly what I'm saying he is. He put a picture of my sister in a newsletter with the goal of humiliating and objectifying her because he thought she was me. And you're still defending him, condoning his behavior. You're just as bad."

"I'm not defending or condoning. I'm just…" He looked like he was at a loss for words. "I will get to the bottom of this and I will make sure no more newsletters go out. That's why I'm on the show—to make sure he doesn't go too far. And that would be too far."

"You know what… I don't know why I was expecting you to be any different than what you're showing me right now."

"Akila, I don't know what you want from me."

"Nothing." I took another step backward. "I don't want anything from you."

Chapter Seventeen

*T*he idea hit me two days later.

I'd trudged through the thirty-seven hours after my confrontation with Carlos like a zombie. I ate, showered, and slept. I didn't cry, but I felt like I was going to break down every time I thought about it. I knew I was going to have to see him on Friday for the Re-Mix staff meeting, and I knew I would have to touch base with him regarding our final projects for photography class, but just the thought of him made me feel unnerved. I knew I needed to harden my resolve and control my emotions before I was forced to see and interact with him.

As I was trying and failing to erase Carlos Richmond from my memory, it was a random thought of him in the wee hours of the morning that inspired my final project for photography class.

"Something that makes a statement," I exclaimed, jumping out of bed. "Holy shit!"

"What are you doing? It's so early," Meghan grumbled from the other side of my door.

"Meghan!" I swung the door open, startling her.

Staring at me as if I'd lost my mind, my best friend clutched her mug in her hand. After a lengthy pause, she took a sip of her coffee. "What the hell is wrong with you?"

I laughed.

"I'm serious." She assessed me, taking another sip out of her steaming cup. "You were moping around yesterday, and now you're up at quarter 'til seven talking to yourself and you have boundless energy." She lowered her voice. "Are you high?"

I chuckled harder. "No!"

She giggled into her mug. "Lies."

"No, I just figured out what I'm doing my final project on for Luca Romano."

"And what's that?"

"Dick prints!"

She sputtered, coffee droplets dropping onto the hardwood floor and her robe. "What?"

"We have to photograph something that makes a statement. This week's lesson is about making a statement. We did a fashion/beauty photoshoot, landscape photoshoot, portraiture, and street photography. So, our final projects are supposed to be conceptual photos that make a statement," I explained with a cheesy grin.

"And the statement you want to make is…you like dick?"

I threw my head back and laughed. "No! Men are not objectified to the degree that women are. But what if they were? What if society treated dick prints like they do cleavage?"

She tapped her chin. "Dick prints *are* male cleavage."

"But we don't—"

"Or male cleavage is the V leading toward the dick. No, no, no it's the dick print." She appeared to be lost in thought. "Because the dick print is just—"

"Are you done?" I laughed, and she joined in. "My point is that women are constantly objectified, but men would lose their shit if they were scrutinized, objectified, and sexualized the way we are."

"And not all dick prints are created equal. Lord knows not every man can make a pair of basketball shorts or sweatpants come to life."

My mind instantly went to Carlos, but I shook it off. "And that is exactly why men couldn't handle it if we did to them what they do to us."

"What made you think of this?"

"The Lost Boys' newsletter actually. I was thinking about the fact that City Boy was telling Country Boy that it didn't matter because the faces were cropped out."

She shook her head and then gestured for me to follow her. "I need to get ready for work."

Trailing behind her, I continued, "The fact that he didn't think it was that big of a deal because he cropped most of the faces out is problematic. And when I heard that, I could only focus on the fact that he knowingly went after me and Alex. But it hit me that if the tables were turned, his reaction would likely be different."

She glanced at me before pulling items from her closet. "I still can't believe he went through so much trouble just to prove your point." She looked at me again. "And his dumb ass didn't realize that he was proving your point."

"He did. He didn't care. Trying to humiliate me was his goal."

"That piece of shit."

"He's not even a piece of shit. He's the whole shit."

She cackled as she laid her outfit on the bed. "I love this idea so much! I volunteer as tribute to assist you during the photoshoot."

"I bet." I grinned. "I'm going to have to find some models."

"So…" She lifted her eyebrows. "I know someone who probably would be perfect for the photoshoot."

"Who?"

"Someone whose phone number you blocked and whose dick you recently rode."

I narrowed my eyes. "If his number is blocked, so is his dick."

"If it's two things I know, it's blocking men and dicks."

"What is wrong with you?" I giggled.

"I'm caffeinated, and I just found out I'm helping my best friend with a big dick scouting session." She sipped her coffee and wiggled her hips. "But really, are you going to talk to him?"

"About what? He made his choice."

"Yeah, but you two still have to work together."

"We were given four dating assignments and two of them have been published. One has been resubmitted to the editor, and I'm finishing writing the last one today."

"So, it's over?"

My chest felt tight. "Yes," I answered softly. "There's nothing else for us to talk about."

"I was talking about the Re-Mix job, but you clearly have Carlos on the brain."

"Oh, no. It's just early." I rubbed my temple and avoided eye contact. "Um, I don't know what is going to happen with Re-Mix. I'll find out at the meeting on Friday. But things look promising."

"Do you need to talk about the Carlos thing again? Sometimes it helps to get it off your chest."

I shook my head. "I told you everything. There's nothing left to say."

"I understand where you're coming from. I do. You two have opposing views regarding something that is important to you. I get that completely. If you don't think it's going to work, you don't think it's going to work." She frowned. "But it's okay to admit you're sad. I can see that you're sad. You felt magic. That doesn't happen all the time."

My eyes pricked with tears. "Yeah." I shrugged. "Anyway…"

She watched me for a second before giving me a sad smile. "Anyway, who are you going to ask to pose for these pictures?"

Grateful for the change in subject, I focused my energy on my photography project. "I'm going to post something on social media and ask if any men want to participate. Then I'll ask them to meet me on Saturday at the Riverfront."

Her eyes widened. "Will they be wet?"

"No!" My voice exposed my amusement. "But that's the only place I can think of that's free and provides a diverse background. I could have one dude against the steps, one on the observatory, one near the water, one near the rocks, one propped against the sign." I raised my arms. "The possibilities are endless."

"And it's free."

"And that's the best part of all."

"What are you going to have them wear?"

"Sweatpants." I wiggled my eyebrows. "And I'm going to call it —Sweatpants Season."

Clapping, Meghan squealed. "That's perfect!"

"I know!" I grinned.

"Okay, I'm going to hop in the shower. But tonight, let's make my grandma's lasagna, watch a badass movie, and scroll through all of our contacts to find dicks to put on display."

I grinned. "That sounds amazing."

I left her to get ready for work. Getting comfortable at my desk, I started writing. By the time Meghan got off work, our lasagna plan turned into ordering a pizza. But we still scrolled through our contacts and decided on a mix of men we knew, men we wanted to know, and men we thought would be nice enough to agree to help me out for the assignment. We sent out twenty-four messages and received a response from twenty-two of them. By the end of the night, sixteen men agreed to pose for Saturday's shoot.

"I can't wait," Meghan expressed while we sat on the couch that night. "This week is going to fly by!"

And it did.

On Friday I arrived to Re-Mix donned in a sweater dress and a pair of knee-high boots. Even though I was anxious to know what Luna Daniels had decided regarding the permanent series writer position, I was more worried about seeing Carlos.

"Akila, may I speak with you for a minute?" Luna asked as soon as I stepped off the elevator.

My eyebrows flew up. "Yes, of course." I followed her into her office and once I closed the door behind me, I asked, "Is everything okay?"

She smiled at me. "Everything is fine. How are you?"

"I'm well." I looked at her uncertainly. "How are you?"

"Today has been a good day." She pulled a paper off of her desk and handed it to me.

It was my article.

"This is good," she informed me.

I was shocked; however, I beamed with pride. "Thank you. Thank you so much."

"How would you like to be our new series writer?"

"Oh my god, yes! I would love that!" I felt like I wanted to scream before giving her a bear hug. I settled on a handshake. "Thank you."

Her lips spread into an even wider smile. "I was hoping you'd say that. Your He Said, She Said articles are done, and I'd like to get you started on some other projects."

She briefly told me what I would be expected to do and bring to the Re-Mix family. After looking at her watch, she concluded that she was finished discussing it with me and that we'd continue on Monday morning for orientation.

I was so delightfully fulfilled that I didn't even think about Carlos until the moment I walked into the staff meeting. I was relieved when he wasn't there, but I was curious. I was happy that he didn't show up, but I was worried. I was glad I missed out on seeing him, but I was disappointed. I was a conflicting mess of emotions when it came to him, but when Luna began the staff meeting, Re-Mix had my entire focus.

Until the meeting was over…

"Does Carlos know I got the series writer position?" I asked Luna as casually as possible.

"No," she responded distractedly.

"Oh, okay."

"But I'm sure he figured it out when I told him I wanted to submit his work as a contributor." She looked up from her phone. "Contributors don't come to the staff meeting if that's what you're wondering."

"I'm not," I sputtered. "I was just trying to see—"

She gave me a sidelong glance and then walked out the door.

Chapter Eighteen

*H*oly dick print.

Only twelve of the men who said they'd come actually showed up. They were all handsome in their own way. Some had great smiles. Some had pretty eyes. But all of them, with their different body types, skin tones, and heights, were aesthetically pleasing.

Too bad no one's face will be shown.

I scrolled through and picked the twelve best shots, one of each man, and on Monday, I arrived to class early to upload my raw images to Luca Romano's computer. I took my seat and waited. With each passing second, my heart nervously rattled.

And then he walked in.

I pretended I didn't notice him and busied myself writing in my notebook.

"Hey," Carlos greeted me as he took the seat to my right.

Without looking at him, I replied, "Hello."

"Akila."

I closed my eyes momentarily as I relished in the sound of my name from his lips. Swallowing hard, I let my lashes flutter open, and I continued writing in my notebook.

"I'm sorry," he whispered. "I called and texted, but it seemed like you blocked me."

I nodded but didn't look his way.

"Please look at me."

Sighing, I turned my head and met his gaze. My heart clenched and I knew it was a mistake. The way he looked at me always did something to me and that moment was no exception. The tremor in my belly was intense. But instead of the intensity spreading through my lower body, it spread through my chest.

"I'm sorry," he uttered. He moved closer, but he refrained from touching me. "I was wrong."

I know you were wrong. My eyes narrowed, but I remained silent.

"I just—"

"Welcome back to class, everyone!" Luca Romano called out from his desk at the front of the room.

Shifting my gaze to our photography teacher, I turned my page in my notebook and prepared to take notes and concentrate on the lesson.

"It's good to be back!" Luca clapped his hands together and then propped himself on top of his desk. "I've seen such great transformation from your initial photos to the photos that you submitted last week. I have no doubt my last video on power shots and perspectives has enhanced what you uploaded today."

He handed each of us a small portfolio of our work that we'd completed and a description of the assignment next to it. Giving us fifteen minutes, everyone poured over their own work and then we were to make our way around the class. As everyone rose to their feet, Carlos reached out for me.

"Akila, can we talk about this?"

His fingers seared my skin and I pulled my arm away. "There's nothing to talk about. And we're supposed to be checking out portfolios right now," I murmured as I walked across the room. I could still feel his touch long after I left our table.

When I returned to my seat, Carlos didn't say a word to me. I didn't know what was worse, the desperate plea in his eyes as he reached for me or the silence that seemed to thunder in my ears.

"Now I want you to pick your favorite image from your portfolio and briefly explain to the class what it is, why it's important, and what you'd hoped to convey." Luca opened his arms wide. "This is what Visual Storytelling is all about."

"I'll go first, Luca," Jennifer raised her hand and then jumped to her feet when he nodded.

"Everyone put your hands together for Jennifer," Luca instructed and light applause followed.

I just sat there. I was saving my applause for everyone else.

Holding up a naked photo of herself, Jennifer grinned. She handed it to someone in the first row and asked them to pass it around. "This photo was from the self-portrait photography lesson. We were told to focus on our natural selves and what's more natural than being nude. I work out constantly since I'm a personal trainer, so staying in great shape is important to me. I take pride in my work and the work I put into my body, so that's why I wanted to showcase it."

I tried not to roll my eyes at her. When the photo got to our table, I took it and immediately handed it to Carlos. Without looking at it, Carlos handed it to the person in front of us. I felt the corner of my lips move slightly.

The rest of the class took turns presenting their photos, and then it was my turn.

"My favorite from my portfolio is the self-portrait. I am constantly working, so I set up my tripod and programed my camera to take automatic shots to capture me writing. Even though I had prettier pictures from when I was mindful of the camera, and I had my smile and face tilted just right, this one is real. This is what I look like when I'm working. This is me fulfilling my purpose in life." I looked around the room as I held my picture higher. "Thank you."

I walked to my seat to the sound of clapping.

"Very good, Akila. Carlos, come on up."

Carlos was very causal in jeans and a grey hoodie. He looked so comfortable and at ease with himself, and there was a sexiness to the way he moved. He flashed the class a smile and my eyes watered.

Get it together, Akila, I yelled at myself. *I can do this. I can do all things.*

"My favorite from my portfolio is the sunrise/sunset dual photos." He held them up. "My partner and I went to my favorite place at the Riverfront. I love these shots because it shows change. Even though the location doesn't change, the two pictures are completely different. So much happened between when one was taken and when the other was taken, but none of that takes away from how beautiful they both are." He paused as he looked at the picture. Glancing at me, he continued, "It's also my favorite for some personal reasons." With that, he walked back to his seat.

Applauding, Luca pushed himself from the desk and took his place in the center of the room. "You all did a fantastic job." He clapped again. "When you're presenting your work, you want to work on your storytelling and your delivery. The work should speak for itself, and you should only say enough to enhance the story your photography is telling. This brings us to your final assignment, which was to make a statement with a series of shots. You needed to tell a story. There needed to be cohesiveness. And I only required a one-page paper for you to tell me what statement you were trying to make and why it's important to you. Your statement should be bold, and the story should be powerful. I should be able to get the same statement from your photographs as I get from your paper."

I took notes and I heard what Luca was saying, but I could feel Carlos staring at me. My skin heated under his gaze and I was distracted.

"…and this is where your partner comes into play. On Saturday, your photos will be showcased at a special showcase at Rich Gallery. I will enlarge them, but keep them pure—no retouching. Before the gallery opens to the public at seven o'clock, we will meet as a class at six o'clock and you will be given the last part of your assignment. You will be paired with your partner for this final part. Please be sure to invite your friends and family so they can see your debut."

Someone raised their hand. "Mr. Romano, do we need to dress up?"

"You need to dress in the way that best encompasses who you are. If that's jeans so be it. If it is a gown, go for it. This is about visual storytelling, and every day you are telling a story about your-self with your wardrobe. So, just be yourself. Any other questions?"

The room was quiet but bristling with excitement. It was apparent that Luca could feel it too as he grinned at us. "Okay, class is dismissed! I will see you on Saturday. Enjoy the rest of this Monday night."

I gathered my belongings and snuck a glance at Carlos. When I saw his eyes boring into me, my breathing hitched. "Have a good night." I turned to walk away, and he was at my side before I could take a step.

"I'm walking you to your car," he told me.

"You don't have to."

"I know."

Without another word, we walked side-by-side to my car.

"Okay, thank you," I mumbled as I pulled out my keys.

"I'm sorry I didn't believe you."

"It is what it is."

Stepping into my personal space, he looked down at me. "I was wrong."

Squaring my shoulders, I made myself taller as I met his gaze. "Yes, you were."

"When I confronted Bryant, he denied it at first and then he told me what he did." Carlos's handsome face hardened. "He told me how he thought it was you and then… He told me he knew what he was doing."

I lifted my eyebrows. "So, he confirmed everything I told you?"

He nodded, only glancing down momentarily to decline a phone call that was coming in. "I'm sorry for that. I've known that man for eight years—since we were eighteen. And I've known you…"

"You've only known me for a month."

"If I told you that your best friend did some shit like that, would you believe me?" His phone rang again, but he ignored it.

"That's the thing… my best friend doesn't have a history of doing fucked up shit." My voice became harsher. "Yours does. So, it wasn't a huge leap. If my best friend was a trash human being and you told me she did something that was garbage, I wouldn't have dismissed what you said. I understand wanting to verify because that's your boy, but I wouldn't have dismissed what you said."

"I didn't think he would do something like that."

"That's not even the point." I shook my head. "You made your choice. What mattered to you was protected, and that's what's important, right?"

He closed the gap between us, cupping my face in his hands. "I'm sorry I hurt you."

My eyes pricked with tears. *Damn.*

He searched my face. "I'm sorry he disrespected you and your sister. I'm sorry I didn't protect you. But more than anything, I'm sorry that I made you feel like you and your feelings don't matter."

His phone rang again.

Irritably, he yanked his phone out of his pocket to decline the call.

It was Bryant.

He gave me a look as he declined the call. All the anger, hurt, and confusion flooded my system, and I needed to get out of there.

"I have to go," I breathed, scared my voice would break even further.

"Will you accept my apology?"

I swallowed hard. "Yes."

He pulled me flush against him and even though I didn't want to, I folded into him as if that was the only place I wanted to be. I buried my face in his chest so he couldn't see my watery eyes. I squeezed him just as tight as he squeezed me.

"I really am sorry. I won't let that happen again. I swear to God," he murmured against my hair.

It had been a long week, and I didn't want to admit that I'd missed him. But in his arms, that was all I could think. I inhaled the sandalwood and vanilla scent and tried to commit it to memory. Every ridge of his hard body, I wanted to memorize. His warmth, I wanted to bottle up for a cold night. And the sound of his voice, I wanted to play on a loop in my ears.

He pulled back fractionally. "Akila?"

Glassy eyed, I looked up at him.

"I miss you," he admitted.

I licked my lips. I wanted to say it back, but I was afraid.

"Do you miss me?"

I nodded.

Leaning down, his lips brushed mine gently. The energy between us was so powerful that I didn't even feel like I was in control of myself anymore. I let out a light moan as I parted my lips and allowed his tongue to meet mine. The passion from that kiss made a beeline to the apex of my thighs. His kiss caused me to shiver.

His phone rang again.

Bryant.

I pulled away. "I can't do this. You and I wouldn't work. I have to go."

"Can I see you later?"

"I can't be around you."

"Can we talk later?"

I had to look away from him. "I don't think so."

"Can we talk period?"

I didn't respond, but I still couldn't look at him.

"Akila, will you at least unblock me?"

His phone rang again.

Untangling myself from his arms, I opened my car door. "I'm sure that's Bryant again. Have a goodnight."

I, at least, made it off campus before the tears started streaming down my cheeks.

Chapter Nineteen

*M*y first week at Re-Mix wasn't the fun-loving, free-spirited walk in the park that I thought it was going to be. I had to work my ass off. I was used to working hard, but I wasn't used to waking up at nine o'clock in the morning and being in one spot all day. There was so much to do regarding training and orientation. While I was blessed to have a full-time job, I missed the easy-going schedule of my unstructured freelance days. By Friday night, I was exhausted.

"Have you heard from him?" I asked Meghan about Derrick.

"No. Have you heard from him?" Meghan asked me about Carlos.

"No."

We sat silently on the couch eating popcorn and watching a movie we'd seen many times before.

"Are you going to call him?" I asked her.

"No. If he wants me, he'll call me. I'm not going to chase him." She put a handful of popcorn in her mouth and chewed. "Are you going to call him?"

"I thought about it on Tuesday because I didn't like how we

ended things on Monday. But I didn't know what to say. It doesn't feel like there's a point." I shrugged, feeling that tightness in my chest that indicated I might start crying soon.

"Has he called you?"

"I haven't unblocked him."

"Why?"

I was quiet for a long time. "Because talking to him is only going to cloud my judgement and make me weak in the knees." I shook my head. "You weren't there, Meghan. I had made up my mind. I was leaving, and I wasn't going to talk to him anymore. And then he walked me to my car, and he looked at me."

"Oh, noooooo," she mocked me with a horrified expression. "He looked at you! How dare he?!"

I laughed, tossing a popcorn kernel at her. "You're the worst."

"All jokes aside, I get it." She paused before giving me a rueful smile. "It's the magic."

I nodded. "I couldn't fight it. I spent a week preparing to see him, and it took a stroll to my car to derail my plan." I chomped on my popcorn.

"And here it is almost two weeks since you blocked him, and you still can't stop thinking about him. What are you going to do if you can't shake him?"

"I don't know. I just… I don't know. We wouldn't work."

"I understand why you don't think it'll work with him. I get it and I agree with your point. But it's hard because I know that you believe in magic."

"I've never felt like this before, but what am I supposed to do? Date a man who is privately one of the best men I've ever met but publicly encourages fuckboys to be fuckboys?"

"He's no City Boy."

"Yeah, but he's still on the show." I paused. "You know Alex hasn't been on a date since that tutor guy. She won't even wear anything lowcut or even remotely revealing. She posted a picture of her and her friends at this social on campus, and she's wearing a dress with a high neckline." I made a face. "Alex is basically wearing a turtleneck every day because she feels uncomfortable because of what happened with the newsletter. My sister is scarred because of City Boy. I was harassed and kicked out of Koi because of a Date Night listener. There are real consequences to the 'advice' they're passing out."

"You're right."

I let my head fall into my hands. "But I can't stop thinking about him."

"Because of the magic between you two." She rubbed my back. "And because of his dick"

I lifted my head and laughed. She wasn't wrong.

"Yes and yes. But it's so much more than that," I admitted before popping another kernel in my mouth and avoiding eye contact. "I've never felt seen by a man the way he sees me. He looks at me and it's like he sees me. He treats me like his equal. He calls me on my bullshit. He can handle being called on his bullshit. He makes me laugh, and he makes me feel special. But he's…"

"A Lost Boy?" Her voice was soft and sympathetic.

I nodded.

"You want someone who can defend your honor?"

"Well, he showed me that he can and will defend me. But when he did it, he was defending me from someone who took advice from his show."

"It's a hard one. What does your heart say?"

"To call him. To date him. To be with him."

"And what does your head say?"

"That at the end of the day, the fact that he doesn't see anything wrong with Date Night will end us before we can even get started."

"So, what are you going to do?"

"I don't know," I groaned, rubbing my temples. "I don't know at all." I dropped my hands and looked at her. "What does your heart tell you about Derrick?"

"Fuck him. On to the next one."

"And what does your head say?"

"Fuck him. Literally. The sex was good." She shrugged as I laughed.

"So, what are you going to do?"

"I'm not going to call and if he doesn't call, fuck it. He's not my soulmate. He's a nice guy, but we don't have much in common. I wouldn't walk away from the man that is meant for me, and the man who is meant for me wouldn't walk away from me."

"True story."

I was in my head for the rest of the night. I went to bed early and woke up late. And around noon I decided that I should unblock him.

"I'm scared," I announced as I ate my salad for lunch.

"Scared to unblock him?"

"Scared to fall for him."

"Ummm…"

I turned my head to look at her. "What?"

"Sounds like it's already happening."

I thought about it. "Yeah." I sighed. "Even more reason to be scared."

"This man has you all shook up." She smiled. "How about you stop stressing about him and think about something that is undoubtable a win. You are about to have your photographs hanging in Rich Gallery at a reception put on by Luca Romano!"

"Oh my god! You're right!" I stuffed my mouth full of lettuce and chewed.

When did I lose my focus?

The answer was obviously when I started catching feelings for Carlos.

"Do you know what you're going to wear? Are your parents driving up? Is Alex still coming? Did you tell anyone at Re-Mix?"

"My parents are coming. Alex is coming. I didn't tell anyone at Re-Mix because I don't know any of those people. I don't want them to come and think I'm obsessed with dicks."

"Ah…true." She nodded. "Good call."

"It's bad enough my dad will be there."

"Yeah. You should've told your dad not to come. That's going to be awkward, and I hope you don't think I'm going to stand with them when you're showing yours." She made a face. "No offense, but I like to enjoy my dick print photos without your mom and dad judging me."

Chuckling, I tried to chew the salad in my mouth. When I finally was able to swallow, I cracked up all over again. "You are free to roam the gallery."

"What are you wearing?"

"I don't know yet. What are you wearing?"

"I don't know yet. But I have this lavender streaked wig that I wanted to introduce to the city."

"Why don't you wear that black bodysuit? That'll be sexy, and it'll draw attention to your hair."

Her eyebrows flew up. "I didn't even consider the black body-suit. I'll be out here looking like a sexy burglar. Is it too much?"

"Not with the blazer. And then if we go out afterward, you can lose the blazer, and you'll be club ready!"

"Yes!" She threw her arms in the air. "Now what are you going to wear?"

We spent four hours figuring out what I would wear, how I would style my hair, and what shoes I'd put on my feet. By the time we'd finished, it was almost time to leave.

"How do I look?" I asked as I stepped into the living room.

Meghan and Alex catcalled as I stepped out in a long-sleeved, plum sweater dress and over-the-knee black, leather boots.

Spinning in a circle, I smiled uncertainly. "I don't know if it'll work for the club, so I'm bringing this, too." I held up a short, tight black dress.

"Oh, that's sexy!" Meghan shouted. "When did you get that?"

"This summer. I haven't worn it yet, and I didn't tell you two thieves about it because I wanted to wear it first."

"I would never!" Meghan feigned shock.

"Well, I'm staying out of your closet for a while," Alex commented.

I knew it was meant to be lighthearted, but I couldn't help but notice the slight edge in her voice. My eyes quickly flicked down and took in her appearance. In a blue sweater dress with plum colored tights, she looked beautiful. But she only wore stuff like that when we were home and going to church. Ever since the newsletter came out, she dressed a lot more modestly. If that were her style, I would've been cool with it. But I hated that The Lost Boys took something away from her and made her feel that she had to completely cover her body.

"Oh!" Alex burst out, looking down at her phone. "Mom said that her and Dad are leaving now."

"Okay, cool." I looked at my dress and then my clutch. "Okay, I have everything, so I'm leaving now. I'll see you guys at seven."

"You're going to be so early," Alex pointed out.

"I know, but I'm nervous, and I need to get myself together beforehand," I explained.

"Nervous to show off her affinity for dick prints," Alex told Meghan in a loud stage whisper.

Rolling my eyes, I giggled. "And on that note, I'm leaving!"

"Good luck!"

"You got this, Kiki!"

"Love you guys!" I waved goodbye and left.

I couldn't decide on what I wanted to listen to on the drive over, and the silence was making me even more anxious. I kept wondering how it would be to see Carlos and if it would be awkward. I wondered if he was going to show up because he had to record Date Night. I couldn't deny that he'd gotten under my skin, and I felt shaken by that fact.

Then it hit me.

The best way to get him out of my head was to focus on the reason we couldn't be together. So, before I pulled out of my parking space, I scrolled to the list of podcasts on my phone and saw that there were two new ones from Date Night. Clicking the most recent one, I prepared myself to be angry. Being angry was so much better than being caught up in my feelings. Being angry made me motivated; being caught up in my feelings made me reckless.

I fast forwarded it through the introduction and then I hit play.

Twenty minutes of bullshit while I was caught in traffic was just the thing I needed to get my mind off missing Carlos. While he was great in person, hearing him participating in the conversation with

City Boy without completely shutting him down or cursing him out felt like Carlos was normalizing City Boy. As much as my heart seemed to call out for Carlos, my mind fully rejected the idea of dating Los Cabos.

"*I think WildStyle1 should approach his coworker,*" *Country Boy stated, his deep voice bursting through the speakers.* "*I mean, it's not like she's his subordinate.*"

"*I think it's a slippery slope. Stay away from coworkers—especially in smaller offices,*" *Carlos advised.*

"*Speaking of coworkers,*" *City Boy started.* "*Carlos worked with anti-Date Night spinster, A. Bishara.*"

"*City, chill,*" *Country Boy warned.*

"*And as you know, we had her in here the other day. Since that podcast hit the airwaves, our email account has been blowing up with questions. Is she blaming our show because she can't get a date? Is she as ugly as she sounds? Does she even date men? Does the A stand for animal,*" *City Boy continued, causing Country Boy to laugh uncomfortably.* "*And since we've had some issues and dealings with A. Bishara, I wanted to spend some time answering your questions.*"

"*What are you doing?*" *Carlos asked with a sharp edge to his voice.*

"*It's fine. Our first question comes from GregCarter and it reads: Do you know her name?*" *City Boy laughed to himself.* "*I actually do know her name. The three of us know her name. But we refer to her under the name she writes under. It's a pen name she hides behind. So, just to clear that up for everyone listening, the name of the woman behind A. Bishara is known by us; however, we call her by her pen name to protect her privacy. She'll out herself when she's ready.*"

"*Okay, let's answer Timothy's email about what to do with the naked pictures of his ex-girlfriend now that they're no longer together,*" *Country Boy interjected.*

"*We will get to the reasons why he should keep them in a few minutes. But first, I want to get through the questions. We have more questions and comments about A. Bishara than anything else, so that's what we're talking about now. The people have spoken, and we have to give the people what they want. So, let's start with the question that kept coming up the most… what does she look like? Fellas, do you want to start or should I?*"

25

"What she looks like has nothing to do with why she was here," Carlos answered through clenched teeth.

"Los, answer the question. Don't think I didn't notice the way you would look at her," City Boy snickered.

"She's pretty. Let's move on," Country sighed.

"I must admit she's hot. But as soon as she opens her mouth, she goes from a strong nine to a low two. The only reason I won't give her a one is because of her ass. Los, calm your ass down. We're telling the truth. Are you denying it? You're saying you didn't notice she was hot and that she has a nice ass?"

"What's your point, City Boy?"

"My point is that the people want to know, so we give them the answers." He let out a growl. "While Los Cabos calms down, let's move on to the next question: does she have a point?"

"Does she?" Country Boy pondered.

"Yes." He paused. "Her nipples," City Boy joked, causing Country Boy to laugh.

"City, chill the fuck out," Carlos barked.

"Come on, guys. We're live," Country Boy reminded them.

There was a moment of silence.

"Let's take a call from the phone line—remember we take calls between eight thirty and nine o'clock every Friday when we can get to it. Okay, Caller, you're on with Date Night."

"Hey, City Boy! What's up, everybody? I'm Matt, and my question is about that Bishara bitch. What's wrong with her? She can't take a joke?"

"Well simply put, we said something that offended her delicate sensibilities and now she spends her time writing columns about how we are what's wrong with the modern man and dating today. Even Los agreed that her ideas that we were toxic, misguided, and communication deficient were bullshit."

"On the other podcast you said that she had a stick up her ass. Maybe she has one up her ass but needs one in her pussy. She sounds like she needs someone to hold her down and give her some dick!" The caller laughed. "That'll straighten her out!"

"If she had some dick, she wouldn't be on ours so much," City Boy added with a chuckle.

"I'll find her and force her uptight ass to take the dick," the caller continued. "That'll calm her ass down."

I felt sick to my stomach. I pulled into a parking spot at Rich Gallery and felt like I was going to vomit.

"What the fuck did you just say?" Carlos roared.

"Calm down, Los. He was just suggesting that she needs to get laid. That's all," City explained, his tone of voice slightly off.

"No, the fuck he wasn't. And then you… You know what? I'm done."

"Thanks for your call. Line two caller, you're on the line with Date Night," Country Boy said quickly as if trying to erase the first call.

"I have an issue with a woman who doesn't know her place. Thanks for always keeping it real with bitches like A. Bishara. You three are heroes!" the caller cheered.

"Knows her place? Are you fucking kidding me? What the fuck is going on?" Carlos was livid. "Is this what you wanted, B? Is this what you wanted?"

"Do you see how many emails we got this week? How was I supposed to know what people were going to say?" He laughed uneasily. "You're going to have to chill out. You act like they're talking about your mom or your girl or something. You don't even work with her anymore."

"Maybe not, but I can't work here anymore either," Carlos responded.

"Los, wait man. At least wait until we're off air," Country Boy pleaded. "Let's talk it out."

"Talk about what? The fact that—I'm not doing this on air. I'm not doing this at all." Carlos sounded done.

"What's the problem?" City Boy asked. "We are answering a listener's question about a woman who wrote an article that talked shit about us. It's fair game. And for the record, you agreed that she was wrong."

"And now I'm telling you that she's right. This is fucked up. Have you listened to any of the bullshit you've said?" Carlos didn't sound like he was near a microphone anymore.

"While Los Cabos cools off, let's head back to the emails and see what else is waiting for us," City Boy propositioned.

"Los!" Country Boy called out.

Carlos's response couldn't be heard.

"You said it yourself. This show is for entertainment purposes only. That was your statement for us." City Boy let out a chuckle "That was our official word, remember?"

There was a moment of silence.

"Okay, that's it for tonight. Tune in next week and we'll answer more of your emails. You don't want to miss it. I'm City Boy—"

"I'm Country Boy…"

"And this is Date Night with the Lost Boys," the two of them said in unison.

Chapter Twenty

$\mathcal{J}$ was so mad and frustrated that I didn't even realize tears were streaming down my cheeks. Because I called out toxic masculinity, I had random men attacking me. I didn't care that they called me a bitch. I didn't care about what they said about my looks, my relationship prospects, or even my opinion. The thing that caused my body to convulse was the fact that the one guy insinuated sexually assaulting me. The thing that brought tears to my eyes was that in standing up for the objectification of women, I was not only objectified, I was threatened.

Using the heel of my hand, I wiped my eyes. Fortunately, I didn't put on any makeup, so nothing smeared. But my eyes were pink, and my face was flushed. It looked like I'd been crying. Since I had a few minutes, I closed my eyes for a while, hoping to look normal again as soon as possible.

"Close enough," I muttered as I surveyed if the two-minute meditation helped.

As I walked to the door, I was so in my head that when I saw Carlos, I was caught off guard. I stopped in my tracks.

My heart skipped a beat. "H-hey, Carlos."

He looked at me quizzically. "Hey."

"Hey," I replied awkwardly.

He wore black pants and a black button up shirt. Something about him in all black was mesmerizing. Just seeing him made the tears well up in my eyes as I thought about everything that happened on the call and everything that had happened between us.

Two people from class walked passed us, and he moved closer to me to get out of the way. I could smell his cologne. I inhaled deeply with my eyes closed, and when I opened them, he was staring at me.

"Are you okay?" he asked.

Looking up at him, I let myself feel the feelings he stirred within me. I wanted to kiss him or at the very least hug him. But I just stood there, staring at him, missing him from a foot away. "I'm okay. Are you okay?"

He licked his lips. "I'm okay."

Our exchange was painfully awkward and brimming with combustible energy. He didn't say anything. He just stared at me. He licked his lips and took a step back, rubbing the back of his neck.

"We should get inside," he declared, turning toward the entrance.

I followed behind him and when he opened the door, he stepped to the side for me to enter first.

"Thank you," I said as I walked passed him. I stopped five steps after entering the building. "Wow."

Groups of photos were framed and hanging on a display wall. A red, velvet rope kept anyone from getting too close, but I could tell there were rows of display walls positioned behind the initial one that greeted us.

"Wow is right," he agreed, standing close enough that I could smell his cologne. As if realizing he was two seconds away from being nuzzled by me, he moved to the other side of the room. He got as far away from me as possible and I felt his rejection down to my soul. I didn't have long to process why it hurt my feelings the way it did because Luca Romano made his grand entrance.

"Hello, fellow photographers! Welcome to your special showcase at Rich Gallery. Whereas one photo can catch a viewer's eye, multiple photos can tell a story. Creating a photo story is the combination of art and storytelling. You begin with planning what story you want to tell. Each individual photo contributes to the theme, the structure, and the message of your final project. Everything we've done over the last few weeks has led us to this." He stretched his arms out wide. "And here we are… your final assignment. Your work is on display and you are going to have to communicate your story to the rest of us. Each of you will have three minutes. By the time we're done, the doors will be opened, and you will be free to show off your talents to your friends and family. Are we ready?"

We moved to the first set of pictures. At first glance it was food, but there was something off about each picture.

Luca opened his arms. "First, we have the work of Lourdes"— we all clapped politely— "But instead of Lourdes telling us about her work, we're going to invite Duke to tell us the story."

Everyone murmured in confusion. Duke walked up slowly, his eyes darted around as if he were still trying to understand what he saw.

"Take a minute and just tell us what story you're gathering," Luca explained, his tone encouraging as he held his notepad poised.

Duke surveyed the makeshift wall of photos. "Lourdes is telling us about food. She's reminding us of where the meat we eat comes from by having the plated dish and the live animal somewhere in the background. Almost like a before and after." He looked over at Luca. "That's all I got."

"That's all you need," he replied with a smile. "Very good. Thank you."

Everyone clapped.

We moved to the back of that wall and there were eight more photos positioned. I tried to find the common link as Lourdes approached the display slowly.

"Duke is commenting on the homeless situation in our country with pictures of people who live on the street?" The tail end of her sentence ended in a higher pitched voice as if she were questioning her own interpretation.

"Are you asking us or telling us, Lourdes?" Luca questioned.

"Telling?"

"Are you sure? Tell us again."

"Duke has pictures of panhandlers with signs. Some look dirtier than others. Maybe some are homeless and maybe some aren't. But all of them are asking for help."

"Very good," Luca commented, clapping. "Thank you."

As a class, we moved through nine other duos before we arrived at mine. I smiled as my classmates murmured.

"Here we have Akila's project," Luca announced. "Carlos, would you please tell us the story Akila is telling?"

Carlos gave me a sidelong look before moving toward the photos. He silently assessed the photos before turning so we could see his face. He stroked his beard before he opened his mouth. "Akila is doing a role-reversal, objectifying men to the degree that women are objectified."

Just the fact that he got it gave me butterflies.

"Excellent!" Luca commented, giving him a huge grin. "Thank you."

Carlos looked at me and the corner of his lips turned upward. The slight smile coiled a knot in my belly and heated my cheeks.

Maybe there's a chance—okay, maybe not.

Carlos turned his back on me so fast that if I wasn't devastated, it would've been almost comical. Pushing my feelings down, I walked around the wall with the rest of the class.

I can do all things, I reminded myself as I moved toward the front since it was my turn.

I took in several eye-catching photos of the same couple.

"Akila," Luca beckoned. "Please tell us what you see. What is Carlos telling us?"

"Carlos used the same two people in each of the shots. It's clear they are romantically linked from the public displays of affection. Each of the locations are different so it's showing different moments in the couple's relationship. Carlos is taking us on a romantic journey between two people who are possibly in love," I offered.

Luca made a notation in his notebook. "Very nice! But what makes you assume they're in love?"

I pointed to the close-up of the couple. Their profiles were sharp as they looked at each other angrily. "This isn't the end of the story." I pointed to the next photo of the couple holding hands watching the sunrise. "And this being the next photo shows that they got through it. That's part of what loving someone is—forgiving them, overcoming obstacles."

"Excellent, thank you." Luca grinned at me before turning to the next wall.

My eyes lingered on Carlos's pictures for a minute before I tore my eyes away. When I turned my head, I caught him staring at me. He only held my gaze for a few seconds before turning toward our classmate.

Each time he pointedly ignored me felt like a punch in the gut. I wanted to talk to him. I needed to talk to him. But after blocking him and walking away from his apology, I understood why he'd ignore me. I understood why he would stand on the other side of the room even though we were partners. But it still hurt.

I exhaled and tried to shake it off.

We finished the final six photo stories and while I politely clapped on cue and stared straight ahead, I couldn't stop thinking about Carlos. I didn't hear the words used to describe what we were looking at because my thoughts kept returning to Carlos's photo story. I glanced over at him. He was the embodiment of physical perfection, and I marveled at how he was also the epitome of complexity. Since I'd met him, he managed to be nothing like I expected, and his final project was no exception. I didn't expect his work to be so romantic although something about his photos nagged me.

We'd made it to the back of the gallery when the sound of people entering the building carried through the space.

"It's seven o'clock," Luca announced. He clapped once and had an excited gleam in his eyes. "Your work is officially on display. We're going to head to the front, and then you are free to greet your guests. I'm going to say a few words, we'll have a champagne toast, and then the show is yours. While I want you to mingle, be mindful that you should remain close to your exhibit so you can interact with those who are taking in your work. Follow me."

Leading the charge, Luca marched toward the red velvet rope that separated us and our work from the people who had just arrived. While it sounded like a ton of people, I knew that most of those people were there to see Luca. We all knew that he posted it on his social media page, and tickets sold out mere hours after he'd posted. But it was still cool that so many people were going to see our work.

As I was about to pass Carlos's work, I slowed to a stop and stepped out of the way of the people behind me. Since I felt rushed when I had only a couple of minutes to describe his photo story, I wanted the opportunity to take my time.

Couple passing notes at a table. Couple at a bar. Couple at dinner. Couple kissing under the stars. Couple in bed. Couple angrily facing each other. Couple holding hands at sunrise. Wait...

My heart rate quickened.

I backed up to get a better look at the entire story, and I noticed something out the corner of my eye. I glanced over my shoulder. Carlos stood with his hands in his pockets watching me.

My stomach flipped.

"Carlos," I whispered.

I didn't know what to say, so I just stared at him. So many things ran through my mind, but I didn't know where to start. For a full minute, the indistinct chatter stopped, and the gallery was eerily silent. We stood in the stillness, both of us waiting for the other to make a move. I couldn't read him. His handsome face displayed no emotion and his brown eyes gave nothing away. It hurt to look at him, but I couldn't bear to look away. My thoughts and emotions were all over the place and even though I couldn't deny how I felt, I couldn't bring myself to say the words.

Suddenly the sound of people broke the trance we were in.

He took a step toward me. "Akila."

Just hearing my name roll off his tongue was enough to fill my eyes with tears.

I tucked my clutch under my arm and brought both of my hands to my heart. I knew there wasn't much time and that people would be surrounding us soon. But when I looked into his eyes, I just wanted to tell him everything I was feeling. I wanted him to know that I missed him. I wanted him to know that I did what I thought was best for me. I wanted him to know that I had feelings for him. I wanted to tell him that I heard the podcast. I wanted to just confess everything to him and let the chips fall where they may. But when I opened my mouth, none of that came out.

Taking a step toward him, my nerves twisted my stomach into knots. "Was I right about your story?" I asked in a hushed tone.

He moved toward me. "What do you think?"

I was quiet for a moment as I took a step toward him. We were only a foot away from one another. "I think I was right," I murmured. "I think it's about two people falling in love."

"It was supposed to be something that makes a statement." He paused. "I can't think of a bigger statement to make."

I swallowed hard. "I'm sorry I blocked you."

"I'm sorry I didn't believe you."

My eyes watered. "I heard the podcast. I heard you defend me. I heard…everything."

Grabbing my face with his hands, Carlos closed the space between us. Capturing my mouth with his own, he kissed me with a tenderness that caused the tears to escape from my closed eyelids. He moved his hands from my face and down my neck and shoulders. He continued traveling down my arms until he wrapped his arms around me. Pulling me flush against his body, he deepened the kiss causing me to whimper lightly. It was so intense, it felt like he was trying to express what he felt for me through his lips.

I slid my hands up his arms until I clasped them around his neck. I started to feel weak as butterflies spread across my belly and through my entire body. My knees weakened in my boots, and he gripped me tighter, holding me steady.

When he pulled away from the kiss, he just stared at me. His mouth hovered over mine and his fingers dug into my lower back. "I quit the podcast."

"What?" I breathed, staring up at him wide eyed.

"After what happened, I couldn't do it. I'm sorry it took so long for me to see what you were saying, but I swear to God I won't ever let anything happen to you." He swept a tear from my cheek and then returned his hand to my lower back. "Akila?"

"Hmm?" I murmured, relishing the way he held me.

"You know I'll protect you, right?" he asked with unquestionable sincerity.

"From toxic masculinity?"

"From everything. Anything you can't handle, give it to me." He kissed me. "I want you."

A smile crept across my face. "Yeah, I can feel that."

"No," he chuckled. "I meant, I want you—all of you. I want to be with you."

I didn't have the words to express what I felt inside, so I pressed my lips against his.

"Ahem!" The sound of my father clearing his voice rang in my ears.

"Kiki?" The sound of my mom saying my name startled us apart.

"Hey!" I greeted my family cheerfully, giving them a brief hug. "We were just… I mean, this is—"

"I'm Carlos," he reached forward and shook my dad's hand first and then went around the group. "It's great to meet each of you. Akila speaks highly of you."

I grinned. "Where's Alex?"

"Salivating over your photos" Meghan's eyes shifted to Carlos, a huge grin on her face. "Carlos, Carlos, Carlos… It's nice to officially put a name with a face."

A little bit of me died of embarrassment. Only to be resurrected and die again when my mom started speaking.

"Oh! This is Carlos, Carlos!" My mom's eyebrows shot up and her smile grew even larger. "Pleasure to meet you! You're so good-looking! We've heard a lot about you."

"Well, I haven't. How do you know our daughter, young man?" my dad inquired.

I knew my dad was joking, but Carlos didn't. "Dad," I admonished him with a smile.

"We actually met in photography class and then we worked together for a little while at Re-Mix," Carlos answered.

"When did this happen?" My mom gestured to the two of us. "Last time I checked, you don't kiss your classmates."

Slipping my hand into his, I stared up at him and smiled. He gazed at me with a look of affection and amusement.

"Carlos!" a beautiful couple shouted as soon as they came around the corner.

He let go of my hand to hug them. Returning to me, he draped his arm around my shoulders. "Mom, Dad, this is Akila. Akila, these are my parents."

I shook their hands and introduced them to my family.

"Kiki, I love it! Oh!" Alex exclaimed. "Hi, everyone." She looked around surprised but seemingly confused. Her eyes found her way to Carlos's arm draped around my shoulder. "Well, well, well, what's this?"

I giggled, looking up at him. "Alex, Carlos and I are—"

"Together," he answered.

"Wait…" Alex's smile dimmed. "Carlos from Date Night with The Lost Boys?"

My stomach tied itself into so many knots that it ached. "Let me explain," I answered.

She turned around and walked away.

Shit!

"What's wrong?" Mom asked, looking around.

Dad eyed Carlos. "What's this Date Night?"

"It's a podcast I used to work with," Carlos answered.

"What?!" his mom cried, putting her hands to her cheeks. "You never told us you were on a podcast!"

"I quit." Carlos rubbed my arm. "It's a long story, but I'm no longer part of the program."

"She didn't know he quit." I looked at my parents. "I'll explain later, but I'm going to go find her."

Alex hadn't gotten that far. I saw her near the door when I started making my way to the front.

"Alex!" I called out to my sister as I maneuvered through the crowd of people and through the entrance of Rich Gallery. "Alex, wait!"

"I can't believe you!" Her voice cut through the gentle October breeze. She folded her arms over her chest and squeezed her eyelids shut. When she opened them again, she gave me the saddest look. "You of all people know what they did to me. How could you be with him?"

"Alex, listen," I stepped toward her. When she didn't recoil, I took another step and wrapped my arms around her. "First and foremost, if Carlos would've had anything to do with that news-letter, I would've never forgiven him. That wasn't him. I found out it was City Boy." Pulling away, I looked into her eyes. "City Boy thought the email was about me and even when he found out it was you, he put your picture in the newsletter to hurt me."

"What?! It wasn't random?" Alex gasped.

I shook my head. "I'm sorry. He was trying to take me down, and you were collateral damage."

"When did you find out? Why didn't you tell me?"

"The night I went on Date Night. I forgot my notebook and when I went back to get it, I overheard City Boy and Country Boy talking. City Boy did the newsletter on his own as a way to fuck with me. I was going to tell you eventually. But I felt so responsible and you didn't want to talk about it, so I waited. I'm sorry."

"You don't have to be sorry for what he did." She paused. "But you should've told me all of this."

"I didn't want to make things worse."

She shook her head. "It actually makes me feel a little better."

My eyebrows flew up. "Really?"

"Well, knowing it wasn't random and knowing there was a reason behind it besides…" She shook her head and wrapped her arms around her middle. "It sucks, and I hate that he would do that to you. But knowing City Boy did that to me for a reason that wasn't just some perverted sexual objectification is better. Not by much, but it's better."

"So, can you forgive me?"

Her head tilted and pulled me into a hug. "Of course." She

squeezed me tightly. "I heard his name and remembered why he looked familiar and overreacted. I'm sorry."

"Don't be sorry. I should've told you sooner."

"I hope I didn't ruin your showcase."

I pulled out of the hug. "Not at all. But I should get back in there."

With our arms linked, we walked back into the building. "Do you think Mom and Dad will judge me if I linger at your wall of photos instead of checking out everyone else's?"

I let out a short laugh. "They won't judge you for looking any more than they judged me for taking them."

She giggled.

We found our parents talking with Carlos's parents. I stopped to join the conversation, but Alex continued walking. When she approached Carlos, I watched silently as they talked. I didn't know what was being discussed, but he listened intently while she talked. He nodded and after he said whatever he said, they hugged.

"What are you smiling at?" Meghan asked, calling me out.

"I'm just happy," I giggled. "Where were you?"

"Bathroom and then checking out your photography again." She smiled. "You're very talented."

"Thank you. I should probably go over and engage with people about the story."

Her eyes widened. "There's a story?"

I couldn't do anything but laugh.

"Looks like they made up," Meghan whispered as she walked with me to my photo wall.

"Yeah. I never got around to telling her what I found out about the newsletter." I glanced over at Carlos and Alex who were both smiling.

"Looks like you two made up as well." She bumped me with her hip.

I felt warm all over. "I don't know what it is about him."

Meghan pointed to the third picture in my photo story and quirked an eyebrow. "D-I-C you have a great balance of light and shadow. Oh, hey, Mrs. Bishara!"

Mom eyed us suspiciously before breaking into a huge grin. "Hmm… you two always look like you're up to no good."

"We would never!" I feigned shock, making Meghan giggle.

"Well, your father and I are going to check out the other exhibits with Carlos's parents."

My eyes widened. "Like a double date?"

"If that's what you want to call it." Mom laughed. "We want to continue talking. Your father and Alberto used to work for the same company and Pam and I love art. What can I say? We hit it off!"

The idea of the four of them becoming friends made me nervous for some reason.

We decided that we were going to be in a relationship and we met each other's families all within the same five-minute timespan. I took a shaky breath. *What if everything blows up in our faces?*

"We'll be back," Mom informed me before walking back to Dad and her new friends, Mr. and Mrs. Richmond.

"I'll listen in on the conversation for you and report back," Meghan murmured as soon as Mom was out of earshot.

I breathed a sigh of relief. "Thank you so much."

Meghan walked off to follow the parents, and Alex fell into step with her. Carlos walked over to me, but I couldn't read his face.

"Our parents seem to like each other," Carlos pointed out.

"I know… which is cool," I replied, carefully choosing my words.

"Very cool."

"But…"

"Weird?"

"Yes!"

We stood there grinning at one another.

"This is Akila Bishara," Luca Romano interrupted, walking over with a woman. "She is the photographer for Sweatpants Season. Akila, this is Joan Stanford. She wanted to meet you."

I reached out and shook Joan's hand. "Hi, Ms. Stanford! Nice to meet you."

"Nice to meet you as well. Call me Joan. I'm interested in

knowing more about your photo story for a writeup for The Herald."

The Herald? The. Herald. The Herald! They wouldn't even respond to my submission requests and now I'm talking to Joan Stanford of THE HEARLD! I internally screamed.

"Oh, wow. Yes, of course." Beaming at Carlos and then Luca, I turned to begin discussing my project with Joan Stanford of The Herald. "Women are primarily the target of objectification, so I wanted to turn the tables…"

The End.

Cuffing Season

I wasn't looking for a man.
I was looking for a mentor.

When renowned photographer Luca Romano returned home to
teach a Photo Storytelling workshop, Hamilton University was
buzzing. But a campus wide email warned us not to approach Luca
if we weren't selected to participate—and I wasn't selected.

I wasn't looking to break the rules.
I was looking to break into the industry.

I knew getting photographed by Luca Romano would catapult my
career. I hoped he'd call, but I had no expectations. I wanted to
converse with him, pick his brain, expand my portfolio. That's all.

Listen… I wasn't looking to be his muse.
But I wasn't going to tell him no.

Broken Clocks Sneak Peek

*M*y Dearest Layla

I don't have many regrets. But I regret not telling you that I had cancer. Please don't be mad at your mother either. I forbade her from telling you. I wanted to tell you myself. But the more time passed, the harder it got. But that's no excuse. I should've been honest with you. But I will say this... Your mother knew, and she shifted from my child to my nurse. She didn't ask me how I was doing to hear my stories anymore. She asked me how I was doing with managing my pain and taking my pills. She worried about me, not because I was still missing your grandfather, but because I was sick. But with you, my lovely Layla, we would sit back and talk about any and everything. With you, my love, I could forget.

This does not absolve me from keeping you in the dark. But I hope that it can show you that I didn't do it to hurt you. I did it to free you. I did it to free us. If I could do it over again, I wouldn't have told your mother. So please, don't hold it against your mother. And please, don't hold it against me.

Even though I'm sure you're angry, please don't hold it against me. Please don't forget that I was there for you as much as you were there for me. Who talked to you about sex and birth control when you were too embarrassed to talk to your parents? When you got caught with condoms, who said they were hers so you didn't get into trouble? Who didn't tell your parents when you stole her condoms?

And if you're really angry, please don't forget who covered for you when I caught you and Jenelle on her birthday, drinking with two boys in my house when you thought me and your grandfather were going to the casino? She may have been twenty-one, but you weren't.

And if you're really, really angry, please don't forget that Nana loves you, and that you are my best friend—right after your grandfather. And right after Rose. But none of the old biddies I had book club or church functions with held a candle to you.

You kept me young. You kept me honest. You kept me company. You were my light, and the moment your mother had you, I knew that you were going to be the golden goose. Not just because you're my only granddaughter. And not just because you look more like me than any of my children do. You, Layla, are something special.

When your grandfather passed away, I didn't know what I was going to do. But I will never forget the day it happened or the fact that I woke up and he had stopped breathing sometime after some early morning canoodling. We had gotten up to have coffee, watch the news, talk on the porch, and then we returned to bed at eight. After a tumble in the hay, we fell asleep and when I woke up, my watch had stopped at 9:27 a.m. When I looked at the clock in the room, it was about 9:50 a.m. I tried to wake him and called emergency services a few minutes later. They were here at 9:58 a.m. He was pronounced dead soon thereafter. They said he'd been without oxygen for at least thirty minutes.

There is no one who can tell me that he didn't die at 9:27 a.m.

For the last three years, I've missed him, but I didn't dwell on it. I knew we would be reunited again. So, I focused on the fact that there is so much life to be lived and I need to take advantage of it. A broken clock is only right twice a day. Any other time, you're just guessing and trying to figure it out. So, seize the day and the opportunities. You don't get an unlimited amount of times to get something right or to capitalize on it in the way God intended. God knows that we're flawed humans, so he gives us a second chance to get it right.

You get two times for the timing to be perfect, and everything lines up just right. If you miss the opportunity the first time, make sure you jump on it the second time. Don't settle. Be patient, and wait for it to come around again. If you do that you'll have few regrets and plenty of stories. You'll have a love life for the ages. And if you're lucky, maybe it'll be with one man. And if you're luckier, maybe it'll be with three. You'll have a job that won't feel like work. You'll have at least one friend you can count on. You will see humor in things and not take yourself so seriously, while at the same time knowing your worth.

I want you to have that kind of life, Layla. You're still going to die at the end of it, but you will have lived. And when you die, you won't be afraid because you'll know that you lived, you loved, and you laughed. So, to my dearest Layla, I leave you my watch that I got from the love of my life to remind you that a broken clock being right twice a day means that in any given situation, perfect timing only happens twice.

I love you. I'll be waiting for you when it's your time. We'll have new stories to tell each other. Because the first thing I'm doing when I get to heaven is kissing my husband. The second is to find Rose because you know she died owing me twenty dollars.

Never forget that Nana loves you.

LOVE ALWAYS,
Nana

Chapter One

I exhaled slowly as I watched William Grayson walk away from me and out of my life forever. There was no way he wasn't going to get that promotion. He had just finished his second interview and from the sound of it he would be the head of the Philadelphia division in three weeks. Not only was he great at his job,

I knew from personal experience he was extremely good at taking charge.

My tongue slowly slid between my full lips as my eyes skated over his six-foot, three-inch frame. The way his black suit stretched across his professional football player build left the promise of an even better view underneath the tailored fabrics. I stared at his close-cut Caesar haircut and let my gaze slip down to his black leather shoes. Even without seeing his smooth, unblemished skin, his straight, white teeth, and his dark brown eyes, anyone would be able to tell he was fine. Sexiness radiated off him from every angle.

I don't think I blinked until he was completely out of the restaurant and the door was starting to close behind him.

"What was that?" Jenelle McFarland practically yelled from across the table.

My head snapped back toward my best friend in shock. My eyes darted from her to the door Will left out of and then back to her. "What? Nothing! Why are you so loud?!"

Glaring at me, a little amused smile played on her lips. "Don't play coy with me. What's going on with you and Will?"

"I don't know what you're talking about," I lied, glancing at my watch. "Look at the time! It's 9:27 already!"

"That watch always says that and has needed a new battery for six years so cut the shit." She pointed at me. "You and Will just undressed each other with your eyes."

I let out a loud laugh. "No, we didn't."

She dropped her fork, and it clanked loudly against her plate. "Layla, it couldn't have been any more obvious that you two want each other."

"That's not true," I argued, my face getting warm. "We broke things off over two years ago. We are just friends now. You know this already. We are just friends."

She shook her head. "Listen to me… I had to avert my eyes at one point because I thought I saw him pull his dick out and put it on your plate."

"Shut up!" I laughed so hard my body shook. "That did not happen."

"Okay, okay." Jenelle's giggles mixed with my own. "But those weren't 'I used to want you two years ago' looks. Those were 'I want you right here and right now' looks. I mean the eye-fucking was so intense, I was about to toss my cookies." She crossed her arms. "And that's not a euphemism… I ate an embarrassing number of cookies this afternoon, so I would have literally vomited cookies all over this table."

My shoulders shook uncontrollably, but I covered my mouth in an effort to muffle my laughter. After two straight minutes of giggles, we both calmed down.

"I needed that laugh," I sighed, still grinning. "It's been a stressful week."

She lifted her almost empty wine glass and gave me a nod. "You've had a lot going on. But it doesn't help that you are repressing your feelings and emotions."

I rolled my eyes. "I'm not repressing anything. Moving is stressful. Starting a new job is stressful. Being far away from my best friend is stressful."

"Yes. Yes. And hell yes! The actual moving part of moving sucks. The uncertainty of starting a new job sucks. And even though we won't be able to yell for each other from the other room anymore, we're only going to be fifteen minutes apart."

"I know. But living with you for the last year has spoiled me. What am I supposed to do without you borrowing my clothes without asking?" I joked.

"And what am I going to do without you singing loudly and off-key every morning before work?" she returned.

Reaching across the table, we squeezed each other's hand and exchanged bittersweet grins. After a breakup with a man I had no business dating, let alone living with, I moved into Jenelle's townhouse and remained for nine months. We'd always been close, but the last year had strengthened our bond.

Sitting back in our seats, she sighed. "Well, at least this can be our Friday night happy hour spot. Hello, Lavo!"

My eyes danced around the trendy new restaurant. Lavo was centrally located between my new apartment and the townhouse

Jenelle owned. Bringing my glass to my lips, I nodded. "I like the way you think because these happy hour specials are on point."

"The entire menu is on point. And when it's warm, they have a rooftop space that overlooks downtown. Next time I'm going to come here hungry, so I can eat what I want."

I pointed at her. "Or next time don't eat all those damn cookies before we go out to eat."

She laughed. "Ah yes, that is what happened. I guess I'm repressing the memory of my gluttonous cookie intake just like you're repressing your feelings for Will."

"That again?" Shaking my head, I took a bite of my salad and chewed. I could feel Jenelle's eyes on me and when I glanced at her, she sipped her wine knowingly. I swallowed the leafy greens. "Fine! Do I still have nothing but love for him? Of course. Do I think he's a great man? Yes. Do I still think he's sexy as hell? Absolutely. Would I still"—I leaned forward and lowered my voice— "fuck him? Hell yeah!"

Lifting her glass in the air, Jenelle gave me an approving nod. "Okay!"

"And even with all that being true, I no longer date men I have no future with… so Will and I are just friends. That's all it can be. That's all it'll ever be."

Jenelle's eyebrows shot up, and she pursed her lips. I waited for her to say something, but she remained silent.

I cleared my throat. "A relationship wouldn't work with us. It didn't work then. It wouldn't work now. And honestly, I'm not even interested in pursuing anything serious with him or anyone. I just want to focus on me. This year is going to be all about making money."

"Yes, but didn't Will say he was up for that job in Philly?"

"Yes…?"

"And if he gets the job, which we already know he will, he's moving to Philly?"

My brows furrowed in confusion. "Yes…?"

"So, next week, he'll be starting a new life in Philly?"

"Yes!" My voice elevated in exasperation. "What's your point?"

"This might be your last weekend to have him blow your back out one more time."

I heard her words just as I was swallowing the swig of water I'd just sipped. Somewhere between my body's reaction to what she said and my brain's memory of what he did to my body that summer, I choked.

"What?" I screeched, the sound garbled by a laugh-gasp that simultaneously escaped.

"Timing is everything... right?" Jenelle giggled as I gave her a flabbergasted look.

"You two look like you're having a good time," the waiter pointed out, appearing unexpectedly. He looked between us with a huge smile as he poured wine into our empty glasses. "On the house," he noted with a wink. "Celebrating something?"

Reeling from Jenelle's words, I just shook my head.

"Yes! My best friend has a new job, a new place." She paused and gave me a look. "And a new opportunity to get her back aligned."

"Congratulations!" The waiter looked between us and smiled. "Very good reasons to celebrate! And you know what... I saw a chiropractor just a couple of weeks ago, and I instantly felt better."

The laughter bubbled up inside of me, and I tried to keep it together. My entire body shook, and it wasn't until he walked away that I could look at Jenelle. As soon as our eyes met, we both cracked up.

"See, go ahead and call Will and let him give you the adjustment you need." She wiggled her eyebrows. "You'll instantly feel better."

I felt the heat on my cheeks, between my legs, and in my chest. "I don't think that's a good idea."

"Why not? I still don't understand why you two even split. I've never understood your relationship. You two had so much fun together and then all of a sudden, you two decided to be friends. Within a month, he started dating that social media model"—she rolled her eyes dramatically— "and you started dating Thomas. And then that was it. You two have been 'friends' ever since." She used air quotes to emphasize her sarcasm.

"We are friends—well, we're friendly. And a relationship between us is not viable."

"But we're not talking about a relationship. We're talking about sex with someone you care about in order to de-stress. We're talking about the hottest goodbye sex. We're talking that post-Valentine's Day dick."

"Oh my God!" I cackled, and then I cleared my throat. "I guess it has been a while since I had sex with anyone."

"A while?" she sputtered. "You're basically a virgin again. You and Thomas broke up forever ago and besides that brief hookup—"

"You mean that quickie that resulted in a pregnancy scare?" I corrected her.

"Whatever. You let that pregnancy scare scare the sex out of your life."

I laughed, but she wasn't wrong. I glanced at my cell phone and then picked up my wine glass. It had been a long time and William really had a way with my body.

I shouldn't though… should I?

"No, no, no… I shouldn't," I answered my own question into my hands as I covered my face. I sighed before meeting my best friend's eyes. "We had our one good summer. Our moment has come and gone."

"Maybe it has, maybe it hasn't." She lifted her left shoulder and held her hands upward. "But what was it your Nana used to say? Even a broken clock is right twice a day." Jenelle delivered her argument in a sing-song voice as her eyebrows wiggled. "Well, let's consider seeing Will again being the second time the clock is right."

I quietly considered what she'd said. Staring at my Nana's watch, I looked at the hands as they remained frozen in place.

She's not wrong…

Jenelle shrugged her shoulders. "But obviously, it's your call. If you really don't think it's a good idea, don't do it. I'm not trying to talk you into anything you don't want to do. I just saw the way the two of you were looking at each other and figured why not climb that tree one last time before he moves away? You'll get the closure you never got, and you'll roll into your first day of work feeling like a new woman." She gave me a small smile. "But I get it. Will is...different."

I swallowed hard, glancing at my phone.

"Anyway, I'm probably just horny since Mike's been out of town," Jenelle continued. "I'm projecting and living vicariously through you."

"How are things with Mike?" I asked, changing the subject so I didn't have to deal with my own feelings at the moment.

Jenelle's face lit up. "Mike is enjoying his time in Japan. The first week was all business meetings, and this week he's getting more time to just enjoy himself. Let me show you what he sent me earlier."

As she messed with her phone, I slipped mine off the table and into my lap.

"Isn't this gorgeous?" She showed me a selfie of Mike with the neon-lit skyscrapers of Tokyo in the background.

"Are you talking about Tokyo or Mike?" I teased as I sipped wine and masked my nerves.

She giggled and stared at her phone.

Quickly, I looked down at my screen and moved my thumb over the keyboard.

Layla: I want to give you a proper goodbye. Will you be home in an hour?

Looking up, I nodded at Jenelle's story. Her entire face glowed every time she spoke about Mike. I didn't even think she realized she was telling me a story she'd already told me before. It was looking as though absence was really making her heart grow fonder.

"So, I take it that you two aren't just casual anymore...?" I asked, distractedly.

Part of me wanted to tell Jenelle I was sending the message so she could help me perfect my flirt technique. But the larger part of me didn't want to have the conversation about what hooking up with Will meant. I didn't want to talk about how Will made me feel. I didn't want to talk about the status of our relationship. I just needed a release.

So, I kept the decision to myself and before I could lose my nerve, I hit send.

"…and it's not just that he's so hot, he's so thoughtful and sweet, too," Jenelle swooned.

"He is. You two seem to make a good pair. When does he come back?"

The phone vibrating in my lap shot directly to my clit. My entire body tingled. I knew it was him before I even looked down at the screen.

William: I've been waiting for this text for over two years. I'll leave the door unlocked.

DOWNLOAD NOW
http://amzn.to/2D2ABBm

Playlist

Sweatpants Season Playlist

Music inspires me. The artists mentioned below wrote songs and lyrics that depict the mood of Akila Bishara's journey in Sweatpants Season. If you haven't had a chance to listen to any of these songs, you should purchase them immediately and listen on repeat.

Django Jane – Janelle Monae
    Just a Girl – No Doubt
    Love Lies (With Normani) – Khalid
    Shotgun – Gallant
    Bad Blood – Nao
    If I Didn't Know Better – Sam Palladio & Clare Bowen
    Haunted – Stwo & Sevdaliza
    Poison – Brent Faiyaz
    Bad Dreams/No Looking Back – Syd
    First Fuck – 6lack & Jhene Aiko
    Electric (ft. Khalid) – Alina Baraz
    8 – Willow

Playlist

All We Do – Oh Wonder
Body (Acoustic) – Sinead Harnett
Between the Wars – Allman Brown
Elastic Heart – Sia
Right My Wrongs – Bryson Tiller

Acknowledgments

Sweatpants Season is a multilayered novel. On the surface, it is an enemies-to-lovers romance that deals with what happens when you have instant chemistry with someone you shouldn't. It's a sexy struggle between what your heart wants, what your mind knows, and what your body calls for. In addition to being fun, sexy, and swoon-worthy, Sweatpants Season deals with real issues.

The sexual objectification of women can be harmful socially, psychologically, and emotionally. I believe the prevalence of sexual harassment, sexual assault, and sexual violence stems from objectification and entitlement. If someone has sexually objectified someone else (male or female), harassment, assault, or violence could potentially follow since they are viewing that individual as an object of sexual desire to which they feel entitled. With the help of Tarana Burke and the #MeToo movement, more people are speaking up and out against sexual assault and harassment which is an excellent thing. Without oversimplifying, I wanted to write something that touched on the consequences of objectification—how it can affect the person in question, how it can influence others, etc. Another major underlying theme is passive acceptance. There is no grey area when dealing with right and wrong. If you are choosing the grey area, that's passively accepting wrong.

To my family and friends who have loved and supported me, thank you. I am blessed to have you in my life. I love you all to the moon and back.

Amy Queau—thank you for creating my beautiful covers time and time again.

Nerdy Girl Editing—thank you for your editing, your feedback, and your comments. They are legit the best!

Michelle Lynn—thank you for being you and for using your formatting skills on my work. I appreciate you so much.

Kumiko—thank you for being such an asset to my book life. You're the best.

Authors, bloggers, readers, thank you. You have changed my life with your love and support. It truly means so much to me. I am floored when I hear people say that they know me and love me and/or my work. I am honored when I read reviews that get it—my stories, my characters, my point, my message. The knowledge that I've moved people with my words is huge to me. I don't take it for granted. From the bottom of my heart, thank you. I can't begin to explain how much it means to me to be able to write and publish my novels and to have you take the time to read them. Sending you all hugs and love.

www.authordanielleallen.com

Also by Danielle Allen

Made in the USA
Las Vegas, NV
15 January 2024

84427446R00154